Marie

John McMillan

Copyright © 2017 by John McMillan.

ISBN: Softcover   978-1-5434-8528-8
          eBook   978-1-5434-8529-5

All rights reserved. No part of this book may be reproduced or transmitted in any form or by any means, electronic or mechanical, including photocopying, recording, or by any information storage and retrieval system, without permission in writing from the copyright owner.

This is a work of fiction. Names, characters, places and incidents either are the product of the author's imagination or are used fictitiously, and any resemblance to any actual persons, living or dead, events, or locales is entirely coincidental.

Any people depicted in stock imagery provided by Thinkstock are models, and such images are being used for illustrative purposes only.
Certain stock imagery © Thinkstock.

Print information available on the last page.

Rev. date: 05/02/2017

To order additional copies of this book, contact:
Xlibris
800-056-3182
www.Xlibrispublishing.co.uk
Orders@Xlibrispublishing.co.uk
756810

Marie

For Lesley
love,
John

28th May 2019

Also by John McMillan

On A Green Island
Summer in the Heart
The Soul of the City
Upstream
The Islander

**Fairest of them all by far
Is our darlin' Marie**

(*Marie's Wedding*—Traditional)

PART ONE

1

Start at the beginning, the precise moment when Marie (pronounced *Mari*) came into my life.

O level maths, the stuffy, dusty classroom high in the old wing of the grammar school. My attention wandered from algebra to the legs of the girl seated a little in front and to the left of me in the next row of desks, under the window.

It was a moment of Joycean epiphany as I fixated on those legs. They came out of the short navy gym-slip and curved down smooth and creamy into the white ankle-socks above the black school shoes.

The quiet girl possessor of the legs leant over her desk, concentrating on her algebra, quite oblivious of those wondrous pins tucked under her. I stared and stared, drinking them in, thigh, knee, calf and ankle. The legs invited your attention with an existence all their own. The legs were everything, a vision of the elegant beauty and desirability of the feminine form, the bearer of life. Now the algebra was nothing, those legs were all I needed to know.

I got a good look at the face later, the face that belonged to the legs. It was a pleasant girl-face, fair complexion, blue eyes, the neat dark-fair hair side-parted and cut to the school regulation collar-length for girls.

I'd had wee notions of girls before, little crushes, the pretty faces had got me. This girl, Marie Kelly, was almost plain at first sight, but it didn't matter, the beauty of those legs was reflected in her face. Sitting there behind her, I watched her for weeks from under a hand shading my eyes as if I were concentrating very hard on the maths books open on my desk. My watchfulness was rewarded from time to time as she shifted about carelessly on the hard wooden seat, revealing more leg and the odd thrilling glimpse of navy cotton pants. I liked to imagine that she knew I was looking and didn't care, that she thought I was worth it!

Slowly my stare travelled upwards, taking in the rounded hips in the pleated skirt, the narrowing to the waist and the long sloping back as the diligent student bent to her work, her bosom nestled in the white shirt under her tunic, head down and hair parting loosely about her bowed nape. With a shiver inside I thought of the incredible privilege enjoyed by the clothes she wore next her skin.

It took a long time but finally I made my move.

"Hi Marie, what way are you going?"

I caught up with her outside the school gates; it was the first time I'd ever spoken to her. My heartbeat had relocated to my throat, half choking me as I squeezed out the words I had been rehearsing all that day.

She turned her face to me, where I had drawn level with her on the crowded pavement. In close-up now it was a stranger's face; I was more familiar with the back of her head. Her fair complexion coloured a little at my words but the light-blue eyes, widening in surprise, did not reject me.

"I take the short cut through the Waterworks," she said, speaking in her quiet voice through thickish lips—a look of Mick Jagger, it struck me. A lot of us looked like pop stars back in those days; I was a hybrid of Paul and George.

"I go that way too. You don't mind if I walk with you?" It sounds smooth written down now, but I only just managed to find the right words and blab them out, I was painfully shy of the opposite sex.

She shook her head, *no*, she didn't mind and lo and behold, it was all happening, we were walking side by side! Could it really be this easy?

Her school shoes went clickety-clack on the pavement, *the legs* were keeping time with mine! It felt strangely natural, a boy and a girl, poetry in motion, as if she had just been waiting for me to join her.

"Do you like Jake's maths class?" I said, thinking up something we shared. The words echoed dully in my ears, I was never made for the chat-up lines.

"He explains things clearly," she said thoughtfully.

"Not like Bronco," I said. "Ever had him? Sulks if the class can't answer a question off the board, leaves you all sitting there sweating it out till the bell goes, then it's your homework, sweating it out more till bedtime."

She shook her head. "All I know is the girls think Bronco's good-looking and want to be in his class."

"Tell the girls to steer well clear of Bronco, he's a monster! It's not that he'd ever hit you; he doesn't need to resort to physical punishment, he's an expert in psychological torture."

I wasn't joking; I was conscious of my rancorous tone as I recalled the two years of misery in Bronco's class, the nervous pain in my stomach going into school every day. It was when I was twelve and thirteen, that was when my eyesight had failed too, which I put down to the trauma of Bronco's teaching.

But catching myself on now, I didn't want a girl to hear me fulminating like this, a bilious boyfriend, when we had only just met, or ever; conversation with a fair maid should be charming and fun, romantic through and through.

"*'Time you buckled down and stopped all your whinging and whining, sonny!'*" Making a joke of it instead, I mimicked the thunderous tone Bronco, a six foot two, fourteen-stone Rugby referee, dragged up from his boots to disguise the paradox of his naturally wimpish falsetto that broke through sometimes like a pubescent boy.

I explained, "I'd complained to the form master that I couldn't stand Bronco's class, that I was learning nothing, and asked to be moved to another teacher. Of course it got back to Bronco and he kept me behind after class one day; I was standing by his desk as he prodded my little fat tummy to emphasise his point—*'whinging'*, poke, and *'whining'*, poke, *'sonny!'* I was a bag of nerves anyway and the pressure of his huge forefinger on my gut caused me to let off a fart!"

I blushed at the indelicacy that had just popped out of my mouth, lads' bottom-talk in front of a nice girl!

But it sent Marie into stitches, the passers-by turning their heads in alarm to look at us. And I knew I had won her over already. Thank you, Bronco!

The little back streets of artisan terraces behind the school opened out at the oasis of the Waterworks. It was the summer term; the enclosing trees were in fresh green leaf, the grass banks sloping to the water that held the milky sky.

There was nobody much around and Marie took my hand as we walked by the water's edge. Now my hand was connected to the hand connected via the arm to the torso connected to *the legs*! I was walking on the clouds of heaven.

"Shall we sit down a minute by that tree?" My voice was shaking.

Marie nodded. Like a gentleman I spread my blazer with the lining on the grass under the tree and we sat on it, squashed up together. She perched there neatly, skirt tucked in, knees sticking up pointy-marbly, almost in my face now. The trees and bushes half-hid us from open view. She leant her head on my shoulder and after a minute I twisted my neck, lowered my head awkwardly and placed a kiss on her lips.

It was a good kiss. We did it again. I kept my arm round her as we sat on quietly for a bit, watching the ducks sail past, the water lapping ever so gently up to the green banks.

"I love the summertime," she said eventually.

"Makes you feel like a different, new person," I said. "Do you go away on holiday?"

"Week in Bangor with Mummy and Daddy and my wee sister Thelma. Same rented house every July, long as I remember."

"We do the same holiday every summer too," I told her, "a week at my aunt and uncle's farm at White Park Bay. Aunt Elsie is Da's sister. Ma gets fed up going there every year. But I love it in the country, it's another world up on that north coast with the Scots dialect and the wind, the turf fires and oil lamps, to bed by candlelight. Electricity's coming now; my old Uncle Willie the farmer wants *naethin'* to do with it! Neither do I. I love going back in time!"

"You're a romantic then?"

"Oh, I'd love to have been around to support Bonnie Prince Charlie!"

"*Ye Jacobites by name, lend an ear!*" she sang, light and tuneful like some long-ago Highland lass. "Bit bloody maybe, for you I mean, Culloden and all?"

"Och, you're not a real romantic till you lose the battle, sacrifice everything, your life for the cause!" I proclaimed weightily.

"Oh, I see." She looked at her watch. "Hi, we'd better be heading, it's getting on for five."

We exited on to the busy thoroughfare of the Antrim Road.

"I go this way," she indicated up the hill.

"I'm straight on a bit. There's no rush, I'll walk you home."

The greening mountainside of Cave Hill loomed up ahead, above the city streets. We turned into Jacaranda Close, a lifeless crescent of neat redbrick semis. She stopped outside the gate to a drive with a garage set back below the gable wall.

"See you in maths tomorrow!" she smiled, waiting. We kissed goodbye, awkwardly, conscious of the squinting windows.

I dropped back down the hill towards home, wings on my heels, the feeling of joy mounting in my chest till I wanted to whoop it out to the world, "*I've got a girlfriend!*"

2

"What are *you* grinning about all over your sleekit wee kisser, lookin' like the cat that got the cream?"

My big sister Audrey was waiting there to make sure I wouldn't have too good a day.

"Now wouldn't you just like to know?" I responded with a playfulness I didn't feel. I just wished she'd stay in her student flat for good, away over at the far side of town.

"Mummy, Paul's got a girl, so he has!" she sang out irritatingly to Ma next door in the kitchen.

"How do *you* know?" I said.

"That silly look on your face! Anyone could tell a mile off, *Paul's-got-a-girl now!*" she chanted.

What's it to you? I thought angrily but an aversion in my nature to open warfare strangled my vocal chords.

"What's her name?" Audrey persisted.

"None of your business," I retorted in a feeble attempt to join in her school playground banter, disliking myself more with every word I spoke, the sense of my male ineptitude against her razor tongue.

Ma came through from the kitchen to lay the table for tea. "Indeed Paul has no interest in girls!" she said, defending me. "He's far too busy with his pals, poker schools and pop music!"

As Ma disappeared back into the kitchen Audrey lowered her voice to me and put on the local working class accent: "*A friggin' wee fruit, are ye?* Ha-ha-ha-ha!" she cackled in a fair representation of a witch. "Our Pauly's a queer! You and Roy Watson, eh?"

I felt my face burn up. Big Sis could always put her finger on the sensitive spot. This one went back a couple of years, when Roy Watson had come home with me after school; the house was empty and he suggested I dress up in Audrey's clothes. I wasn't a transvestite or trans-anything but the actor in me wanted to have a go.

There was rain on the windows and we'd been feeling cooped up and bored. We went in Audrey's room and wardrobe and I chose a narrow emerald green skirt I liked the look of, like the kilt of a male Irish dancer, and a black cotton top like a boy's singlet. The fit wasn't bad, my sister was four years older than me, we were the same height and I was going through puberty, narrow of shoulder and broad of beam.

I was rather taken with my reflection in the full-length mirror on the wardrobe door. What a transformation! I might have been a kilted Gael or maybe Bonnie Prince Charlie disguised as a girl; I had a good head of black hair and a soft pink, pretty-boy face to set off the costume.

"You look flippin' great, Carroll!" Roy encouraged me. I'd a girl's name for my surname and all. I wondered about Roy's sexuality but didn't really care; whatever he might be it was harmless enough.

I sat on the side of Audrey's bed and crossed my legs. The skirt moved up my thighs; below it my knees and calves acquired an androgynous sort of smooth elegance and looking down, admiring them, I couldn't help wondering if I'd have made a better-looking girl. I was finding myself sexually attractive, for God's-sake!

Roy was smiling, lapping it up, I wondered if he was going through some homo stage in his adolescent development, though he was a muscular Rugger captain, not at all effeminate. I enjoyed his attentions and was happy to play along with him. There were no girls in our lives yet.

"*Wh...what in the name of God!...is going on in my bedroom?*"

Audrey stood in the doorway, screeching, aghast. She was in her school hockey uniform, her fair hair sticking out in bunches, thunder thighs going up under the brief maroon gym-slip into those big black gym-knickers with a pocket in them.

Roy and I froze. It was as if we'd been woken from a dream. What *was* going on?

"Dressing up!" I said cheerily. "Hope you don't mind me borrowing your stuff a minute?"

"Oh, of course I don't mind some wee boy smelling of dried pee trying on my clothes! Have you got my bra and panties on under that attractive ensemble?"

"Of course not! What do you think I am, queer or something?"

"Well, now you mention it..." And at that point she dissolved into a laughing fit. "Wait till I tell them all at school about this!" she shrieked.

"Don't you dare, Audrey, I'll kill you!" I said, assertive for once, imagining a thousand eyes on me at morning assembly, *Hi, did ye hear about Carroll? His sister caught him trying on her clothes!*

"Sure I'm only pulling your leg, you vindictive article!" Audrey snapped coldly. "Do you think I want to be known as the transvestite's sister? Now just put my clothes back where you found them!"

She went back out the door, closing it firmly behind her.

"Try the bra and panties next time?" Roy panted, leering over me, and I could see he was only half-joking.

So back or should I say forward to that first day I walked Marie home from school and Audrey's mocking, "*Our Pauly's a queer!*"

I wanted all that kind of false rumour put firmly behind me now.

"Well, if you must know, Miss Nosey Parker," I told Audrey, "I *have* got a girl now, as a matter of fact! She's called Marie."

"Oh, *Maa-ree! Step we gaily, on we go, heel for heel and toe for toe!*" Audrey had a decent singing voice, if nothing else, I had to admit. "Mummy!" she called out to embarrass me. "Mummy, do you hear that? Paul *does* have a girl, after all, I was right, she's called *Marie*!"

Ma looked cautiously round the door.

I said, "It's true, Mum. She's a really nice girl."

"I'm sure she is if you have chosen her, son! You are a really nice fellow after all!"

"Oh, listen—Mummy's wee pet!" Audrey sneered, spitting out the *pet!* "Marie must be a bit hard up for a boyfriend, more like!" she scoffed.

"Like you, you mean?" I tried a bitchy riposte.

"Not at all," she dismissed it airily, "I'll have you know I have *three* fellas *mad* about me at the minute: B J, Niall and Colin. The only problem *I* have is *which* boy to choose!"

When she had gone upstairs Ma said, "Those fellows don't know what they may be letting themselves in for, Paul, eh?"

"Aye, the taming of the shrew!"

We had a good snigger till we heard her footsteps coming back down the stairs. Funny the way we were all, even my parents, afraid of her like that, and she only a young girl. It had always been so.

I lay on my bed in the light of the long clear evening, sparrows twittering on the coal-house roof under my window. I had abandoned my homework and was reading a novel, or trying to, for the thoughts of Marie kept rising between me and the page. I had a *girlfriend*, oh the glory of it, and it was everything now!

I heard the phone ringing below in the hall, Ma answering and then calling up the stairs to me,

"Paul! It's Marie!"

My heart leapt for joy. I was nervous too. I tumbled down the stairs, almost tripping over my own feet, and picked up the heavy black receiver.

"Hello."

"Hello!" Girl-voice: wondrous *she*!

"That you?"

"Marie."

"Hiya. How's things? Much happened since five o'clock?"

"Done my homework. Listening to Luxembourg and filing my nails. What are you up to?"

"Reading a novel, *Franny and Zooey*, by J.D. Salinger."

"Any good?"

"Disappointing after *Catcher in the Rye* but it's just different basically and gets better the more you get into it, he's my favourite writer. What are you reading at the moment?"

"Somerset Maugham, *Of Human Bondage*."

"Oh God, I loved that!"

"Romantic, the way you like? Fated, hopeless love!"

"That's right. You understand me well!"

"It was nice in the Waterworks today," she said warmly, with a touch of mischief.

"We could do it again tomorrow if you like?"

"Okay. It's nice there in the summertime. Have you done your algebra for Jake?"

"No, I couldn't concentrate."

"I'll see you in class then. I have to go now, read my wee sister a bedtime story! Enid Blyton again, *Five do something or other*! Thelma says she's like George and I'm like Anne!"

"Enid Blyton's good. *The Castle of Adventure* was my favourite. Okay, see you tomorrow then. Bye."

"Bye."

The girl's voice, quiet and intent, lingering in my ear, left me full up with the promise of strange complete happiness she had brought into my life.

I lay on my bed in the last long fading light of the evening, just holding on to the thought of Marie, the two of us kissing under the tree. The obsession with a pair of legs had crept up to encompass the whole girl, body and soul, that in turn was connected to the whole world.

3

I woke to Ma's morning call and images of Marie flooded my slowly dawning consciousness like the sunshine through the window as I pulled back the curtains. Now every day would bring this joy of *girlfriend*. The world was a different, marvellous place with Marie in it.

I turned along the busy Antrim Road in good time for school, ducking down Duncairn Gardens to the smokers' club, the shop that sold single cigarettes, Gallaher's Greens, manufactured in the great mill just down the road, tuppence each in the shop. The figures of Ralph and Frankie, fair and athletic, like handsome twins, who came on the train from Jordanstown each day, were over in the corner sneaking a morning smoke.

I got my fag from the obliging man behind the counter and joined the two lads. We stood there puffing away between the stands of American pulp fanzines and the humming freezer with its ice-cream and lollies. You felt a little dizzy, nauseous with the inhalation of nicotine and carbon dioxide, but you persevered, it was the sociable conspiracy of smoking that was so appealing—it was strictly forbidden by the school.

Frankie said, "We were talking about the group, Paul."

"Getting everyone together for a practice sometime," said Ralph.

"Beatles, Searchers, bit of Buddy Holly, some of my stuff," said Frankie, the singer-songwriter.

"Sounds wonderful," I said. The idea of starting a group had germinated that summer term in the course of long afternoons in the art room.

"Saturday morning at my place?" said Frankie. "Dad's away and we'll have the house to ourselves."

"Great!" I said. "I love Jordanstown! Charlie and I'll bring our guitars, and we have Mike on the drums."

"I have a basic drum kit there," said Frankie, "and the old piano if anyone fancies a plonk on it."

"Charlie's the boy can fairly tinkle the ivories," I said. "And Ralphy-boy here on bongos?" I smiled. "And looking cool as ever!"

"I'm the boy to pl'ase yous!" It was a Ralph catchphrase.

Time was getting on. We stepped out on to the street and flicked our cigarette butts away into the gutter. A short cut through an alley between the backs of the houses brought us out on the Antrim Road at the Phoenix pub and the pedestrian crossing to the tree-lined avenue that climbed to the school.

"Hi Paul, saw you walking with that wee-girl yesterday!" Ralph grinned.

"Marie!" I smiled proudly. I wanted to tell everyone she was my girlfriend now and we were in love, but it was a bit soon and anyway lads didn't say those soft things that left you vulnerable.

I said, "I walked her home via the Waterworks."

"Oh, I see! A court on the way?" Ralph persisted—"court" pronounced *coort,* a snog.

"Well, a wee court anyway."

"Marie a good wee court then?"

"Not half!" I said smugly and to shut my mate up.

The massive dark frontage of the Victorian school building loomed up behind the line of tall green trees screening it from the road. The bell was tolling for assembly.

Knowing she was there somewhere in the crowd that packed the assembly hall and afterwards poured along the corridors and up the wide central staircase to fill the classrooms changed everything about the school day. It seemed to welcome me now.

I cast about for a glimpse of *my girl*, the dear face in the crowd. Even the crowd seemed tender now, an extension of Marie.

And there she was at last, Jake's class in the afternoon; she acknowledged me with a wee smile as I slipped into my usual desk behind her. That was all, then she kept her head down, working away conscientious as ever. I sat and stared at her, more openly now, the unconscious beauty of the legs under the desk, her nice profile as she turned her head and lifted her eyes to Jake's instruction from the blackboard.

Legend had it that Jake was a Desert Rat in the war; he was a funny little man, horn-rims and big nose like a joke-shop disguise, high corrugated brow packed with theorems, smoothed-back wavy grey hair. His false teeth glinted in the demonic cold little smiles of a sadist as he posed another equation to the class. He liked to stand there by his desk with a foot up on his chair, heavy-duty *Tuf* shoes with tractor-tyre soles, the short leg crooked in half-mast baggy grey flannels with turn-ups. He favoured roll-neck bottle-green knitted pullovers under a light-green checked suit-jacket. Jake *was* mathematics: it was in the pores of his greyish skin, the fine coating of chalk dust ghostly on his clothing, the rictus of his dentures.

Unlike Bronco before him, Jake *could actually teach*, with the right simplified, slow-motion approach for idiots like me. But better *watch-it, you-boy!* The master's faint "I-know-the-answer" cute smile that tied our fates to his could vanish like the sun behind a cloud at the classroom window. I watched in cringing horror once as he descended on one harmless boy who had jokingly addressed him as "Jake" and blattered the lad around the head with the hardback *O level Arithmetic,* snarling, "I'll have none of your gutter boy expressions here!"

It seemed a funny way to talk about your own name. The blattered boy's eyes swivelled in their sockets as he was almost knocked unconscious. Corporal punishment had been abolished under the school's proud liberal regime, so textbooks were a handy substitute, the heavier the better.

Jake liked the girls, however, he was a complete charmer to them, addressing himself mainly to a little super-attentive circle of goody-goody ones who gathered at the front under his nose.

Marie was not associated with the goody-goodies, I was pleased to observe. She seemed curiously independent, quiet and self-contained; it contributed to her aura of feminine mystique.

She smiled at me again as we packed our books away at the end of the lesson.

"See you at the gate?" I said and she nodded and went off, smiling to herself.

At ten to four we drifted hand-in-hand through the Waterworks in the twittering afternoon sunshine. There was that lovely tiptoeing tenderness of new love between us, that words might only spoil, so we walked in silence mostly. When we got to the courting tree and I slowed down, hint, hint, she said, "Come round my house today, Mummy wants to meet you."

"You told her about me then?" I was nervous but pleased at the idea.

"She saw us outside the house yesterday. She said you look a nice boy," Marie grinned.

"Wish she'd tell that to Miss Savage!" I said, referring to the headmistress—yes, that was her real name. "She cornered me in the entrance hall a while back and yelled at me, her face turning purple in a kind of apoplectic fit, *Get that hair cut, Carroll, you look like something that crawled out of the gutter!*"

"Our school seems to have a thing about the 'gutter' and 'gutter boys'," said Marie. "But you'd never see anyone like that in the school, we're so carefully vetted. So what are they worried about, I wonder?"

"This is an industrial city, so I suppose there's always the threat of Communism at the gates! You know, *free beer for all the workers!*"

"*When the Red revolution comes along*! The Red scare!"

We sneered and laughed but yet I liked the cosy sense of *earned* privilege of the grammar school, primarily dependent *not* on your folks' money or your postal address, but your very own individual efforts in the eleven-plus qualifying exam. Only hard luck if you were one of the minority, it was, who actually *wanted* to go to grammar school but failed the qualify'n'. If your parents couldn't fork out the full fees then it was a near-death experience, at least until you could sit the review exam at fourteen.

"My daddy's only a glorified workie," said Marie. "Runs his own business, haulage contractor. He earns plenty of dough, think that's what attracted Mummy to him in the first place, certainly wasn't his looks, '*Wee Reggie, he's so ugly!*' she jokes." Marie laughed with the casual cruelty of adolescence. Yet her honesty impressed me.

"My da's a senior clerk at the Gas Board," I told her. "Went in there straight from school in the nineteen-twenties. Studied seven years at night school for the Chartered Institute of Secretaries. I don't think he's ever liked his job that much, he's a bit of a literary man on the sly, short stories he neatly hand-writes in school jotters and files in a corner of the bookcase. All drawn from everyday life, the characters he's met along the way, Lyn Doyle kind of thing. Da knows Joseph Tomelty who wrote *The McCooeys* for the wireless."

"Oh, brill!" said Marie. "I don't think my daddy's ever read a book in his life. But he keeps Mummy, Thelma and me in the style we've grown accustomed to, so nobody's complaining really. *Where there's mook there's braass, laad!*"

"That's a good impression of Tom Courtenay in the *Long Distance Runner*," I said. It wasn't really, it was a bad one, but cute as anything.

I felt nervous as we turned into Marie's close. The immaculate semi-detached houses with their uniform frozen facades, their drives and garages—the French *gar-age*—and neat front gardens, seemed to challenge visitors: *Are you good enough to enter herein?* They were a judgement on the council estates or ratty Victorian street warrens that housed the city's broad masses. Our house, an old redbrick semi stuck down an ashy unmade lane the wrong side of Antrim Road, seemed sunken and seedy, a dirty secret in comparison with the proud social progress of Jacaranda Close.

I followed Marie in the front door. The hall was bright and uncluttered, with dove-grey, wall to wall fitted carpet that also covered the staircase. The house smelt warm and clean, like one of the big furniture stores in the city centre.

Mummy came through from the kitchen at the back. Perfect bobbed blonde hair, carefully made-up attractive face and fashionable clothes, she looked almost young enough to be a big sister to Marie. I had to blink at her to believe my eyes.

"Hel-lo, everybody!" she called out, smiling with those appealing kind of big teeth with a pink slice of upper gum. Instinctively I wanted to flirt with her.

"Mummy, this is Paul!" said Marie. "I told him you'd like to meet him!"

"*Hel*-lo, Paul," she said. "I looked out the window yesterday afternoon, wondering what was keeping Marie at school and there she was, kissing one of the Beatles out in the street!"

I blushed as her widening eyes scrutinised me. She said, "Oh, no need to feel embarrassed, Paul, I could see you were a nice boy, not too old and you were wearing the school uniform. It's just that you're the first, Marie's never had a boyfriend before."

"Not a steady one," Marie corrected her, not wishing to sound unattractive or uncool.

"Come on through to the kitchen and have a cup of tea, Paul," said Mummy.

"Thank you, Mrs Kelly."

"Call me Eileen, I'm not forty yet," she said.

The spacious fitted kitchen overlooking the lawn at the back was bright with the afternoon sun, with a pine table where we took tea and buttered brack. Not like our rat-hole of a scullery, I thought.

"You live close by, Paul?" said Eileen.

"Off Antrim Road," I replied cagily and dropping my voice added, "Nettle Soup Lane." I was sure Eileen's face fell at the street name with its suggestions of paupery or a gypsy encampment, though she just wagged her pretty bobbed blonde head and looked puzzled, no one ever seemed to have heard of our shabby-genteel backwater, which was always a relief to me.

"Tell us about your people, Paul," said Eileen.

"Dad's an accountant at the Gas Board, been there all his working life; there's Mum, and I have an older sister, Audrey, doing teacher training at Stranmillis."

I wanted to impress Eileen but my family sounded so boring: public service, the conscientious husbanding of resources at work extending naturally into our frugal domestic life. The Kellys were entrepreneurial, thrusting spenders in the vanguard of a new consumerism. There were quite a few "business" families like them represented in the intake at the grammar school, the progeny of shopkeepers and tradespeople, always with pocket money to spend at break-time in the tuck shop on coconut snowballs and Tayto crisps, so they could never finish their school dinners. And usually a bit thick with it. Funny how I managed to feel inferior to them whilst looking down on them at the same time.

"Oh, Marie is thinking of teaching, aren't you, dear?" said Eileen.

"If I can't think of anything else, that is," said Marie sulkily; Mummy seemed determined to make her sound square. "Teaching the wee ones, maybe. Wouldn't fancy having to control stroppy teenagers in a classroom!"

A door slammed in the hall.

"Speaking of which…" Eileen's eyes swivelled in that direction. "Right on cue!"

"Thelma!" said Marie. "The dear little sister from hell!"

She came flouncing in, a bedraggled, lumpish thirteen-year old in the school uniform, though I'd never noticed her among the hundreds of uniformed girls; it didn't help that I was myopic and never wore my glasses. She glowered at the stranger in her kitchen.

"Thelma, this is Paul!" said Marie sharply.

To my relief, the pouty, heavy dark face looking me up and down registered somewhere between indifference and mild acceptance and she spared me a grudging nod.

"Ah'm starvin'!" she announced. "What are yous atin'? Hi, can I have a piece?"

"Speak properly, dear!" said her mother.

Dark and chubby, Thelma looked quite unlike Marie; two years younger, she already sported a large bosom. Coming to the table, she thickly buttered a slab of the currant brack and fothered it into her, shedding crumbs about her blubber lips.

"What are *you* lookin' at?" she challenged Marie rudely from a full mouth.

"Not much!" said Marie, well able for the brat, and looked away stiffly. "Paul, I'll see you out. Daddy will be home for tea in a minute. You can meet him another time!" she grinned knowingly—*meet Mr Ugly*!

"Bye, Eileen!" I'd never called an older woman like that by her Christian name before, without an "Auntie" in front of it; it was kind of forward and I experienced a small *frisson*.

"Paul, you can come and babysit Thelma with Marie," said Eileen. "That would be most helpful!"

"I'm not a flippin' *baby*!" Thelma protested, while managing to sound just like one.

"*Language*, Miss!" Eileen waved an admonitory forefinger in her younger daughter's sullen mug.

Marie and I stood on the polished red front doorstep breathing the early evening air. She leant into me and we kissed.

She said, "See what I mean about Miss Piglet?"

"Oh, she's young," I said, all of sixteen years myself. "I have a twisted sister of my own, I'm well used to it, except mine's older than me and should know better by now!"

A last clinging kiss till Marie broke off and glancing round the cul-de-sac said, "They'll all be gawping at us from behind the net curtains! Ring you later, wee-lad!"

"See ya, wee-doll!"

4

We spent ages talking on the phone to each other, rambling, witty chats, neither of us big talkers but we squeezed some interest out of every little thing.

We both loved the bluesy music that was coming up, the Yardbirds, the Animals and local group Them.

"We must go and see Them at the Jazz Club," she said.

"I'm not much of a dancer," I confessed straight out; the Twist had come in but the fashion was still strong for the horrible puppet gyrations of jiving and I couldn't do it.

"Oh, nobody dances when Them's playing," she said. "They're too cool for that, you're supposed to just *listen*!'

"That'll suit me! Marie, you must come along to our group practice on Saturday, Frankie's at Jordanstown."

"I'd love to!" she said.

Marie and I had a couple of dates before that. There was the local Capitol cinema we could walk to—not that we saw much of the film, it was a quiet Wednesday night and we ensconced ourselves in a back seat in the dark and kissed for two and a half hours through the Pearl & Dean ads, the B-film, Pathe*tic* News and the big picture, John Wayne I think.

We felt really close afterwards as we walked up the Cavehill Road with our arms round each other. The bay windows of Jacaranda Close shone warm and golden in the soft blue, neverending twilight of the June evening. The manicured lawns and the rose bushes smelt of fresh hosings. We stood by her gate kissing a bit more, it was insatiable, addictive.

"Are you ready for Monster Girl on Friday?" she asked me. Mummy and Daddy were going out and we were babysitting Thelma.

"I told you, I'm already living with her," I said. "Your wee sister will be a walkover after Audrey Carroll!"

I got there at eight on the warm, sunny Friday evening, the glory of the weekend stretching ahead, with the feeling of life opening out to me at last in the beautiful dream-sensations of a summer love.

At the door of 14 Jacaranda Close I was met by Marie's arms and lips. I had a rosy vision of being married to her in a not-too-distant future, being met like this coming home from work every evening.

"Come on through!" She pulled my hand towards the sitting room. "They won't be back till twelve. Thelma's gone to her room, she's not allowed down here with us."

The smile that was half-girl, half-woman, like her application of eye shadow and mascara, shone from her face like the love of life itself, the simple profound joy of being alive and female—what more could you ask for?

Her hair was freshly washed and blow-dried, soft and shiny. She smelt sweetly of shampoo and perfume and the underlying natural heady scent of *girl*. She wore a sleeveless blue denim dress with big buttons all the way down the front and her legs below it, *the legs,* were summer-bare, smooth and tan, sticking out in front of us as we settled on the sofa and moved into our habitual clinch. Being here in charge of the house gave you a feeling of licence.

But the sitting room door burst open and Thelma stood there gawping at us like a half-witted intruder.

"I thought you had homework to do, Miss?" said Marie. She would make a teacher all right.

"Finished!" said Thelma. She was already in her nightie, a skimpy pink Baby Doll one, what a sight.

Marie said, "Do you not need to put on a dressing gown when you come downstairs?"

"It's too hot!" said Thelma. She looked at me boldly. "Are you Charlie's friend?"

"Charlie Hutton? Aye!"

"Charlie's lush!" she said. "Can you introduce me to him sometime?"

"If you like…"

"No!" Marie intervened. "You're too young for sixth-form boys, Thelma. Just find someone your own age. Don't pester Paul and his mates; run on up to your room now and settle into your Enid Blyton. Paul and I are a *couple,* in case you didn't notice and we have things we need to *talk about.*"

"'*Talk about'*! A new name for gropin'?" she called out before exiting hastily, slamming the door behind her.

Marie was on her feet, calling out harshly, "*What* did you say?" And chased after her into the hall.

There was a baby elephant commotion on the stairs and landing as Thelma secured her getaway, Marie's hard, brisk step in pursuit. A bedroom door slammed.

Marie's knuckles hammering. "Open this door!" Then after a minute. "Right, *you are in trouble*! *I'*m telling Mummy and Daddy what you said, your filthy language, and you will be *in for it* now, Miss!"

Thelma's wailing retort from behind the door: "Then *I'll* tell *them you* and your boyfriend were carrying on on the settee when I unsuspectingly walked in on you!"

"You wee fibber, I'll kill you!"

Marie came back, flustered. "Honestly, that wee bitch!"

"Och, let her go," I said. "She'll grow up one day. Sit on my knee?"

First she knelt down and stuck a record on the blue gramophone under the bookshelves in the chimney breast recess; it was the Tymes, *So Much in Love,* and I cried out in joy, "Oh, perfect choice, Marie!"

She closed the curtains on the lingering daylight over the close and settled herself on my knee. The sweet and tender enchantment of the music washed over us as we kissed on the sofa. The lovely roundness of her bottom squirmed into my lap.

She broke off gently and said, "Would you like tea? Mummy left a supper tray for us."

"I'm *so hungry for love...*" I sang a snatch of the Searchers.

Marie said, "Listen, she's still moving about up there, going to the loo. She might conk out soon with a bit of luck. We'll have our supper now."

She got up and smoothed down her denim dress, turned on the light and fetched the supper tray from the kitchen. We were sealed into comfort with our pot of tea, sandwiches and sponge cake. Eating together was another shared intimacy; there was so much to enjoy with a girlfriend.

"Gone quiet upstairs at last," Marie breathed. "Shall we watch *The Avengers*?"

"Okay."

She turned on the telly, turned off the ceiling light and we sat holding hands in the ghostly luminosity of the black and white screen. I had no real interest in the silly spy drama or whatever it was, the bowler-hatted toff and leather-clad cat-woman with her ju-jitsu acrobatics, frankly ridiculous, but I sat there in a state of utter contentment, filled with the magic of the summer night and my summer girl beside me on the couch.

We heard the car in the drive just after the TV transmission shutdown at midnight. The front door opened, voices, man, woman; Mummy and Daddy were back. They came in the room, Eileen ultra-glam in her evening gown that flowed like surf about her ankles; they had been to a dinner dance.

It was my first meeting with Reggie Kelly, short rotund body and football-shaped head, waddling in a penguin suit. Bald egg head, big glasses, rugged more than ugly, he wasn't a Quasimodo or anything. He stuck out his big hand and shook mine powerfully, like a test of my manliness or a blow of the cane back at primary school.

"And this is Paul!" I think he approved; I looked so harmless, I suppose. Which I was, grammar school boy and someone he could trust with his daughter. "He looks like whadayamacallim outta the Beatles! Aye, another Paul! D'ye like football? Whaat team?"

I didn't like to say I hated football and indeed all sports except rounders. I nodded dishonestly and said the name of a local team, "Glentoran."

"Okay, okay! Everyone has his cross to bear, ha-ha-ha-ha! Linfield, me! The blues and nothin' but the blues! Ha-ha-ha-ha!" The belly-laugh revealed a single upper front tooth, nicotine-stained, stuck there like a rusty nail.

"*The blues...*" For a dislocated moment his words gave me an image of Howlin' Wolf or Muddy Waters, the old blues singers that were enjoying a revival, older men not unlike Reggie Kelly. But no, he meant Linfield's colours, Conservative and Unionist true-blue. My brain went stupid meeting people for the first time.

Marie and Eileen—how alike they were, daughter and mother—were looking on in wry amusement.

"He'll bore the pants off you now, Paul, with his blessed football," said Eileen.

"Daddy, we play Rugby at the Academy, the gentleman's game. We leave soccer to the hooligans!" Marie chided.

Daddy gave her a look—I noticed how much he resembled his other, younger daughter, Thelma, the coarse-and-uglies of the Kelly clan! Yet ugly-lovely in a way, like frogs. Then he turned to me and said, "Paul, I'll take ye down to the Linfield Supporters' Club on Sandy Row one night for a dhrink, give us a break from these here weemin!"

My heart sank at the prospect but I feigned a manly enthusiasm. I could see Reggie had the drink taken tonight and maybe, please God, would have forgotten all about this invitation with tomorrow's hangover.

Marie saw me to the door. We stood on the step a minute kissing goodnight. We were becoming a joined-at-the-lips couple.

5

We took the green diesel train from York Road station, beating out under the shadow of Jennymount Spinning Mill, past the hummocks of the refuse tip on the seaward side, and out under the grey sky along the Lough shore. Down below us, waves washed the sloping wall of the railway embankment; the tall bridges of the shipyard gantries stood up beyond. Inland, across the canal, the flat, ordered rows of prefabs ran endlessly beside the railway.

Four of us and two guitars, we had an old-fashioned compartment to ourselves on the mid-morning train, Marie and me, Charlie and Mike. We were at it already on the train, harmonising on *Sweet Little Sheila,* the Tommy Roe take on Buddy Holly, while Mike used his hands to beat out the complicated jungle rhythm on the musty seat cushion between his thighs.

It was lovely having Marie singing along there beside me in the window seat, her legs crossed under a summery skirt. She came through strongly and afterwardsCharlie said, "Hi Marie, we could use you on one of those girl-group numbers like the Shangri-Las."

"Och, away on, I'm not *that* good!" she protested.

"Neither are we, it's just about havin' a go."

"A girl in the line-up would be fab," said Mike, "really make us stand out."

"Aye, c'mon Marie," I said, "we'll audition you at Frankie's!"

"Oh my God, what'll I sing?"

"Anything you fancy, long as it isn't more than three chords, so we can play it."

The train left the shoreline at bleak Greencastle halt and burrowed inland between high, steep grass embankments, through a tunnel and under three bridges, to emerge at Whiteabbey station. It was a short run then; after Bleach Green halt the railway divided with the sandstone viaduct of the Portrush line and the other, iron bridge of the Larne line that we crossed, high over the river down in the densely wooded, sinister green gorge of the Valley of Death.

Into Jordanstown station. We got down there, exiting through the ticket barrier by the level crossing gates, turning up Jordanstown Road with the open fields on one side. When the train had gone, snaking away through the patchwork fields below the mountain, you felt the green country silence dropping around you. The sun was struggling out.

Jordanstown had a leafy gentility about it; I'd like to have lived there with its sense of a smaller, kind of village community, nice people in nice houses, cool friends like Frankie and Ralph, and the plenitude of girls I heard you'd meet at the badminton club...At least, I had thought that until Marie.

Ralphy-boy was there at Frankie's, sporting a pink denim shirt and bell-bottom jeans, his thick golden hair over his collar, as long as he could get away with at school. Winningly short and dapper, cheeky grin, the blue eyes lit up when he saw I had Marie in tow and he sang us a snatch of *"Paul and Marie!"* to the tune of *Love and Marriage,* swinging his arms like a conductor till he broke off in a fit of mad, mocking, delighted laughter.

Ralph was full of wicked fun. He wasn't especially musical but he looked cool and was happy to come to the practice and bang on the bongoes, shake a tambourine or maracas, anything not to be left out of the craic.

Frankie shared the roomy house with his father; the mother had died of cancer not long before, the older brother James gone in the Royal Navy. Having to look after himself made Frankie sensible and mature for his age. But he was able to lose himself in his music. The cleaning lady commented, "You sound like Cliff Richard!"

"I'm not *that* good!" he told her modestly.

Frankie was a prolific songwriter, sixty songs to date, he counted. His idol was Buddy Holly, a big influence on the Beatles.

Charlie and I were more Buddy Guy, *First Time I Met the Blues*. We had seen John Mayall and the Bluesbreakers playing in a club in Bournemouth when we were over there washing dishes in the beach cafes the previous summer.

"Pretentious crap!" Frankie dismissed the blues revival. "Give me Bobby Vee any day!" Frankie spoke with a kind of mid-Atlantic accent, though the family hailed from Birmingham.

"*Bouncy-bouncy!*" Charlie and I chorused in girlie falsetto.

Frankie gave us a dirty look; making music was a serious business to him. He was the undisputed leader of the group, in truth the only real talent among us lads, the rest of us in it for the craic; if you loved music why not have a go yourself? It was simply fun. And incidentally, we liked Bobby Vee too, a lot. *Bobby Vee Meets the Crickets* was one of our favourite LP records.

Frankie was the last one of us to comb his hair over his brow in a Beatles' fringe. He was good-looking but never narcissistic; he didn't bother with fashion or bohemianism, the music was all.

The other female there that Saturday morning was his steady girl Jennifer, pretty in a pallid, willowy way, bouffant blonde hair surmounting her soft features, long slim legs descending from her skirt. I had asked her out once back in the fourth form, before she was Frankie's girl; I stopped her in the crowd after class one day, blurted out an invitation to the cinema and got a straight "No" for an answer, no "thanks" either. I wasn't hurt or anything; once a girl registered her lack of interest in me I went straight off her, like a light-switch turned off, no hard feelings or anything, just a complete indifference as if she no longer existed. I only wanted a girl who'd love me with everything she'd got, and I would love her in return. I was a bit of a narcissist, I suppose.

We practised in Frankie's big living room. The piano and drums were there and a microphone borrowed from his dad's golf club. Frankie had connected his acoustic guitar to an old wireless set, producing a mellow amplification. His dad was away on a business trip but he was asking to listen in on one of our practices soon with a view to *managing* us. That was thrilling; I could just picture our group on *Top of the Pops*, our bright young faces projected into every living room in Britain and Ireland!

That morning we kicked off with the Beatles' *I Saw Her Standing There*, its wake-up, powerful beat with my baritone under Frankie's tenor, Marie coming in strong on the chorus, the piano, guitars and drums bashing away and Ralph adding his tambourine and *woo-hoos!* to the melee of sounds.

Jennifer Grimshaw—"Pretty Grim" as Frankie wryly named her when she'd put him in a mood—sat there demurely pretty, a near-smile hovering close to her lips. But in no time at all quiet little Marie was up jumping about and singing along. The music animated her and brought out this other extravert entertainer who lived inside her.

We played it all back on the reel-to-reel tape recorder, it was exciting like hearing your own record; we were in good fresh form that morning, the singing got you high and it sounded wonderful.

"Marie coming through a treat there!" said Frankie. "How do you fancy being our girl singer?"

She shook her head. "I'm not photogenic enough," she protested dully.

"*Singer,* I said—not photographer's model," Frankie insisted. "You look cool anyway. What do you think, lads?"

"*Hey, Super-girl!*" Mike serenaded her.

Charlie looked her up and down like a horse at a fair, ticking off her attributes: "Vocals, hair, clothes, legs, face—you'd be just right standing up there in front of the group!"

I said to Marie, "You know Ruby and the Romantics, *Our Day Will Come,* don't you?"

Marie nodded—I'd seen it in her record collection and everyone knew and secretly loved, in their heart of hearts, the old-fashioned, beautiful song. Charlie fiddled a little on the piano keys, struck out the opening chords and we were off, united at once in its richly sentimental, romantic vision, Marie opening the lead vocal with such quiet sincerity and assured modest power, the tender, reflective poignancy of lyric and melody playing out, that seemed to say it all for young love, *for Marie and me!* I was *sen*t like some swooning fan, her voice was so pure and natural, so warm and true, it spoke so directly to the heart.

As we played it back on the tape recorder I held her hand, I was trembling with emotion; when it finished we all looked at Frankie.

"You're hired, Marie!" he said. "Your voice has such clarity and most of all you sing the words as if you really mean them, that's the difference between a good singer and an average one."

Marie stood there, the cynosure of eyes, looking bemused but visibly grown in stature, a shining new star.

It was Buddy Holly time next; at Frankie's request Marie took the lead vocal on *Well All Right* with the three guitars pounding out the driving, bittersweet chord changes.

That led into a medley of Frankie compositions: the ballads *Missing You* and *Heart on a String* really did capture the pathos of teenage love, the story of Frankie and Jennie. Then the mood changed with the up-tempo *Sugar Lips and Shapely Hips*—could that really be all about his reserved, willowy Jennifer?!

The cleaning lady had left us a luncheon of sandwiches and coffee we took on the back patio in the sunshine, Afterwards we sat on, smoking cigarettes.

"Anyone fancy a cider?" said Frankie. "There's a flagon of scrumpy left over from Dad's party for the golf club, it's the real thing from the Spanish Rooms on the Falls."

We sweated under the hot sun, drinking the thick bronze liquid from tall, straight glasses.

"Like sucking warm vomit through a sweaty sock!" said Charlie.

Marie squeezed her eyes shut pulling a face at the first taste, but then seemed to take to it. It went straight to your head, got you happy in minutes.

"As if the bit of your brain that worries has gone AWOL," said Mike. "And you're adrift on a sea of mindless contentment, ahhh!"

"They say scrumpy kills off the brain cells," said Ralph.

Ralph made some phone calls and the local crowd came round, boys and girls, armed with more booze. It was a dream come true; here I was at last, in with the Jordanstown set, relaxing in their aura of privileged refinement and the sort of sexiness that went with it.

I was conscious of the girls' warm, well-modulated voices and eager expressions, a prevalence of soft, bouncy hair, tanned legs in tennis skirts. The worse for drink by now, I found myself standing next to one of them, chatting her up.

Selena was struggling with her O level English: "I just don't know what to do with my gerunds! I never will! Help me somebody, please!"

It was my cue: "Stop worrying about them!" I counselled her. "Write the way you think and speak, just get it down on the page, that'll ring true and impress the examiner far more than your gerunds ever could!"

"Oh, do you really think so?" She gave me a lovely trusting, blinking look. She was so clean-limbed, fair and wholesome, sweating lightly, straight off the courts. A classy bird and interested in *me*, I could tell!

But with a jolt I remembered *you've got a girl, Paul*: a doty-pet called Marie. Guiltily, I wrenched myself away from Selena and cast about desperately for Marie in the animated, babbling crowd.

A couple of the local lads who'd dropped by were somewhat less than refined. One I knew a bit, Guy, a talented guitarist, was a happy-go-lucky bloke who had failed all his school exams and gone into the Royal Navy as a rating— swabbing the decks, swilling rum and shinning up the rigging to the crow's nest, all that kind of thing, just short of walking the plank—who now larded his newly anglicised speech with compulsive effing: "Ah'm facking telling you now, you never facking saw the facking likes of them Hindu women for…"

You can guess the rude rest. And I was no innocent, I had read the paperback *Kama Sutra* that was doing the rounds of the school toilets of the day, great to learn of other cultures. Guy was from a posh Jordanstown home but he couldn't stop effing now, even in front of his parents and *the vicar*, Ralph told me.

Then there was Billy, tall and good-looking, not a bad fellow in spite of his Unionist views like the threat posed by university students and Communist waiters in Chinese restaurants to "our wee Ulster". He remained psychologically in the Teddy boy era still, his black hair brushed back in a high crown, oil-slicked into a d-a (duck's arse) after his idol, Liverpool's own Elvis: "Could yous not include a Billy Fury medley in your set?" he insisted of our group. "From *Wondrous Place* to *Halfway to Paradise*. Billy's still the greatest. Even the Beatles weren't good enough to be his backing group. Hi Marie, bet you like Billy Fury? All the girls are dyin' about him, I know!"

Marie nodded, politely noncommittal, why ruin someone's day?

The guitars struck up, saving us from further drunken fatuities and we sang Peter, Paul and Mary. Sausages sizzled on the barbecue. It felt like California and our group raised a Beach Boys' chorus, the heavenly nostalgic harmonies of *All Summer Long*.

Before you knew what, it was evening, a mellowing and golding of the light that seemed fused with the scrumpy and Harp lager glow. By this stage the lads all seemed awfully likeable and witty and the girls irresistibly charming and pretty. I put aside my guitar and put my arm round Marie and kissed her. All I wanted really was to kiss Marie all the time.

Frankie and Jennifer had gone upstairs. Marie and I followed hand-in-hand up the broad staircase and along the bedroom passage. Muffled sounds, bedsprings, gasps, came from behind a bedroom door, must be Frankie and Jennie. Another door stood open, with a single bed neatly made; it looked like absent sailor brother James's room, shipshape, with a model yacht. I closed the door behind us and we lay down together on the single bed against the wall.

We kissed till we passed out.

When we woke up the room was in darkness. The house had gone unnervingly quiet. Marie found the light and consulted her watch.

"Look at the time!" she exclaimed. "We're going to miss the last train!"

It was a scramble then to get out and down the Jordanstown Road. We made it just as the glow-worm length of carriages pulled into the station. We sat in an empty compartment, our reflections looking back at us from the blackened window as we went out over the night fields.

"We fell asleep," said Marie. "We were pissed."

"I've got a headache from the scrumpy." I only acknowledged it now. "And a burning thirst."

"You left your guitar behind," said Marie.

"Safe with Frankie," I said, "till the next practice. Hi, you were brilliant, wee-girl. You're one of the group now! *Lead singer* actually!"

"If you all say so. I thought I was crap!"

"That's crap. Marie, you have star quality. You've got a powerful voice and you look the part and all."

The train emerged from the dark of the deep cutting and the lights of Belfast were sprinkled out like stars before us.

"I'm awful late getting home," said Marie worriedly. "Mummy and Daddy will be furious!"

"You can blame the boyf for keeping you out past your bedtime. I'll apologise and suck up plenty to Eileen and Reggie, it'll be okay."

"They think you're an awful nice, good kind of fella who'd always look after their wee Marie."

"Yeah, like getting you pissed on scrumpy, and us falling into bed together?"

"Well, you didn't exactly have to twist my arm."

It was ten past eleven on the Belfast station clock and York Street was unnervingly quiet in the late dark. We waited five minutes at Duncairn Gardens to see if a last bus would materialise. No one else at the stop. Traffic dying out. Sinking feeling.

"Oh, this is hopeless!" said Marie. "C'mon, we'll walk it!"

We cut across Bentinck Street and up the steep cobbled brow of Lower Canning Street on to North Queen Street. The

Moyola Fish Salon on the corner of Upper Canning Street was in darkness. A bad sign. On along North Queen Street, our hurried footfalls resounded in its enclosed dark, narrow channel that seemed to curve away down forever. At last we emerged on Limestone Road and began the ascent to Cavehill Road.

It was midnight when we got to Jacaranda Close. A light burned in the hallway of number 14. Eileen came to the door in her dressing gown and curlers, looking put-out and severe.

I blurted out the lines I'd prepared on the long night-walk: "Ah'm awful sorry, Eileen, the practice ran over, we lost track of the time, but hey, your Marie is a star and she will be joining the line-up now as lead singer, with your permission of course!"

There was hoarse smoker's laughter behind her as Daddy appeared. "Long as music is all yous are playin' at till this hour of the night!" he cracked.

"*Reggie!*" Eileen glanced round at him in snapping disapproval, then confided in us, "Someone here has been on the Scotch! Never you mind his crudity!"

I felt like kissing Reggie for putting Eileen on our side. I bade a cheery, wholesome, "Goodnight, everybody!" and turned away homeward with a guilty stiff, measured tread.

6

"That was good at Frankie's yesterday," she said. "Especially kissing on the bed!"

I blushed into the telephone receiver. : "Y-yes. We were drunk!"

"We must do it again soon—get drunk, I mean!"

I gulped.

"Hello?" she said in a smiling voice, teasing me along.

"Yes, I'd like that," I said.

I wasn't totally inexperienced, I had done some courting prior to Marie. Most significantly there was Naomi, the farmer's daughter, next door to Granny's at Islandmagee where I would visit in the school holidays.

It was a couple of years back, I was at that tragic Mr In-Between age, with no friends outside school. I moped about, home alone in the long summer vacation. At least I was reading, Carson McCullers and James Herlihy were favourites, books about lonely young people like me, and I was writing my own literary scraps in a jotter, poems and novel openings, if I got past the title page, that was. I had a penchant for catchy titles: there was *The Sixteenth Summer of Eugene Shannon*—Herlihy meets McCullers—and *All the Merry Morons,* an obvious tribute to Salinger, as well as an attempt to justify my own increasing oddity.

Sometimes I went downtown on my own to catch a matinee at the cinema, Marlon Brando or the latest Elvis film—*Follow That Dream* in which he was a budding writer, I liked that idea, and

Flaming Star, playing a Native American, versatility in a wooden way but it didn't matter, he was Elvis the King of Rock, larger than life up there for you on the technicolor screen. I had the brushed-back black hair and soft features to model myself on the King, adopting his dark moody persona. The Brando influence, my favourite actor after the late James Dean, lent an intellectual edge to that.

My tormentress Audrey had thankfully gone away with a crowd from the sixth form, across the water to can peas at Smedley's of Wisbech. At last I could enjoy being an only child but I think my kindly ageing parents got fed up with me mooning about the place and as August came in they suggested I take myself off for a short break to Granny's at Islandmagee.

I treated the trip as a bit of an adventure, like the opening to a novel, everything heightened and meaningful with anticipation, David Balfour goes to the House of Shaw. Mine was a living book, the story of my life. The train journey from York Road station continued on past Jordanstown to historic Carrickfergus and thence to Whitehead which with its promenade and swimming pool was the nearest thing to a holiday resort this side of the Lough.

From Whitehead a green country bus took me out along the peninsula of Islandmagee. It was a beautiful remote patchwork landscape stretched out on the water but the atmosphere turned sinister somehow as the bus penetrated its hinterland. You remembered the place's history of witchcraft.

In 1711 eight local women had been found guilty of witchcraft and sentenced at the county court. But that was not the end of witches on Islandmagee; now, two centuries on, the newspapers reported that evidence of a contemporary black mass had been discovered in a cave of the rugged Gobbins cliffs.

I got down at the stop for Granny's. The bus pulled away with a decisive roar and I was the only person on the lonely, tree-arched road. I entered the old farm loaning, the lane that climbed up to Granny's cottage.

Making my way up the half-overgrown summer loaning I felt my solitude as a kind of heroism. I was young Paul Carroll on a mission to the middle of nowhere. With its history of witchcraft, smuggling, and the revolutionary activity of the brave United Irishmen of 1798, the remote locality contained all the ingredients of classic adventure in the tradition of Robert Louis Stevenson, with shades of Edgar Allan Poe mystery and imagination! I carried, slung from one shoulder, the army-surplus satchel that served me as a schoolbag but now contained a change of clothing, toilet bag, novel and notebook. The young adventurer, I floated freely on the spirit of life's endless possibilities.

At the head of the loaning the wind was blowing in the heavy dark-green foliage of a stand of tall deciduous trees that sheltered the farm buildings. My mood changed abruptly as I felt the chill breath of the sea coming up over the Gobbins cliffs below; a shudder of supernatural menace went through me like a curse and I had a momentary inclination to turn back whence I'd come. But no, that would be worse than the spooky strangeness here, I decided; it would be a defeat of the imagination.

At the cottage where Granny abided, in the shadow of the tall old farmhouse, I opened the gate in the low whitewashed picket fence and went up the path through the summer flowerbeds to the front door. It was all so neat and attractive, like an illustration from a book of fairy tales. The door opened and my stout little grey-haired grandmother was smiling and holding out her arms to me, "Ah, Paul!"

She hugged me to her plumpness in the black widow's weeds she lived in, her massive softness and rosewater fragrance bringing a rush of happy childhood memories to my brain.

Inside the cottage there was a single living-room with doors leading off to the scullery, toilet and two bedrooms. The living room, pleasantly cool in this summer weather, smelt of cleanliness and baking. Her home had the uncluttered feeling of simple traditional country living; Granny was not someone who gathered possessions about her. Widowed at only twenty-five with two little daughters, she was at least comfortable for life on her clergy-widow's pension and had never remarried. She had moved around a bit, down to Drogheda, back up to Ballintoy, and now here, to be close to her younger daughter Mary. She had always lived in old country cottages that I thought of as "granny cottages", like this one.

Every night she said her prayers aloud kneeling at her bedside; through the day she would hum a Sankey-Moody hymn as she went about her chores or rested by the fireside, her small shoe tapping out the rhythm on the linoleum. She would not entertain a television set in her home, the very idea of sitting there goggling at a screen when you should be up and about your endless domestic chores.

Visiting Granny's was to step back into a quieter, simple homely past. I was beginning to resist its cosiness of childhood days for the wilder promise of the teenage years. But once I had got here and was drinking a cup of her tea, I was already settling back into the magic of Granny-land.

After a soup lunch we sat out on deckchairs in the backyard sunshine.

"And how are Mammy and Daddy?" she enquired.

"The best thanks now. Daddy wasn't so well for a while, he got wheezy on our stay at White Park Bay in July and we had to come away early."

"The cold, damp climate of that north coast would put you in an early grave; I was glad to move away from it," said Granny.

"Mammy and Daddy met each other up there, didn't they?" I said. "The place has sentimental value for them."

"Aye indeed," said Granny. "Your daddy was staying at Elsie and Willie's and he saw your mammy for the first time in Lisnagugnogue church. On that Sunday afternoon the girls and I were down at the Slough pool at Dunseverick harbour when your daddy turned up for a swim, and the rest is history, as they say!"

I was intrigued by these odd flashbacks of my parents' early days together. Old snaps, 1930s, pictured the two of them in various seaside holiday settings, Termonfeckin or Bray, though always fully dressed, looking like film stars, he very dark and striking, with the big straight nose and wavy black hair, rower's blazer and white trousers, she pale, strawberry blonde, a girl still, with the gracious smiling charm of a clergy-daughter, posing elegantly, raincoat open, her hand resting inside it on the curve of her hip.

Later photos, 1940s into 1950s, showed Audrey with bucket and spade in the sand around their feet, then I the baby growing up, the four of us on holiday, posing in front of a converted railway carriage we stayed in at Ballycastle, our parents looking middle-aged now, Daddy wrinkly, grey and rumpled, the worse for wear, in declining health but smiling in round horn-rims; Mammy bespectacled too, her body heavier and face careworn with parenthood, though still with that air of the parsonage, a benevolent kind of superiority.

Granny had acquired that aura too, a simple farm girl turned parson's missus. She was asking after Audrey. "And your sister away in England now!" she exclaimed. "The young ones get around these days, I'm telling you!"

"Students can earn big money canning peas in Smedley's factory," I told her. "They have to work long hours, all-night shifts—gives Audrey big biceps for beating me up when she comes home!" I half-joked.

"You must miss your sister, gone all summer like that?" said Granny.

"Not too much."

Granny didn't detect the irony in my voice.

The back garden of the farmhouse next door was adjacent to ours. A young girl came out wielding a full laundry basket.

"Hello, Naomi!" Granny called out to her.

My heart lurched as the girl, in a faded cotton summer frock, turned her head to look over the fence at us. She was beautiful in a strange gypsy way, eyes dark and deep-set in an olive-skinned, intense, bony face, her lank dark hair framing it.

I was smitten from the moment I first laid eyes on Naomi. I watched her pegging the washing up on the line and go swinging back into the house with the empty basket, her movements deft and purposeful like a little housewife.

I kept an eye on the door, hoping she might come out again. And sure enough, not long afterwards she reappeared with more wet washing piled in her basket. She was looking over the fence at us. Was she looking at me? My heart beat up hopefully.

Granny called out to her again, "Is your Mammy any better, Naomi dear?"

"She's in her bed," Naomi replied. "She's getting up for a while later."

"Well, I can see you are a big help to her, you're a great girl altogether!" said Granny. She turned to me and explained, "Mrs Blackhall has not been at all well lately."

I imagined the coal-black eyes over the fence might be taking me in, we were just the right age for each other. But could you ever really tell with a girl? Apart from the odd bold one they were so separate and far removed from us lads. Could you ever really know a girl?

"Naomi, this is my grandson Paul," Granny introduced us.

We looked stupidly at each other, boy and girl of an age, like dumb animals over the fence. To look at, you might have taken the girl for a poor tinker's daughter, yet there was a sort of refinement of old nobility about the brow, the cheekbones and the aquiline profile. I told myself she must be a descendant of some ancient dispossessed aristocracy.

She turned back to her chores and I observed her swift, sure movements as she bent down and stretched up to hang out the washing. In strange intuitive flashes I pictured her as a magical being out of mythology or fairy tales.

7

After tea that evening I took a walk down the loaning that continued through the open fields at the back to the Gobbins. The hedged fields sloped to the edge of the cliffs, with not another soul in sight. It was the solitude that made you feel special in the country, as if you owned the land, or were the only boy in the world. But I was a teenager now and another part of me longed for company, for friends my own age, for...a girl?

Over my shoulder I caught a glimpse of someone following some way behind, the figure of a girl, the blowy, pale summer frock and long dark hair. Naomi! I slowed down to let her catch up with me. My heart thudded sickeningly; what would I say to her? Half of me wanted to run and hide.

I came out from the lane on to a hay-cut field that ended at the clifftop. Under a dull sky the Irish Sea stretched away towards Scotland. I waited there pretending to admire the view. The opaque grey-green water came running in, white-crested wave upon wave, breaking with a thump away under me at the foot of the tall cliffs.

I felt the atmosphere tainted by my awareness of the caves in the cliffs below, where the black mass had been celebrated. *Hail Satan, Prince of Darkness!* My lips moved on the hideous words that signified the trashing of Christ's compassion, perceived as a form of weakness; in its place the unimpeded worship of power for power's sake. The evil was a real living force, you only had to look around at all the suffering in the world for confirmation of the fact.

There could be little doubt that there were witches living hereabouts, in the scattered quiet cottages and they would be watching me, *the interloper*. The Carrickfergus trial had not ended an ancient tradition here; rather, it had left an open wound, a bitter grievance and the desire for revenge.

"Paul!"

I jumped at the girl's voice on the wind as she came up behind me. My name sounded special on her lips. I turned to face her, at a complete loss for words.

Face to face in the open landscape, she looked meagre and poor in the washed-out rag of a frock, the faded cardigan about her thin shoulders. The beautiful, bony yellow face could have been Romany.

"Going for a walk?" she said.

"Aye." Full stop. The shyness had taken my tongue. But I turned my full attention on her instead, my whole being focused on hers. I was overcome with the reality of her physical presence.

"Are you looking for the caves?" she asked.

"Aye." Why not? Now I had company they didn't seem so scary.

"C'mon, I'll show you."

We had to walk in single file down the narrow perpendicular cliff path to the shore, a drop on one side, the girl in front of me with her lank hair about her dark nape, her slim brown calves, the small feet nimble and sure as a goat in her old gutties. I stared at her back, this goddess-being, *a girl,* as I hurried after her like a dog.

We came down on to a shore of big smoothly rounded stones that clattered under our stumbling feet, then I followed the girl up over black barnacled boulders to the path that wound round the base of high, dark, rugged-faced cliffs, to the black mouth of a cave.

I followed her inside, it was cavernous, receding into dark shadow; she stood and looked about her as if she were inspecting the interior of a stately home. It was horrible here, dark and dank, smelly and slime-dripping, echoing with the eery whispering sound of the sea. I imagined vampire bats swooping at your hair, or the roof caving in, the tons of earth above your head burying you. But people had lived here once.

"This is where they hold the black mass," she said. "Look, one of the candles!"

She picked it up and held it out to me, a stump of black wax. There was no way I was touching that!

She pointed at the floor. "See the row of small rocks? That marks out the circle, with four candles outside it. The altar is in the middle, it's laid with incense and two candles for the God and Goddess and a chalice for the wine, like in a church."

I made myself look though I couldn't see much.

"Do you believe in magic, Paul?" She lifted the dark hollows of her eyes to my face and I had to look away.

"Dunno, maybe…" I liked to believe in stories, that was all; it made life a lot more interesting.

"*I* do," she pronounced solemnly. "I even know a witch!"

"Who?"

"I'm not allowed to tell. But she lives not far away, I can take you to meet her sometime. Only don't say I told you about her or we'll both be in for it."

I couldn't wait to get out of that black hole in the cliff. Real witches or not, there had to be something queer about anyone who'd choose to spend time in there.

It was a relief to sit out under the sky, on a boulder in the clear evening light, watching the steady advance and retreat of the waves, rattling over the round stones on the beach.

Naomi sat beside me, watching from our rock, perhaps as the original cave-dwellers, the earliest inhabitants of Ireland, had done on this very spot. It was strange having a girl for company. Not just stuck there like a sister at home or a girl in your class at school, you ignored each other like part of the furniture, but *with you*, close to you, this strange…*creature*, she was really, like an alien being. That you wanted more than anything else in the world.

I sneaked glances at her profile as she stared out to sea, the curtain-fall of dark hair with the blade of aquiline nose; the smooth brown kneecaps below the hem of her skirt. It was the *difference* that intrigued and captivated, the natural refinement of *girl*.

I thought of something to say at last. "When can I meet the witch?"

"Maybe tomorrow," she said. "I must get back now, Mummy's not well."

"I'm coming too." The long summer's evening light was failing. The last thing I wanted was to be lost in the bewitched nightfall.

We walked in silence together back up the loaning. The long grass leant out from the banks and grew along the middle of the lane between the cart-tracks, dew-wet on our shoes and legs; Naomi brushed a snail from her calf without fuss—Audrey would have screamed the sky down at the slimy contact and blind crawling ugliness.

We came out on top behind the farm buildings. The girl paused. I wondered should I kiss her; I badly wanted to. But no, I couldn't possibly do that. I was too shy. She might not want me to. How could you ever tell what a girl wanted or not?

"Night-night," she said, soft as the dropping dew, and slipped away through the little gate to her back garden. The pale frock flitted through the twilight and was gone in the back door. My heart sank, as if I had been shut out from life.

But the yellow electric light burned warmly in Granny's window. Inside, the peat fire was lit against the evening chill. An orchestral medley was playing on the Light Programme; the old HMV wireless had a mellow tone, filling the cottage.

"Hot chocolate?" Granny was this lovely reassuring fixture in my life. "Bread and butter?"

"Oh yes, please, Granny!"

She baked her own soda bread, a fresh crusty loaf daily, served warm from the griddle and well-buttered, tasting like cake. Eating supper off a tray on a stool as we sat in the two armchairs by the fireside, I said, "I met Naomi down the loaning."

"Now what was *she* doing there?" said Granny archly.

"Out for a walk, like me."

"Oh, aye?" Granny smiled as if she knew something I didn't. "Well, it's hard on a young girl like that, a child still, having to look after a sick mother and do all the chores for a houseful of men. Her father and brothers are busy out on the farm all day. She could just do with a bit of company her own age."

"She showed me the witches' cave at the Gobbins. There was a black candle they'd left behind."

Granny gave a shudder. "I hope you didn't touch that! Oh, the witches are about here still, two hundred and fifty years on from the trial of that coven of them that cast its evil spell, with witches' knots and poltergeists, on a poor young woman they took against. The devil sees his opportunity in the dreadful malice and spite that's in women, especially towards other women. They never die out, you know, the witches, their badness is handed on down to the next generation; they'll lie low for just as long as it takes then pop up again when they see their chance."

I knew Granny believed in the banshee, she'd often heard it on Rathlin as she lay in her bed at night, a hag keening along the island roads before a death.

"Were there any bad witches out on Rathlin Island?" I asked her.

"Aye, surely. If you crossed one of those ladies they'd put the evil eye on you. But you could protect your house from the eye by hanging an ass's saddle and harness in the window."

I had heard enough and changed the subject. "It's lovely and cosy here, Granny, with the fire lit, I'm glad I came to visit."

"Sure don't I love having you, Paul. Speaking of fires, did I ever tell you about the time my hair caught fire?"

"Tell us anyway."

"On Rathlin. I was a teenager with this lovely long hair, it was all the fashion at the time, the turn of the century, with the long dresses, and I'd wash my hair and dry it in front of the fire at Kenramer. Till one evening, *whoof!* My head was on fire! There was this horrible sizzling and the scorched smell, my lovely shiny chestnut tresses gone up in flames! I was screaming the roof down and Ma came running and threw a basin of water over me. I escaped serious injury, thank God, it was just my beautiful hair ruined. I sat there in a puddle on the kitchen floor, with the burnt hair, crying my eyes out.

"'*Look at ould Burnt-Head!*' they jeered after me on the road to school."

"That wasn't very nice of them," I said.

"No indeed, Paul, people aren't very nice if you've anything wrong with you! It took a while for my lovley hair to grow properly again."

We went early to bed, in our bedrooms at opposite ends of the living room. The last light was draining from the western sky as I looked out the small window. An upstairs light shone in the farmhouse next door. Could that be Naomi's bedroom? I wondered with a quickening heart. I stared up at it a minute willing her to appear but saw no one, before drawing the curtains.

My bedroom was small, like a room in a doll's house, with a patchwork quilt on the narrow brass bed; there were always those touches of olden days about Granny's. I had shared her bed when I was younger, the two of us saying our prayers together kneeling at the bedside, then sleeping "bum to bum" as we called it, giggling at our rudeness in the secrecy of the dark.

I read by the little bedside lamp, George Eliot, *Silas Marner*, a lovely book and just right for Granny's country cottage, I could feel myself back there in time with "the weaver of Raveloe". I always wished I had been born a century earlier; I was visited by strong sensations of those times, especially in the countryside or the older parts of the city. I even thought and sometimes spoke in the archaic language of the Victorian novel.

When I turned out the light in the bedroom the black-darkness enclosed me like a hood. I could hear the wind gathering, rising and falling in the trees. I was drifting into sleep when a bang woke me. The noise, like an item of furniture falling over, brought me wide awake. It came from the empty dark living room between Granny and me. I thought of the poltergeists those witches had sent to plague the poor young woman. It might even have been here at Blackhall Farm, the house was old enough.

I lay there wide awake and terrified, listening hard. Had I dreamt the bang? Now I thought I heard an armchair moving next door, castors rolling on the linoleum. The short hairs prickled on the back of my neck. I could hear the ticking of the mantelpiece clock in the living room, matching the beating of my own heart. I lay there frozen with terror.

8

When I drew back the curtains the morning sun climbing in the eastern sky twinkled and flashed through the windblown trees and shimmered their leaf-shadow on my bedroom wall.

Washed and dressed, I took stock of myself in the dressing-table mirror. I wore my school rugby shirt, red with a white collar, over black jeans and baseball boots. I was still a bit of a pudge, the consequence of the 1950s' "body-building" diet, chiefly dairy produce and potatoes, I had been put on after a long run of the childhood illnesses had left me a washed-out weakling. The crown of my black hair stuck up in a short, spiky crewcut, like the teeth of my plastic bebop brush.

"Handsome in a chubby way, like Elvis or Cliff," I told myself, thinking of the impression I would make on Naomi.

And oh God, had big sister Audrey really gone to town on me with the "fat boy" verbal abuse, leaving me with dysmorphia for life, only lucky to avoid a fatal eating disorder.

I went through to the sun-filled living room. There was Granny's home-ground oatmeal porridge and Ormo bakery fresh pan loaf with butter and homemade damson jam and a pot of tea at the table under the window overlooking the backyard.

"You eat up now, Paul, you're a growing lad!" Granny encouraged me.

"A fat lad," I joked.

"Och, nonsense, sure it's only puppy fat, natural in a pedigree. It'll drop off as you galavant through your teens."

She was right, as it happened. The notion of *pedigree* set me up; I was a right wee snob, proud to be a scion of the illustrious Armstrongs of Armagh. It wasn't about money—that was vulgarity, like the sweetie-shopkeepers' sons at my grammar school with their bottomless pocket money. No, I looked to culture, the poets, painters and pianists who came out of the gentry but were likely to die penniless and coughing in some garret.

Granny was just a small-farmer's daughter who had married into the Armstrongs, it was the kind of thing that happened in the Anglican church fold with its socially mixed congregations of gentry and farm labourers; she'd been dispatched to finishing school before wedding my late grandfather, the Reverend Henry Armstrong.

Full of it now—delusions of grandeur if you will—I was buoyed up for the day, master of all I surveyed. After breakfast Granny and I walked down the lane to the little rural housing estate by the main road, where my aunt lived.

Auntie Mary and Uncle Frank were childless but had six cats who occupied the comfortable council house with them. The cats each had a proper human name, a personality and sometimes personality disorders requiring counselling.

"Clarabella's just a bad article!" Aunt Mary declared in frustration with the fat tabby, a bandy bully who gobbled up the other pussies' dinners after she'd scoffed her own in double-quick time. "We've tried everything and she just won't stop! Spoken to her nicely, shouted at her! The other cats, especially Hildegard, hate her, but is Clarabella bothered? Not a bit of it!"

Clarabella looked up at Mary and miaowed, as if she'd understood every word that was said and was either agreeing or protesting her innocence.

Auntie Mary, my mother's younger sister, was like a domestic cat herself, a nice easy one with her purr-miaow and soft, stealthy movements. My ma wasn't keen on her sister for some strange reason, old sibling discord of some kind, certainly nothing in the present that I could make out. And Audrey hated Aunt Mary, *of course,* in keeping with her instinctual mistrust and jaundiced disapproval of all kinds of people, or what you might call *just being a bitch.*

But I *liked* Auntie Mary, the harmless, relaxing way she had about her, like the cats other than Clarabella. Yet my aunt had suffered nervous trouble and mental illness in the past, I knew. There was no shortage of that in the family. It had marked her broad, round-cheeked, pleasant face with a raw, ravaged aspect under the fading red hair.

Uncle Frank Little, son of an Anglican clergyman of County Mayo, was a retired civil servant. He had tried teaching after he came out of Trinity College Dublin, but he was an odd fellow with a severe facial tic and pebble glasses and the youngsters made a monkey of him and a misery of his life till he had to pack the job in.

Frank Little liked his *Reader's Digest* and Player's Please cigarettes and an old, scratched, crackling 78rpm record of the Luton Girls' Choir, *Londonderry Air* he played on an ancient little black wind-up gramophone. He drove an old Morris Minor; he was always supportively at his wife's side in a touching childless relationship. I liked Frank too, the easy way he included me—perhaps he had taught some nice boys of my age—and his satisfied air of contented retirement, the baggy flannel trousers and comfy tobacco-smelling tweed jacket with leather elbow-patches. He had a residual sort of topknot of grey hair above the high corrugated brow, his round horn-rims and toothbrush moustache like relics of the wartime.

"*As a matter of fact, the mater...*" my da would mimic the catchphrase he attributed to Frank, lifted from conversations with him when they had first met. You never heard the rest of that sentence, what Frank was saying about his mother, the alliteration and 1930s' expression was everything.

Da liked almost everybody; I think my mother and sister saw that as a bit of a weakness in him, too soft for his own good. Together they made up for it.

"Did ye just hear that skitter Frank Little sittin' there drinking our tea and contradicting every word Daddy said?"

Audrey fumed after one Sunday afternoon visit from Frank and Mary.

"Aye and Daddy far too nice altogether for the contrary wee wart!" said Ma, her ire aroused too.

"And Frank Little that *mean*!" said Audrey. "You know, I have *never ever* seen him offer his cigarettes around in company. And Uncle Tommy and my Edward sitting there, both of them smokers. Frank Little will be bringing his fags out lit next!"

"Never as much as, 'Have you a mouth on you?' to anybody. Och, sure he's just *dirt*!" said Ma, her last word on the subject.

It was strange, the bitter contempt of those two for the harmless, dacent sort of freak that Frank seemed to me. I didn't get it at all. Was I just too naive and trusting, only seeing the good in everyone, like my da? Probably. I would certainly pay for that softness as I struggled through life.

The two women, Ma and Audrey, would gang up on Da sometimes, feeding off one another in a coven-like ritual persecution of the male. Audrey would start it, a niggling opposition, and draw Ma in, then they'd needle away at him till he blew his top—that consisted of taking himself to the sideboard, opening the drawer and shaking the cutlery box in sheer exasperation. Once I heard him say "Fuck" under his breath—he never swore normally, he was after all married to a clergy-daughter. He never responded by having a go at the women, there was only his mild implosion and the controlled clashing of the cutlery box; he maintained a strict sort of old patriarchal dignity from the Edwardian era: a gentleman didn't lash out like a frustrated woman.

The worst rows at home had been between Ma and Audrey during the girl's pubescence, when she hit a peak of nasty wilfulness, *she would rule the roost,* and there were screaming and scratching matches, so bad that for a time we lived in the shadow of the Asylum as Ma came close to certification. That is no joke; only Da's unfailing kindness and steady support saved our mother from the loony bin.

Back to Islandmagee and that sunny day of the summer holidays, it was hard to imagine such a thing as family discord.

There was Granny and Mary and Frank and me, and the cats, the sleepy little housing estate under a blue and white sky in the remote green countryside. It was a cosy feeling, a homely feminine domain, Frank and I just tagging along happily after the women.

9

Granny picked up her messages from the Spar grocer's on the estate, sliced ham, tomatoes, and we wandered back up the lane to her cottage for lunchtime.

"There's no one about," I said to Granny as we passed under the windbreak of trees at the top. I was looking out for Naomi.

"No, they'll be inside now for dinner, filling their faces with big platefuls of meat and spuds," said Granny. "There's Mr Blackhall, and the two sons, Aeneas and Carson. With Mrs Blackhall not well now, Naomi will be run off her feet waiting on them all like a wee slavey." I heard the tone of her resentment of a woman's lot, the endless thankless servicing of others. That was what my mother had found so hard.

Back in the cottage Granny washed a lettuce from her back garden to have with the ham and tomatoes. There was a dollop of Heinz salad cream, and pan loaf and butter, and the ubiquitous pot of tea. We sat at the table with the door open to the midday sunshine. It was a lovely airy feeling of the countryside and summertime.

"I like being here with you, Granny," I told her.

"Och, do you now, Paul? Well, I like having my grandson's company!"

We didn't talk much, nor feel the need to. Granny had the refined air of the clergy-widow but at heart she was still the simple country girl she had been before she met Grandfather.

There was just this quiet contentment resting between us. After lunch we sat out on the deckchairs in a sunny corner sheltered from the wind. I read my *Silas Marner*; Granny flicked through her *Women's Realm*. She wasn't a serious reader like my mother. Her late father, a farmer and churchwarden, was illiterate.

I liked those women's magazines with their descriptive, cosy little stories, with evocative line drawings. *Women's Realm, Woman* and *Woman's Own, Woman's World*—my mother took them all— with their front cover photo-portraits of attractive women, nameless models of a calm, smiling, natural beauty, wholesome, mature role models for the woman reader. I liked to flick through the magazines, the problems page, fashion and beautification, they were an opening up to me of this world of woman, of aesthetics, relationships and homemaking, an emotional intelligence that got left out of any curriculum I knew of.

Ma had stiffened into withdrawal when I asked about one of the advertisements: "Mum, what's *Nikini*?" There was the image of a young woman, floaty and carefree, but nothing to tell you the nature of the product.

Audrey had to intervene, usefully for once. "It's a new kind of sanitary product, for women's menstruation," she explained sensibly.

I had heard of women's monthly periods or "moons" and their "jam-rags"—anything intimate was made crude like that, the flip-side of prudery. What Audrey told me was fine, sensible, so why the secrecy surrounding a normal, natural, reproductive bodily function?

Ma's prudery came out too with some of the language and scenes "of a sexual nature" on TV, which were fairly restricted in those days.

"Well, I don't think that's very nice," she would say, averting her face from the screen.

There'd be this excruciating embarrassment in the living room; you closed your eyes and prayed the sex would be over quick. In Ma's eyes it was a dirty secret that should be kept that way; that is how I took it anyway and it made me shy away from the whole business. I'd not started wanking like some of the other boys at school and I hated the wet dreams I was beginning to have, that left a telltale stiff white stain on your pyjama bottoms.

Yet I was strongly attracted to girls. A face, a look—not necessarily great beauty: if I had to say what attracted me so instantly to Naomi, it would be her girl's features, yes, but more than that, an indefinable individual special aura surrounding her femininity, something subliminal, sort of magical, that drew me like a magnet.

"There's Naomi!" said Granny. I was lost in my wonderings, *Silas Marner* open on my lap, unread.

I looked up with a thrill; she was pegging clothes out on the line again, her thin back to us, bending and stretching.

"Coo-ee, Naomi!" Granny called and the girl twisted her head round to see us, a half-smile lightening its habitual gravity.

"She has no youth at all, that little one," Granny whispered to me after Naomi had darted back inside. "Why don't you ask her out for a wee walk this afternoon, Paul? That'll give her an excuse to be out in the fresh air in young company for an hour."

Granny's suggestion set me all atremble. I sat there pretending to go on reading my book. At last I said, "When should I ask her out?"

"Try half past two, the dinner will be cleared up by then and she could be back from your walk to give them afternoon tea at four."

"Half an hour's time," I said, looking at my watch. The nervous pain in my stomach grew as I waited there, till I had to go and sit on the toilet. Maybe I could beg off sick?

Then Granny called to me, "You'd better go on now, Paul, while the coast is clear; the men will have gone out to the fields."

I pulled up my knickers, as they say in boxing, washed my hands and splashed my face, raked the plastic spikes of the bebop brush over my scalp and went out, passing Granny in her deckchair, and round to Naomi's back door.

I knocked and waited with thumping heart and churning tummy.

The door opened and she was standing there. She wasn't a smiler but the narrow, dark, aquiline face registered a sort of openness or interest that signalled approval. Instantly the slow-death torture of chronic anxiety lifted from me and I had a pleasing image of myself in her eyes: not the obese monstrosity that Audrey made me feel, but only a bit chubby really, with nice clothes and a nice-looking baby sort of face under the spiky black hair.

I had been rehearsing under my breath the words I would say to her, in case I got dumbstruck on her doorstep and unable to remember them: "Hello Naomi, would you like to come out for a walk?"

But there was no need for them after all. Naomi said, "Hang on, Paul," and went to shout up the stairs, "Ah'm goin' out a wee walk, Mammy, Ah won't be long!"

And in a trice we had exited her garden gate and were dropping down the back loaning to the long dark horizon line of the sea. It was a heady feeling of escape and freedom.

A big black-and-white ship was making its way out of Belfast Lough into the open sea.

"Is that the *Ardrossan*?" Naomi cried, excited perhaps by this vision of a wider world.

I was a landlubber with no idea about ships but I pretended to be thinking hard, I hated to disappoint people or look stupid.

"Think so..." I said safely. She'd see the ships passing every day and would know.

She looked different now in the wide open sea-light. The face, though beautiful to me, was not a young girl's face, but more the face of a woman, a young mother.

Without looking at me she said, "Mind I said I'd show you Peggy Drumm's?"

"Peggy Drumm?"

"Aye, the witch."

"Oh...Aye, I'd like you to..." With Naomi I was like someone still learning to speak, the words dragged out, awkward.

We walked in silence, down to where scattered white farms looked out over the bay. We went down another unmade lane towards the sea. We passed a farm cottage then the lane dropped away with a disused appearance, narrowing and weed-choked as the overgrown banks closed in.

The sun had gone behind silvery clouds, but it was humid in the sunken lane.

"Here," said Naomi.

I saw the corrugated asbestos roof and smoking rusty tin chimney. It wasn't much more than a hut, half-buried in the bushes and trees by the side of the loaning. It had a single small window, a front door and a water butt. The lumpy walls were a dirty faded lime-wash, the woodwork a scabby blistered green. Perhaps the building had a deteriorated certain fairy tale charm. A lot of the things you saw hereabouts seemed touched by that fey quality.

Naomi went straight up to the little window and peeped in, the dark pane reflecting her serious little face.

The door opened and an old woman stood there looking out at us. Perhaps she wasn't that old, it was just the grey hair and the old-fashioned clothes she wore. The eyes that regarded us were cunning little chinks of sky-blue sunk in the fat cheeks reddened by the sea-wind and turf fires. She looked like a farmhand, someone who milked the cows, more than a witch.

"Och, tis you, Naomi!" she cried hoarsely, coughing. "How are ye the day, daughter?"

"The best thanks," Naomi replied woodenly.

"How's yer Mammy?"

"Still no weel." Naomi had lapsed into the vernacular; with those words her face clouded over in solemn resignation.

"Ach, tis a shame! And who's this gude-lookin' big fella? Is't yer boy, Naomi?"

The compliment made me warm to Peggy Drumm; I grinned in a good-looking way, like Edward Kookie Byrne, *Lend me your comb*, through my blushes. Naomi didn't look at all put out by the suggestion that I was her boy.

"Paul is doon frae B'lfast staying with Mrs Armstrong, she's his granny," said Naomi.

"A gude wumman, Mrs Armstrong, the Raghery minister's widow."

I bridled a little: we didn't have *ministers* in the Anglican Church of Ireland, *minister* was Presbyterian—any more than we had *priests* like the Catholics, for we were Low Church too. We had *clergymen* and by the same token they were *Mister* more than *Reverend*. But I didn't dare to correct Peggy Drumm.

"Yis'll drink a cuppa tae?"

An alarm bell went off in my head: what if she put something, poison maybe, in the tea? But I saw Naomi nodding and then we were stooping under the lintel into the hut-like low-ceilinged darkness smelling thickly of the turf that glowed on the fire.

You couldn't see a thing for a minute, you groped your way through the cramped dark shapes of heavy old furniture to a seat next the fire, to sit on the made-up single bed along an inner wall, Naomi and I perched there side by side.

The reptilian green eyes of a black cat fixed us. Peggy poked the fire to life and put the blackened kettle on the flames. She rattled cups and saucers.

Naomi leant forward to stroke the cat and mutter to it, "Hel-lo, Hector!" A big black tom, it purred like an engine and hopped up heavily on to her lap. We both stroked it; the luminous round green eyes burning in the dark seemed to stare into your soul. The witch's familiar, better be nice to Hector! Naomi put him back on the rag mat when the tea came.

There was pan bread and butter to eat with the strong tea Peggy Drumm gave us. She sat herself on the rocker. We huddled round chewing and sucking, a weird little tea party there in the firelight with the witch of Islandmagee! I certainly wasn't being short-changed on holiday adventure, on my living novel.

"Are yis goin' for a swim in the tide?"

"Haven't the time," said Naomi. "I must be back to get the men their meat."

"Aye, it's growin' up fast ye have to do now, daughter, helpin' your poor Mammy. It's a hard ould life in sowl." She turned to me. "And what about you, Pawal? What's it like in B'lfast with the millies and dockers and the whole crowd of them, the trolley-buses and department stores, the dance halls and pitcher houses?

Ah've heerd al aboot it though Ah've niver bin, and I niver will, Ah'm tellin' ye, for the ruckus of it wud drive me mad!"

"I prefer it here in the country," I said. "You're not just one o' the crowd, you feel more special like."

"Ay-ee!" Peggy nodded, rocking gently, pleased with my response. "Folk might luk at me in thus wee hoose and feel sorry for the poor ould wumman but I have the peace that they'll niver know, with naebodie and naethin tae bother me iver. Isn' that richt noo, Nai-omi dear?"

Naomi nodded emphatically. You would hardly disagree with a witch in her own parlour.

"Isn' Nai-omi the great wee one noo?" said Peggy. "See you, Pawal, an' luk after your girl!'

It brought tears to my eyes to think of Naomi as *my girl* now. It was as well it was dark there, so no one could see me greeting like a big cissy.

"We need to go," said Naomi. "I have to be back. Thank you for the tea, Peggy."

Peggy saw us off from the door. It was funny out in the clear afternoon light under the wide sky, like coming out of the matinee into the city streets, a queer feeling of unreality.

"Do you like Peggy?" Naomi spoke quietly in her normal voice again.

"Yes, I did! She was complimentary to me, it was nice!"

Naomi turned her face close to mine and stage-whispered, *"She's the High Priestess!"*

An involuntary kind of raspberry-laugh exploded from my lips; I just managed to convert it to a dissembling cough as Naomi looked round sharply. I'd had a fleeting image of hefty old Peggy in a witch's hat and cloak, astride her broomstick.

As we headed back over the fields together, in silence again, I was conscious of Naomi turning her head to look at me; she did it several times, till she caught my eye and said, "Did ye hear what Peggy called me?"

"She said you were my girl."

"And am I? Your girl?"

"Aye."

"Oh, Paul." She linked my arm and we swung along together. It was the greatest feeling I'd ever known.

Before we got to the farm she said, "I'll see you again—down the loanin' after tea?"

"Aye okay!"

I watched her run up the back path, the brown calves and soiled white gutties below the swing of hair and skirt, and disappear in the door, afraid of being late.

10

"Do you believe Peggy really is a witch then?"

We came out of the loaning on to the fields before the clifftop and the sea spread below. The day had brightened up at last as evening came on.

"That's what they say," said Naomi. "And that black cat Hector is her familiar."

I had to laugh. "She seems such a harmless old one! And Hector's just a big fat stupid ball of fur!"

Naomi smiled faintly. "If she *is* a witch, then she's a good witch. She knows cures from nature for all kinds of ills and they work too: she gave me a twig off the bog to suck on for a sore tummy, it tasted like liquorice and made me better. I wish she had a cure for Mammy."

"People must be grateful to Peggy Drumm then?"

"She can tell the meaning of your dreams and everything. But people don't trust her, they say she could as easy turn her powers against you, if you got on the wrong side of her like."

Once we were out of sight of the houses Naomi slipped her wee hand into mine. A feeling like the blessing of heaven settled on my head.

"Peggy taught me a spell," she said.

"What did she teach you?"

"I'm not allowed to tell anybody, not even my boy."

I had an idea. "Is it...something...anything that affects me at all?"

"I said I can't tell."

"Is it a kind of love spell?" It *was*, I decided, I could *feel* it. I had gone all funny, besotted and stupid over a girl. Naomi had put that spell on me!

"If I told you, the spell would be broken!" she said. "Come on, bate ye the race to the gate thonder!"

The gate to the next field was about fifty yards ahead. Naomi took off, hair and skirt flying, knees pumping, gutties skimming the grass. I raced after her, I mustn't let a girl beat me! But she stayed in front.

She hung on the top bar of the rusty gate, out of breath, turning here face to me as I came flying up seconds behind her. "Beat you the race, I told you!" she laughed.

Her hair was wild, the black eyes glittering like a moonlit sea. I couldn't stop myself anymore and I kissed her on the flushed cheek, then the lips. She returned the pressure of my lips and pressed into my arms; I felt the contours of her body through the thin cotton frock.

We kissed a minute or two, then wandered on in the dream of new lovers, arms round each other, down along the shore, every now and again stopping for a kiss. The eternal rhythmic washing of the sea and the cries of the gulls was the music of our love. We walked back together in the strange enchanted peace, through the blue-grey twilight gathering over the expanses of fields and water.

The walk continued in a dream through my night's sleep, Naomi and I together, looking for Peggy Drumm's cottage again but it seemed to have vanished, or we had taken a wrong turning, or had Peggy Drumm been only a dream? It was a relief to waken from the frustration of it and know everything was real again.

The following afternoon the weather broke. The cottage grew dark and the rain pounded down, the commotion of it rising to a deep-throated roar, the windows blind and streaming. It was cosy being inside, reading, but I wanted to see Naomi.

When the rain eased a little I told Granny, "I'll just pop to Naomi's and check she's alright."

"You're not going to drag her out in the wet now?"

"No." I dodged round the puddles to her back door. It was still raining hard, like walking under a changing-room shower with all your clothes on.

Naomi opened the door and laughed at the sight of me. She was frequent smiles and laughter now. "Och, look at you there, Paul, like a drownded duck!"

She waved me inside and bobbed up to peck me on the lips; it was brownie points for me for pure effort.

She said, "Come on in to the fire and get dried out!"

I'd not been through her door before; there was the heavy damp yet homely smell of an old farmhouse, a lofty hallway with stained glass, an imposing banister going steeply up. I thought of atmospheric old houses in literature and the girls who lived in them, Cathy's Wuthering Heights, Lorna Doone's family home above the waterfall on Exmoor.

Naomi showed me through to the drawing room; its sunken fusty dimness thrilled me, like going back three hundred years in one step. The fire was lit, an old leather three-piece suite arranged about it. A stag's head mounted on the wall stared down glassily.

"Granddad shot him in Scotland," said Naomi.

A big oil-painting in a heavy gilt frame caught my eye: a fat bald man with a walrus moustache, dressed in a military officer's uniform of the last century.

"Who's that?"

"The general, my great-grandfather, Algernon Blackhall, Madras Staff Corps. He was a politician after the army, Conservative and Unionist. He bought the farm here."

"This is fantastic, Naomi!" I declared. "Like travelling back in a time machine. I love old houses. Antique and junk shops put a spell on me. I wish I had lived back in the old days."

"Would you like a cup of tea?" she asked. "Mammy's asleep in bed and the men have gone to the Larne market. We have the place here to ourselves this afternoon."

While Naomi was out in the kitchen I prowled around like a visitor in a museum. There were old books in a glass-doored bookcase that covered one wall, dry old volumes of law mostly till I found a row of Victorian Christian novels that were inscribed as Sunday School prizes to the Blackhall children, dated through the 1870s. I opened one of them in the middle and shoved my face into it, closed my eyes and inhaled deeply, letting the musty smell of the pages fill my brain and transport me magically back to the last century.

There was a small organ against the wall; I slid back the lid on the keyboard and sat on the stool to press my feet on the pedals and finger out the opening chords to *Abide With Me*.

Naomi brought a tea-tray, tea and toasted Scotch pancakes, the butter running on them. We sat close together on the couch, leaning over the tray on an occasional table before the fire as we ate the pancakes and drank the tea. There was the cosy feeling like a little married couple; I had already found the girl who one day would be my wife!

"Oh, I'm full!" Naomi groaned, sitting back and patting her tummy.

The rain was falling in a cloudburst again, the roar of it rising like a flood filling the old house.

I sat back and Naomi leant in to me. I turned my head and kissed her on the lips. She pressed up to me in a long embrace.

A voice was calling faintly from upstairs.

"It's Mammy!" Naomi jumped up, straightened her frock and hurried out of the room. I heard her footsteps ascend the steep staircase and her voice calling out, "I'm here, Mammy, I'm coming!"

She was gone ages. I could hear laboured, stumbling footfalls over the high ceiling above my head.

I browsed along the wall of bookshelves again till this time old local history titles caught my eye; my hand alighted on Samuel M'Skimin's *History and Antiquities of the County of the Town of Carrickfergus*. It ran from earliest records till 1839. I turned the pages excitedly to the year of 1711. March 31, the county of Antrim court at Carrickfergus, the trial of eight women "for witchcraft".

Their names and addresses listed; there were five Janets: Janet Mean, Janet Latimer, Janet Millar, Janet Liston and Janet Carson; and Margaret Mitchell, Catherine McCalmond, Elizabeth Sellar.

From addresses at Carrick's Irish-quarter and Scotch-quarter, one from Kilroot, and four from Island Magee (sic).

Their alleged crime was acting together in a coven to torment 18-year-old Mary Dunbar at the house of James and Mrs Haltridge, Island Magee. The house had become haunted by evil spirits. Mary Dunbar found an apron in the parlour that had gone missing before and was tied now with five strange knots which she loosened.

The following day Mary was seized with a violent pain in her thigh and afterwards she fell into fits and raving. On recovering she said she had been tormented by several women who had appeared to her. She gave a minute description of their dress and personal appearance.

Soon afterwards, once more seized with the like fits, she accused five more women of tormenting her and described them in detail too. When the accused were rounded up to be brought before her, Mary suffered extreme fear and additional torture as they approached the house.

The poltergeist struck: strange noises, whistling and scratching, were heard in the house and a sulphurous smell observed in the rooms. Stones, turf and the like were thrown about the house. Bedcovers removed and made up in the shape of a corpse. A bolster walked into the kitchen with a nightgown about it.

In a fit Mary Dunbar vomited feathers, cotton yarn, pins and buttons; it was testified that three strong men were scarcely able to hold her down on the bed at times. At one point she slid off the bed and was laid on the floor as if drawn by an invisible power.

The afflicted Mary Dunbar was dumb during the trial proceedings and could not give evidence. However, she did not suffer any fits there.

The defence for the accused women—it included three reverends—testified that the accused were "mostly sober industrious people who attended public worship, could repeat the Lord's prayer and had been known to pray in private as well as public, and some had lately received the communion". Judge Upton stated that real witches could not "so far retain the form of religion" as that and maintained that the jury could not find the women guilty upon the sole testimony of "the afflicted person's visionary images".

Justice Macartney, however, for the prosecution, insisted that the jury could "bring the accused women in guilty" of witchcraft from all the evidence that had been laid before them—which they accordingly did.

The trial ran from 6am to 2pm on that March 31st 1711 and the women were sentenced to 12 months' imprisonment and "to stand four times in the pillory in Carrickfergus. Tradition says that the people were much exasperated against these unfortunate persons, who were "severely pelted in the pillory with boiled eggs, cabbage stalks and the like, by which one of them had an eye beaten out".

It was that last little detail that sickened you. And you wouldn't know what to believe. On the face of it, seen through 20th century eyes, you were inclined to go with Judge Upton. You thought of grudges, grievances, hatreds and revenge, of ganging up and bullying rather than the supernatural. Yet reliable witnesses had testified to Mary Dunbar's terrible fits and the poltergeist activity. The common people, not always wrong, had been ready to believe the women were guilty. They were different times, there was a different consciousness. It was the worship of Satan, the ridicule and inversion of the Christian mass by the black sabbath, that struck terror into the human soul in those hard days long ago when life was short and death ever-present.

With still no sign of Naomi, and left feeling shaky and paranoid by what I had read, I sought refuge in one of the Christian novels from the bookcase. I needed that sense of the transcending power of love and goodness. I read *Stepping Heavenward* by the licking flames while the rain drummed incessantly. I felt sealed in to cosiness; the tragic world brought to life on the pages just reinforced my own sense of comfort and security in the present.

The book had evocative grey-gloss full-page illustrations, *frontispiece* and for each chapter, depicting the Victorian English industrial streets, a rat-infested slum close with ferocious drunken men, brazen baggages of gin-drunk women or impoverished, desperate mothers nursing ailing babes, a dark satanic mill, and within, rows of men, women and children tending its grinding infernal machinery.

In the midst of it all a beautiful poetic sickly boy, about my age, Tom Huddersfield, who, the story told, had been orphaned in a tenement fire, could find neither shelter nor work, was sleeping rough and slowly starving and freezing to death.

Enter *Naomi*! Good God, what a coincidence, the name of the girl in the book. She rather resembled my Naomi too, dark, slight and grave-faced; she was dressed in the heavy ankle-length clothing of Victorian women, with a cloak and bonnet. She found poor Tom slumped under a lamppost on the cobbled night-street.

She knelt to him and told him softly, "Wake up, boy, you cannot sleep there, you'll catch your end!"

And Naomi took him to her comfortable home, to warmth and sustenance, did her best to revive him with soup but he was fading fast, it was too late to save his life, it was only the matter of his soul now.

"I have come to my sad end," the waif pronounced faintly.

But at last the good news as Naomi informed him there would be no end, only the life eternal in Christ Jesus. So Tom must come to the Christ now, before drawing his final breath.

And here was the happy, the glorious ending to his story as Tom opened his heart to the Saviour and the boy's eyes were filled with the Light of the World, the figure of the Christ appearing to him, arms open wide welcoming him to the Everlasting Kingdom of Heaven, a safe, caring, loving, compassionate, beautiful place, where there would be no more loneliness, no tears, no more hunger or hurt or injustice. And the story ended there as Naomi prayed and Tom, who had found peace in the end, closed his eyes for the last time on this cruel, sinful world...

I hastily wiped a tear from my cheek as Naomi's slippered feet came slapping up the hallway.

"I had to help Mammy to the toilet," she said, entering the room. "She was taken bad. Then I made her bed and refilled the jar and got her a cup of tea. What are you reading?"

I held up the front cover. "It's got a girl called Naomi in it!" I said. "It's very moving, she tries to help this poor orphan starving in the gutter but it's too late, but she brings him to Jesus in heaven in the end."

"I think they named me after that book," said Naomi. "Mammy read those books to me when I was growing up. They are sad but beautiful old stories, like the Bible itself."

She sat beside me on the sofa and I kissed her again, but she said, "It's time for me to start getting the tea now. The men will be back soon from the Larne market. I'll see you later down the loaning, about seven?"

"Okay."

But it was raining steadily as I walked down the loaning after tea, in a borrowed Pakamac and galoshes, over the drenched grass and muddy cart-tracks. I came out on the wet yellow expanse of field edged by the cliffs, with the grey swirling blur of sea and sky beyond.

There was no sign of Naomi this evening. I hung about getting wetter and colder, hoping against hope for the sight of her bobbing down the lane behind me. It was far too wet to be outdoors anyway.

The light was failing early under the charcoal sky. I turned back up the loaning, defeated, disappointed, the water running off my ugly plastic coat.

"Put your wet claes on the horse, by the fire," said Granny. "They'll dry there overnight."

I got into my pyjamas and drank a cup of chocolate with her before going in to bed. She let me tune the wireless to Radio Luxembourg; they played *Bomp-bomp-abomp, A dangodong dang, A dingadongding, blue moon...*

"Dear me," said Granny, "how to ruin a good song!"

I didn't like to argue but I thought it was really exciting jazzed up like that, the cool way they sang it a cappella on New York street corners.

In bed I read another chapter of *Silas Marner* then turned out the light and lay there awake a long time, listening to the patter of the rain on the leaves of the trees. Images of the day passed before my mind's eye, random but vivid as slides projected on a screen: Peggy Drumm's dark cabin, kissing Naomi for the first time by the gate, the fixed stare of the stag's head from the wall, Naomi on the leather couch...Remembering, I felt the warm, vital connection growing between the girl and me.

11

The August wet had settled in, it was another gloomy, teeming afternoon.

"We can go in the barn," said Naomi. "I have something to show you…" She gave me a knowing look.

She led the way with a firm, purposeful tread, skipping over the farmyard puddles. A storm was blowing up, tossing in the treetops like a chorus line swaying, kicking and bowing in an accompaniment to our wild youthful escapade, Naomi and I and the trees all part of the same vital force of nature.

I followed the girl into the shelter of the gloomy, high-ceilinged barn where farm implements, coils of rope and sacks of meal were stored.

"Up here!" she said. A fixed ladder went up to a hatchway high on the inner wall. She started to climb it. "Come on!" she called down to me.

I followed under the proud swing of her hips, up the ladder and through the hatch into the darkness high on the stacked bales of hay in the adjacent shed.

We settled ourselves on the bedding of loose hay on top, under the roof. The big sliding doors were bolted shut, with a long sliver of daylight at the bottom. The rain drummed noisily on the tin roof above our heads as we knelt up in a close embrace.

After the kissing we lay back on the hay, talking in the dark, feeling very close now.

Naomi said, "The same way we have weddings in a church, the witches have the Great Rite. The priestess joins the couple in a *hand-fasting* with the words, *Lord and Lady, all fruits of the earth are fruits of your union, your womb, your dance.* Beautiful, isn't it? The man and woman are God and Goddess, who together create all life."

"Pre-Christian, paganism," I said, "but the same celebration of love and procreation."

"I'd love to have your baby," she said.

"What, now?"

"No! When we are married."

The glow of intimacy bound us, raised us up.

"I'd love that too," I said. "For you to bear my child." There was a biblical ring to the words that I relished, filling me with a sense of my male power.

"You love me, don't you?" she said. "I can tell you do!"

"How can you tell?"

"It's on your face," she said. "I love you too!"

To love and be loved like this, it was everything.

"Think the rain's stopped. They'll be looking for you," I said, suddenly anxious.

We climbed through the hatch and back down the ladder. Outside in the soaking farmyard we blinked dazedly in the twittering grey vacancy of the declining afternoon.

"See you later!" Naomi darted off to the house to start the tea.

There was the emptiness when she had disappeared. I thought of Poe's *beautiful Annabel Lee,* the thirteen-year-old cousin he married, who had wasted to death in his arms while they lived on stewed dandelions from the garden of their humble poet's cottage—*my darling, my life and my bride.* There was the terrible drama of a man's love for a woman, *that you might ever lose her* like that. I would count every second till I saw Marie again.

"Mammy says for you to come and have tea with us."

It was the next day, an invitation to six o'clock teatime that I took to signify her family's acceptance of me as her boyfriend. But I was a shy boy and dreaded meeting them all at once like that.

"You need to look tidy for the Blackhalls," said Granny primly. "Did you bring a tie?"

"Not in the summertime," I said.

"I'll find you one of Henry's. I keep a few of his old things in a drawer as mementoes of him, there's a tie and a cravat, not that he wore them much, he had his dog-collar of course."

The tie was a Black Watch tartan; I really fancied it, sort of lord of the manor going grouse-shooting. I had a white shirt and my brown tweed sports coat and grey flannels. Even if my family wasn't much now on the social scale, we had no need to be fit-ons, we were genuinely of the tony ascendancy after all, at least on my mother's side, right back to Henry the Eighth and the Earls of Meath, and certainly fit to take tea with the Blackhalls.

The semi-invalid mother, Mrs Camella Blackhall, looked frail and haggard in a distinguished posh way, like a fading duchess or horse, a bony old nag, her skin the yellow of fusty pages from their bookcase, long thin pointed neb like a dagger, exophthalmic eyes rolling like golf balls in their sockets. But she greeted me courteously and looking into her face I could see my Naomi there and softened to the mother.

"Naomi hasn't stopped talking about this boy-next-door, Mrs Armstrong's grandson Paul," she joked. "I thought it was high time we met him! And he is a good-looking boy, I see!"

She gave me a feeble, indulgent little grimace of a smile.

"Paul is smart too, Mammy," said Naomi. "Brainy like. He reads loads of paperbacks and he writes things himself."

"What books do you read, Paul?" Mrs Blackhall wanted to know.

The contemporary literature I read usually now, mostly American, didn't sound right for this old house of poshies, so I said some of the classic authors I loved: George Eliot, the Brontes, Dickens and Thomas Hardy.

"You have good taste then, Paul," said Mrs Blackhall. "Did you know the Brontes were Irish? Their father the Reverend Patrick Brunty of County Down."

"Yes, I know the Bronte children in Yorkshire spoke with Irish accents from their father and that Charlotte, for one, like Jane Eyre, preferred to think of herself as Irish."

"Do you know," said Mrs Blackhall, "when Dickens visited Belfast to read from his works at the Ulster Hall, he walked to Carrickfergus and back that same day, to view the great Norman keep above the harbour."

Not to be outdone, I said, "Thomas Hardy wrote a poem, *Donaghadee*, although he never actually went there! He had an Irish friend there. He just liked the sound of the name, Donaghadee, like an Irish jig!"

Mr Terence Blackhall, the father, olive complexion and soft brown eyes, was smooth as 3-in-1 bicycle oil and spoke in a refined, slightly nasal anglicised voice he had acquired at Eton, Oxford and service in the Irish Guards:

"What abight Lyn Doyle, *The Shake of the Bag* et cetera? Sure you can't beat that good old Ulstah creck!" he commented.

"Yes, I've read his short stories," I said, "I like the local expressions he writes in them. He was a bank manager, posted all over the country districts."

There were the two big brothers of Naomi: Carson the dark younger one, a dour fellow in the John Calvin mould and Aeneas, a loud, outgoing farmer, chubby red cheeks and curly-fair, speaking a put-on, down-among-the-people Ulster archaic:

"Och, ye cannae bate the Ulstermon for that great mordant wit! D'ye ever listen to the *McCooeys* on the Home Service? Shur ye couldn' whack thon with a big stick for the sheer crack!"

"My father once met Joseph Tomelty who wrote the *McCooeys*," I said, "they were staying at the same hotel in Bundoran."

"Tomelty, aye! A Roman Catholic too. The good ones can be very talented sometimes in the fields of drama and music," Aeneas conceded.

"Sure we are all Ulstah here together," said Terence. "Citizens of the province of Ulstah!" The name filled his mouth smugly, with a seductive syrupy coating of gentility.

Ulstah! God's own country, a portion of the earth wrested from the levelling of democratic progress, small but significant and ver' precious, the Union Jack flown with equal pride from big house and back street, it had to be right and good. Though the history books told a different story, of the machinations of British colonialism, with Ireland's native electoral majority cheated of their birthright.

Naomi and the help girl, Annie-Elizabeth, brought the platters of tongue salad through, hard-boiled eggs and tomatoes, and a bowl of steaming Cyprus potatoes, with glasses of milk to wash it all down.

The dining room was dim and low-ceilinged, its sagging tiled floor sunk below the level of the adjacent kitchen. There was damp-stained yellowing wallpaper with a pattern of small red roses. On one wall hung a large framed picture of *Little Lord Fauntleroy*, the rich hues and precious living of a vanished aristocratic rule; on another wall a framed print from the English civil war, *When did you last see your father?*

Whatever the intention, if there was one, of this choice of pictures, probably plain human interest, the feeling they gave you was of the precariousness of lives in the shadow of political power, that you could be a lord one minute, an outcast the next.

"Have you been to the Gobbins to see the witches' caves?" Camella enquired, smiling at the idea, indulging the folksy quaintness and colourful eccentricity of native superstition.

Thinking it better to steer clear of any mention of Naomi in this context, I commented jovially, "It is said they are still practising their black arts there, all these centuries on from the witchcraft trial at Carrickfergus!"

Terence addressed the table in the cultured, liberal, slightly nasal, whiny tones in which he must have read the lessons from the lectern at the Church of Ireland:

"It is sed that the 'witches' were in fect nathing mor' than unfortu-nate de-luded hags desperate for a seppeosed self-empowerment, with a genging up in thet malicious way that women are prone to—yet ultimately pathetic creat-ures, mor' to be pitied than anything else. There is even talk now in some 'progressive' quarters, ahem, of a commemorative plaque to honour the ould biddies!"

Black Carson gave the father a blacker look and spoke out sharply at last: "Aye and what next, you wonder? As far as we can tell, and going by the convincing evidence against them in a court of law and the background of satanic worship all across Europe at the time—not to mention the apparent evidence of continued dark rites not half a mile from this table where we are sitting eating our tea, who are we to be talking of honouring the work of the devil himself, the foul rottenness of witchery? I tell ye, this province of ours is going to the dogs, like the rest of the United Kingdom! Wake up, Ulster! The next thing you know, Sinn Fein will be sitting up at the Stormont parliament telling us loyal British subjects what to do!"

Sinn Fein, Irish for "Ourselves Alone", meaning independence from Britain, had a shameful sound about it in English-speaking mouths, like "sin" crossed with "profane".

"Oh nevah, nevah!" Terence shook his fine head dismissively at his son's extremism. It was a sleek, shapely, gentleman's head, a liberal head. "Thet could nevah heppen, not while there is still a single loyal Ulstahm'n left to draw breath! The Cethlics wouldn't want it either, they are far too well looked after here with their big femilies!"

Carson dropped his black head and harrumphed into his glass of milk. He had said his piece for one day.

"Maybe the witches weren't all bad?" Naomi piped up contentiously. "Maybe they were misunderstood?"

"Aye, you're still a wee girl, Naomi," said Aeneas. "What would you know about a coven of jealous ould hags with their hoard of malice and grudges against dacent respectable people?"

"I'm not a wee girl anymore, I'm a woman now!" Naomi insisted proudly, then blushed as the meaning of her words redounded upon her, the bloody secret revealed to all now, like waving her knickers in their faces.

"I think we've heard quite enough now," Camella intervened stiffly. "Would you like another slice of tongue, Paul? Cyprus potatoes? C'mon, ye boy, they're delicious, let's get em all eaten up, ataboy! Pass Paul the butter, Naomi!"

I beamed like Bunter of Greyfriars as they piled up my plate again; I think we were all grateful for the change of topic, the switch of attention to the primacy of the inner man.

There was tapioca pudding with rhubarb jam, tea and a Peak Frean biscuit assortment. When we had finished eating I sat there ignored and bored stiff with the men talking weather and crops and cows while daughter, mother and Annie-Elizabeth cleared the table and washed up.

At last Naomi came back and said, "The sun's shining, Paul. Will you walk me down to the Gobbins?"

I jumped up, delighted to get away.

The sun, on course for the western horizon, glittered like diamonds on the upright blades of wet grass as we made our way down the loaning.

Naomi said, "They treat me like a wee dope still and sure I know more about some things than they ever will."

"Like the witches?" I said jokily.

"Aye indeed," she said, straight-faced, meaning it. I looked away with a slight uneasiness; I was a little afraid of her at times.

"Carson can be a bit scary," I said.

"Aye, he's kind of a political fanatic. And Aeneas is just a big bully!"

"Your ma and da are nice though?"

"I'm sure they seem so to visitors but you should just hear them having a go at me sometimes! Like when they found out I was going to Peggy Drumm's."

"What did they say to you?"

"That Peggy was linked to the current outbreak of witchcraft and I was turning into a witch too if I wasn't careful and how I needed to find some proper friends my own age…"

"How were you 'turning into a witch'?"

"Losing my temper and screaming at everybody. But that can happen when your moons are coming on or maybe it's just I have so much to do running after them all, with Ma in bed most of the time—I have no life of my own at all…"

She stopped and burst into tears. I put my arm around her thin hunched shoulders that shook pathetically while she cried into her little lace hankie that was soon a wet lump in her skinny fist.

"Don't worry, Naomi," I tried to soothe her. Her tears made me feel clumsy and inadequate, too masculine, then an overwhelming rush of compassion and suddenly I was kissing her, all over her face like a big dog licking away the salt tears.

"Och, my poor wee witch!" I said, making her laugh through the tears.

She started to brighten up as we walked on hand-in-hand towards the long horizon of the sea. The sun was going down in flames, setting the waves on fire. I had a sudden magical feeling, as if we were two figures in a *Rupert Bear* book, walking on Nutwood Common, Rupert and Rosalie!

12

It was with Naomi that I had come to the great joy of first love.

The wet days passed and the sunshine returned, we bathed in the afternoon at our private beach, as we called it. You went round the base of a headland, clambering over rocks, and there it was, tucked away, a little crescent of pure sand washed by the tide, our secret place, with only the shadows and beady eyes of passing seagulls. It was sheltered from the stiff sea breezes, warm in the sunshine. You lay back on your towel, shut your eyes and let the lazy summer rhythm of the sea beat in your ears, like some desert island.

I wore my old red itchy woollen trunks, a bit tight on me now, Naomi in her bathing costume; I was conscious of her womanly curves, the long, smooth bare legs. We walked holding hands to the edge of the tide and paddled there. We swam a bit, but the water was painfully cold. Teeth chattering comically, we hurried to our towels spread side by side on the white sand, to dry off in the intermittent sunshine.

I turned to her lying prone beside me, and kissed her cheek; she cocked an eye open at me and showed her teeth in a dazzling little smile in the dark face. Turning on to her side, she crooked an arm around my neck and we kissed. In our ears the waves broke and unrolled, withdrew again. Intermittent cloud shadow swept over us, cold, warm, cold. We had an hour or so together in the mid-afternoon before she got the men their tea.

I could no longer be alone; I went in thoughts of Naomi all the time we were apart, dreamt of her all night, opened my eyes in the morning and couldn't wait to see her again. Everything else was forgotten, my life in the city, my family; Granny seemed happy for me to stay on indefinitely with her and my parents weren't complaining. I only wished that I might stay forever; it sounds callous but I fantasised my parents dying and then I would have to come and live here at Granny's, fitting into her easy, homely routine, and be with Naomi all the time, my country sweetheart, travel on the bus to school with her every day, we'd do our homework together; it was my dream of an earthly paradise.

Our time together was of necessity limited, there were her strict domestic obligations with a sick mother, so we packed as much as we could into the ecstatic minutes spent together.

As the days and then weeks passed into the second half of August the rains returned, long heavy downpours, and we retreated to the warmth, darkness and secrecy of the hay-shed again, our lovers' heaven.

Till the day came when suddenly the bolt was shot, the long iron one that secured the hay shed door on the outside. The big corrugated iron door was slid grinding and rumbling open and the wet grey daylight poured in on the girl and I sitting, arms round each other, halfway down the high steps of hay bales.

The voice from the silhouette in the doorway cried out harshly, "What in the name of God are the pair of yous up to in here?"

It was Carson!

I had our excuse ready, all false mateyness: "Och, hello there, Carson! We're sheltering from the rain, that's all!" I pitched for just the right tenor of teenage gormlessness and innocent jollity, Eden before the Fall.

But the no-nonsense, dour Ulster voice, like a man with the flu, came straight back at me in disgusted reproof, "Ach, whaddaya take me for, I wasn't born yesterday, y'know! Didn't I hear yous at it like a couple of all-in wrestlers? Well, let me tell you, I wasn't born yesterday and I know fine rightly what the pair of you are up to in here! Filth and depravity! And what have *you* got to say for yourself, Miss? I don't doubt for one minute it was you leading the poor fella on!"

I almost jumped out of my skin as Naomi let out a scream at her brother: "Och, shut up, Carson, it's *your* dirty mind, that's all! Go away and leave us alone, will you! Paul told you the truth, we're drying off in here after a wetting, that's all! We like to sit here and talk, on our own, it's not a sin, you know. Mammy and Daddy allow me to go out with Paul. I have no other friends, I'm too busy running after you and the other men and tending to our poor ma lying up in her sickbed!"

"You-ou we-ee *Jezebel*!" Carson's voice trembled with fury. "It's a witch out of hell you are! The divil's own daughter! Well, *I know* you have been dabbling in the diabolical rites going on down in those cursed caves of the Gobbins! You and Peggy Drumm and God knows what other ould bitches sittin' round cuttin' straws with your backsides, with scores to settle and nothing better to occupy your minds. When you should be down on your knees prayin' for deliverance outta sin! It should be the ducking stool in the village pond for the pack of you, like olden days, then we'd get to the truth at last!"

"Och shut up, get out, go away!" Naomi was furious. "Aye, ye're right, Carson Blackhall," and now her voice changed, *"I am a witch and I'm proud of it! It's the only thing gives me any hope to live for! And I'll putt a fuckin' spell on ye, so I will!"*

There was more out of her, that I don't wish to remember and cannot clearly recall anyway, I'm not even sure whether it was English or Irish, it was like nothing on earth, blood-curdling vile profanities, verbal projectile vomiting of hideous bile, her face all screwed up about the foul spitting mouth like a wildcat and as I stared aghast she wasn't my lovely sweet girl anymore, she was *this creature;* the ugliness of it cut through me and killed something in me stone dead.

Carson beat a hasty retreat, ramming the barn door shut behind him. We were in the dark again. Naomi was sobbing pitifully, I should have consoled her but something held me back, I was too scared of her now.

We stood up together; she was in the pale cotton frock, the washed-out cardigan about her stooped shoulders, hair hanging limply around the grubby face scored with tears.

She turned to me pathetically and sank her head on my shoulder. I stood there unfeeling as a wall, I couldn't bring myself to hold her. I sort of hated her—or rather the glimpse I'd had of this other diabolical Naomi, twisted with the malignancy of some dark power. I couldn't even pretend to be kind.

She lifted her tear-tracked face and looked up searchingly into my eyes. "Paul, d'ye not love me anymore?" she moaned. It was truly pitiful but her voice grated on me like a knife now. "It's the time of the month comin' up to my moons makes me like this," she explained, "like the devil's got into me. It'll be alright soon, now I'm bleeding."

I thought of the happy, carefree girl in the *Nikini* advert in *Woman's Own*, why couldn't my girl be like her?

I would never forget that heartfelt pleading look she gave me and my hard-hearted response to her in the time of her need, her physical and psychological suffering that, after all, stemmed from the same root as the love she gave me, the feminine principle.

I got down the ladder to the ground fast as I could, waited with a last shred of courtesy till she had come after me.

"Paul..." she began but I couldn't bear another moment in her company and I was off across the yard to Granny's, in the vicelike grip of this fuming revulsion towards her.

In truth, it was I Paul Carroll whom the devil had got into. I had failed in love, fallen at the first hurdle, the first challenge of a loved one's needy humanity, this was the only sin that had been committed, the trashing of love by yours untruly.

Coming away from Blackhall Farm to Granny's cottage was to enter a different world, the cumulative sheltered calm of the long, confined domestic years, the old lady pottering about humming a hymn and getting the tea.

I burst out, "Granny, what time's the morning bus to Whitehead? I have to go back to Belfast."

"Why, all of a sudden?"

"I remembered the Junior exam results are out today and I need to go into school and get them!"

"Don't they post them out to you?"

"That'll take a couple more days. I'm too worried about my maths results."

"What's happened with you and Naomi then, did you fall out?" Granny smiled at the idea, imagining some sweet lovers' tiff.

"Oh no, nothing like that, it's just I forgot about the exams!"

"Well, Mammy and Daddy must be wondering where you've got to. You came for a couple of days and stayed four weeks! It's been nice for me having a young person about the place."

I cringed now to think of my wild plan to come and live here to be with Naomi, even kind of plotting my parents' murder! Had that been part of her spell on me? I couldn't wait to put the miles between us now. I was soon packed and ready for the off first thing in the morning.

That last evening I finished *Silas Marner* at the fireside and went to bed early. Free of Naomi I experienced a new strength in myself that was like a form of cruelty, the freedom of no real conscience anymore. I didn't sleep much that night, I kept waking and feeling secure in the callousness, the loss of conscience I could still feel there inside me, buoying me up.

It was a blowy dark morning with the bleak feeling of impending autumn and school. That was alright now, it was the normality I craved. I had my porridge and toast and tea, and was off down the lane in a light shower with my haversack over my shoulder, in time for the 7.37 bus to Whitehead. The wind drove in a hard flood through the dense leaves of the big elm tree. I would miss the smell of the country, that was all, the wet fields, the turf-smoke and the cold salt-sea.

I didn't even turn my head to look at Blackhall Farm, it loomed there, a forbidding gaunt, gloomy presence in the corner of my eye, the house of my shame—the musty sitting room under the dead eyes of the stag, the dark hayloft with the rain on the roof. I was afraid to look up lest I should glimpse the accusatory blade of Naomi's face at the window.

The little rural housing estate below looked so peaceful, its chimneys smoking in the light rain as another quiet day began for the simple rural folk who dwelt there, and Uncle Frank and Aunt Mary and their cats, the great contentment of country life *as long as you kept yourself to yourself.*

The green bus with its early birds collected from the length of the peninsula whisked me away, tyres swishing on the wet country road under the archway of green branches, the neat patchwork quilt of fields slipping away down to the sea on either side. I couldn't wait to be back in the city again, to wander in its liberating anonymity.

But you didn't escape the dark spell of a girl as easily as that. Your first love too. As I sit here writing this down, all these years later, I am still haunted by Naomi, still attached to her under the spell of a funny unreal kind of undying love. And I a happily married man who loves his wife above everything in the world.

There was nothing evil in Naomi at all. The terrible thing was that she gave me the precious gift of first love, real love and I threw it away. I wasn't ready for it; with the hindsight of maturity I can see clearly where she was coming from. Naomi, just into her teens, had to take her dying mother's place in the house, there would be no youth for her. There was little love lost between Naomi and the oily father and thoughtless brothers, the one, Aeneas, a bully, the other a fanatic, Carson, puritan and modern day witch-finder general.

I suspect Peggy Drumm *was* a sort of witch, or fancied herself so, but also a true friend to Naomi at a desperate juncture in the girl's life, that her influence on Naomi may well have been an empowering one. And anyway she was an intelligent girl, she would surely grow out of any superstitious nonsense.

At the time I could only think of those chilling words on Naomi's lips, to her brother Aeneas, *"Ah'll putt a fuckin' spell on ye"*, the babble that came out of her from some black hole deep in the human soul, the ugly contortion of pure hate on the face I had loved. PMT, the thought came to me, "the curse" they called it, and there was something in that.

I feel only compassion for Naomi now, it was me she put a spell on, a beautiful one; we were only kids, I know, but that spell taught me the love of a woman, a wholeness of the physical and spiritual, the love at the very root of human existence. It was the everlasting shame of my rejection of that love that taught me the saving heartfelt compassion I was able to bring later to my marriage.

13

The summer of Naomi was followed by two years in the wilderness before Marie. During that time Naomi lived on vividly in my head, she came to me in my adolescent fantasies before sleep, the naked girl in the hayloft—you could not have made up anything quite so piquant, so wonderful. I even imagined looking Naomi up, the two of us together again, but Granny died the following spring, Frank and Mary moved away and I never returned to Islandmagee till after my marriage.

I went youth-hostelling the following summer with Mike and Charlie from school, who I'd taken up with, proper friends at last. The friendship and holiday seemed only to lead to juvenile delinquency however. We got drunk on whiskey in the Harbour Bar at Ballycastle, snogged girls on the bunks at Moneyvart hostel in the Glens (the only good thing we did, arguably) and travelling south to the Mournes where Charlie took a queer antisocial turn and, unbeknownst to Mike and me, chucked a lighted fag-end on a bunk at Bloody Bridge as we were leaving. Looking back from the road below we saw clouds of smoke rising from the hostel high on the long steep mountainside. Two hearty outdoor types on racing bikes overtook us and informed us that we had been identified as the arsonists responsible for the hostel fire and were now in deep trouble.

Instantly barred from the YHA we had to spend that night sleeping rough in Newcastle, County Down, squashed into a phone box for shelter, sitting knees-up on the concrete floor, with the door opening every time someone moved, then transferring to the railway station where we could stretch out on the square of hard wooden benches under the big central clock.

In the morning Charlie phoned his da who was in the motor trade, who came down from Belfast and picked us up; I was sick over the back seat of his fast new car. I arrived home in an awful state, finished with life.

We got off with a warning from the YHA disciplinary board, we seemed such nice middle-class boys, I suppose. It was the music that saved us in the end. It began with our vocal harmonies competing with the flushing of cisterns in the acoustics of the school bogs, Everly Brothers, the Crickets. The Fab Four were just coming up, *She Loves You, yeah, yeah, yeah,* we saw their concert on stage at the ABC cinema, a wall of screams between us and the music but never mind, they were up there alive in front of you.

After school we mooched around the record and book stalls in Smithfield market and were soon tempted by the musical instruments that were on sale there too. Charlie and I bought cheap Spanish guitars, Mike picked up a basic drum kit, we all had old pianos in our front rooms—and we were a group, *The Fringe,* Belfast's answer to Liverpool's Big Three. Charlie and I had Teach Yourself Guitar manuals and we started group practices in Mike's front room on the Crumlin Road.

Back at school we teamed up with Frankie in the art class and we were in business. Ralph, Bob and Marty joined us in due course, it was surprising how musical everyone was in our school friendship group. It wasn't about great talent, except perhaps Frankie, it was the fun of having a go and enjoying making music, getting right inside the music, a natural extension of passive listening to it.

And then along came Marie, our girl singer! Marie and I were sixteen though she was almost the whole school year younger than me and it felt just right, like being born for each other. That first long hot summer together was touched with the magic wand of new young love. We lived so near each other, we could meet anytime at one or other of our houses, or halfway for a stroll in the Waterworks.

We were townies, we turned our backs on the mountains behind the city, on the seaside in front of it, and took the bus daily into the centre. Marie liked the buzz of the crowds, the shops, the style. She'd point out some item of men's clothing for me in the window of one of the new Mod boutiques, tab-collar shirts and hipster trousers were in for men that summer. I never quite made it as a dandy, new clothes were too uncomfortable; I preferred to watch my girlfriend parade in a short skirt and ask me, "What do you think?"

"You look terrific, Marie!" My enthusiasm was tinged with eroticism, her leggy steps and the game twitching of the cute butt, as the Catcher said.

When our feet got achey, mid-afternoon, we'd pop into the Lombard Restaurant. Mike and Charlie would be settled in there already, tucked in one of the booths along the wall, expecting us.

A uniformed waitress brought tea, Mike passed round his twenty-pack of Piccadilly Filter. The tall windows were open, the long orange curtains blowing, flapping in the cooling summer breeze, it was a feeling of luxury and expansiveness. We could sit there for hours over a cup of tea which was a lot cheaper than coffee, talking about God knows what, I don't recall a single word of it now, a lot of wishful thinking no doubt; our music bonded us and there was always talk of the latest records and whether our group might cover them.

Sometimes Van Morrison, Billy Harrison and Them would come in and occupy a table. How cool was that, but if you think that sounds like party time, you'd be wrong, they were a subdued, silent little bunch—well-mannered, nice boys, the waitress informed us. They were regulars at DJ Dino's Plaza lunchtime sessions, the Maritime Hotel and the Jazz Club. The Belfast Sixties scene was quite something: musical, fashionable, vibrant, and I imagine just as with-it as Manchester or Dublin. And we were just the right age to feel a part of it all.

"Are you coming to Marlene's tonight?" Mike enquired.

"Party?" said Marie.

"Kind of," said Charlie. "Every night at Marlene's is a party. Jennie Sloan will be there, so it should be lively!"

"Just the two of you and the two girls?" said Marie. "Is that all?"

"And you two! We'll *make* it a party!"

"Okay then, we'll bring a bottle. Marlene has some good records."

Charlie said, "She's got the new Stones and Geno Washington and the Ram-Jam Band, and some great older stuff, Sinatra with Nelson Riddle, *Songs for Swingin' Lovers* and the *West Side Story* soundtrack."

"Oh, I love that!" said Marie and sang, "*Mar-ia, Mar-ia, Mar-ia!*" in an alarming effortlessly operatic voice that turned heads around us to identify its possessor.

Going back home on the bus in the late summer's afternoon, Marie asked me, "Which one of the lads is Marlene with now, I wonder?"

"Mike, I think, she decided Charlie was too young. He can have Jennie."

"Sure Marlene's only fourteen!" said Marie. "She's wild, that girl, with her ma away in Liverpool half the time and that flat all to herself. I don't know how many boys she's had through there"

As we parted I said, "I'll call for you at seven and we can walk over together."

Memories are made of this…

Picking up Marie from Jacaranda Close on a sunny summer's evening of the long school holidays. The evening world is a warm golden place.

My almost-straight black hair has grown long enough to turn heads in the street, invite the disapproval of older or square people, or the momentary passing interest of the cooler girls, hopefully, hip lads too. Not that I need a girl, I've got one, God has blessed me with Marie Kelly.

I sport a retro-bohemian look, I call it, my old brown tweed sports jacket, a bit short on the cuffs and a bum-freezer now but too comfortable to abandon, worn over a navy shirt with a button-down collar and lime-green cord trousers, a bargain 19/6 by mail order, and the slip-on shoes I wear to school, down-at-heel comfy like the soft old jacket.

I know somehow, deep in my heart, that life doesn't get better than this, to be sixteen and meeting your girl on a fine summer's evening.

She opens her door to me, she is all freshened and pretty, perfume that goes to your head, she's yours, it's understood, and ready to go. Residual warm cooking smells of teatime follow her out the door. Even a cool teenage girlfriend has that lovely feminine domesticity behind her, beckoning you into its creature comforts, feeding and love, and on to family and the life eternal.

Twisted sister Thelma hollers from behind her, "Hi yous two lovebirds, can I come to the party?"

Marie pulls a face, shakes her head firmly, n-o, no, calls over her shoulder, 'Wait till you've grown up a bit, wee girl!"

Marie is dressed for the glamour of evening, sweet little face carefully made-up under the helmet of chopped, straight, sun-bleached fairish hair; the smart new pinafore dress picked up in a summer sale that day, the legs descending from her skirt, smooth bare summer-browned skin, curving down into stilettos that click-clack over the Belfast pavement as she links my arm, *my girl.*

"I wish these summer days would go on forever, you 'n' me, babe, just groovin'!" Her voice is soft and breathy with the intimacy we share.

"Doesn't Belfast look beautiful with this evening sunshine painting everything gold?" I pronounce. "Cave Hill above us there and the Lough stretched below. This hot weather turns the city into a foreign, exotic place, it could be somewhere in France or Italy."

"We need to pick up a bottle of Bulmer's from the off-licence," Marie reminds me, as if I'd ever forget *that,* the key to ever greater abandonment and fun.

But it is always a nervous moment entering the small off-licence attached to the big redbrick pub on Antrim Road. They must know me by now as a fairly regular customer but the woman serving there avoids eye contact or pleasantries, tight-lipped as she wraps the tall bottle of cider in a sheet of plain paper and grabs the money quick.

Outside again I say, "There's no way I look eighteen really, is there?"

"Not with that baby face," Marie smiles and kisses it. "When are you going to start shaving?"

"I have started!" I declare indignantly, referring to the fuzz I shave off my upper lip with Da's shaving soap, brush and safety razor weekly.

It's a short walk on along the Antrim Road then left-turn, up a winding old narrow kind of lane between high garden walls and trees growing over them and out of the pavement.

A little way on the trees open out on a fine detached house set well back from the road with a circular drive around a neat expanse of lawn. Marlene's. It looks American somehow, as does she. Across the road through the trees there are tennis courts, balls popping and white figures leaping, voices calling beyond the hedge in the pinkish evening light, delightfully middle class.

"Oh, very tony round here!" I remark. "Did you ever play tennis?" I ask Marie.

"No!" she responds firmly. "*Ho's fo' tennis?* I don't think so! Compulsory hockey in the junior years was bad enough! I like swimming, but not races, only for fun."

"Rounders is my favourite game," I tell her. "Whacking that soft ball high, high up into a blue summer sky and making a mad dash for it round the circle!"

"Oh, I forgot rounders, I love it too!" she enthuses, we always agree on the important things in life. "It's not really recognised as a proper sport though, is it?"

"Too civilised and enjoyable," I rejoinder caustically.

We proceed crunching up the pebbled drive to the detached house as I comment, "It's like Hollywood coming here, I feel like John Kerr or Troy Donahue and something unexpected and passionate is going to happen inside that house."

"Oh, Paul, I live in hope!" She squeezes my hand and giggles. "Please Troy, can I be your Sandra Dee?"

Jennie Sloan answers the doorbell, a tubby five footer, generously curvy, pretty little face framed by long, shiny chestnut hair, greeting us with the gay laughter she lives on as others need oxygen, hard to imagine a dull moment with Jennie around.

"Look at you two!" she exclaims. "Paul and Marie, the golden couple! Where did you get that dress, Marie? You look *a mill-ion doll-ars, hon-ee!*"

"One pound seventy-five, summer sale at Robinson and Cleaver's!" Marie chirps up, constant shopping pays.

"*Ah, g'wan!*" says Jennie. "And look at Paul! Nancy Savage would throw a blue fit if she saw your long hair now! What have you been up to then, you two love-birds?"

"Let me think," says Marie, stroking her chin meditatively, super-cute. "Shopping of course! Afternoon tea at the Lombard. Pictures the other night, Rock Hudson and Doris Day, *Move Over Darling*, it's a quare geg, I'm telling you! A bit of singing with the group in front rooms, though we're limited with Frankie away in Eastbourne on the buses, just Paul and Charlie strumming or plonking along, Mike tapping on the drums while I sing a Helen Shapiro medley. All I need is the beehive: *Plee-ease don't treat me, bap-bapbap, like a child!* Protest music, you see!"

"It's all right for you students!" says Jennie in mock protest. "Rockin' and a-rollin' while us shorthand-typists slave away all summer in our offices, isn't that right now, Marlene? We hardly see the light of day!" Marlene has appeared, grinning like a chipmunk at Jennie's shoulder.

We follow the small figures of the two girls through to the cavernous living room of the ground floor apartment, cool and green like a forest glade in the summer's evening light. High moulded ceiling and the tall windows hung with floor-length green velvet curtains, a smart three-piece suite in matching green velvet, plump seat cushions like magnets to the bum, arranged about the big marble fireplace with ferns in a pot on the tiled hearth and our heads reflected in a huge gilt-framed mirror over the mantelpiece.

Charlie and Mike are already settled in, comfy on the cushions, fags on, glasses of the golden ambrosia in hand, cider of course, our poison of choice. Rolling Stones' EP on the record player, *Can I Get A Witness?*

"Let me chill your bottle in the fridge," says Marlene. I follow her through to the long fitted kitchen. She is a nice dark Jewess, lots of sex appeal with the big brown eyes and thick black hair. She exudes a *femme fatale* quality, taking a fancy to every attractive boy she encounters, giving generously of herself by all accounts, then dropping them just as quick, the boys that is, leaving the pathway from her door strewn with broken hearts, and she not yet fifteen.

Tonight she bats the long mascara'd lashes at me and fixes me with her charming big-teeth smile.

"Have you finished writing your book, Paul?" she enquires. "What was the title?"

She speaks with a sort of mid-Atlantic accent, she's spent some time across the bigger pond.

I like to be asked about my "book".

"*The Sixteenth Summer of Eugene Shannon,*" I announce proudly, such a brilliant title, would do justice to Tenessee Williams or Truman Capote. The only problem with my book is getting past the title to the story itself, I have filled wastepaper baskets with false starts.

But seeking to impress Marlene now, with that shining, admiring look in her girl's eyes, I lie, "Yeh, I've got a rough first draft. Sort of *Tea and Sympathy* meets *Catcher in the Rye*. There's Eugene, see, my protagonist. Bit of a Holden Caulfield figure, or Clinton Williams from *All Fall Down*, lonely and misunderstood kinda thing. Anyway he fancies this girl Shelley but is too shy to approach her. He's convinced he'll never get a girl the way he is going. Then his sixteenth summer of the title comes round and he goes to cut the grass of a neighbour, Leila, a mature married woman who gives him tea and sympathy, sort of. Leila is lonely too, her husband is away in the navy with a woman in every port. Now Eugene and Leila, two lonely people, fall for each other, even though she's nearly ten years older than he..."

"And...?" Marlene's big brown peepers are popping with anticipation.

"That's the end bit, I still have to work that out," I tell her disappointingly, watching her face fall. "But I think she seduces him..."

"Oh yeh?" Marlene brightens up again.

"Yeh, but it's all pretty traumatic for the both of them and I think it's going to end in tears. Leila and her husband make up and Eugene runs away to sea, or something..."

"What about Shelley, the one he fancied in the first place?"

"Oh, maybe she turns up and saves him in the end! Just as he's about to board ship." I had quite forgotten about Shelley.

"Paul, your book sounds super, I can't wait to read it!"

Her eyes shine with something like fan-worship as they gaze into mine and I feel a bit of a phoney. She is standing very close to me in the kitchen, just the two of us there. Oh God, she *is* attractive right enough, the big white gnashers splitting her wee face in a come-on smile. And all those boys she's...done whatever with, if you can believe the half of what they tell you.

She stands the large Bulmer's I hand her on the shelf inside the door of the tall American refrigerator—we still make do at home with a cold cupboard in the scullery and in the summer heatwave week the butter and milk standing in a bucket of cold water. The Golds, Marlene and Mum, are sophisticated, cosmopolitan, they keep salami sausage, coleslaw and other delicatessen treats in the fridge, that Marlene serves as snacks with the big Mazzo crackers. I love anything ethnic like that, especially the girls.

Plonk, plonk, plonk, fizzz! Marlene pours me a glass of cider from a chilled half-drunk bottle out of the fridge, heaven in a glass! And one for me to take to Marie next door. But I gollop mine straight back down the hatch like lemonade on a hot summer picnic, not thinking. It's nerves, and Marlene laughs, "Gosh, you were thirsty! Here, let me pour you another one to take!"

I go through to the sitting room, already a bit unsteady on my feet and hand Marie her drink. She complains, "You were ages in there with Marlene! Leaving your girl sitting here with my tongue hanging out!"

"Marlene was asking me about my book."

"Oh, thought you were still on the first page?"

"Aye, I started imagining what I could write and told her that."

"I'm sure she was impressed." Marie gives me a look, she isn't the jealous type but she knows the games Marlene plays.

I let it go. Marie and I are on the couch. Mike and Charlie occupy the big armchairs either side of the unlit fireplace, Marlene and Jennie, respectively, on the floor, backed up between their lads' knees. There are witty comments, gay repartee and laughter in a golden cidery glow that blends with the sunset at the window.

Slowly the daylight is fading in the rather grand room. I feel the cider pincers pressing on my temples, numbing the monkey-brain. I am filled with a gloating sense of life's pleasures, booze, girls...

"Right!" Jennie claps her doll-like hands. "Is everyone up for the kissing competition?"

Certainly nobody demurs.

"You've gotta kiss the boys or girls you're *not* with, then the one you *are* with, and then write down the name of the best kisser and put it in the hat! Then the prize: the two winners get to kiss each other! Okay, everybody?"

There is a little whirlwind of excitement in the room as we circulate. There's a naivety about it all, far removed from the *News of the World* reports of "wife-swapping" parties, I am quite happy with Marie kissing my best friends Mike and Charlie, like the matey sharing of a sherbet dip. I have absolute confidence in Marie, that there could never, in the immortal words of Ricky Nelson, be anyone else for her but me.

Jennie Sloan is a champion kisser, her full lips open, moist and pliable on mine, rhythmical and insistent, holding nothing back. She has made a thing of teaching boys to kiss. Making a meal of it, we squash into a corner of the sofa.

Jennie transfers to Mike; Marlene comes sweetly smiling to me, her chocolate-brown eyes deepening to black as they hold mine; something naughty and unspoken, knowing and conspiratorial passes between us. An inch smaller at four foot eleven and slimmer than Jennie though with equally big bazookas, Marlene's firm round bum sinks in my lap, her skirt sliding up revealing most of a pair of shapely little pins.

I don't know what has got into me, as they say—the drink mainly, with the dark sexy foreign aura I attribute to Jewess Marlene, the tales of her multiple couplings...her odalisque eyes as she tilts her face up to mine...And I cover her wide open mouth with a greedy long, lascivious, desperate kiss. Her big eyelids, darkly shadowed and lashed, shut rapturously, tremble, and her breathing comes heavily. She returns the pressure of my mouth on hers, pokes her tongue between my teeth, French kissing, I am almost swooning!

But Jennie Sloan's kissing-with-confidence tuition has upstaged her friend. Marlene's lips, though wide and full, are hard and unyielding somehow, like rubber more than tender feminine flesh, and she holds her mouth and jaw a little too rigid, perhaps an involuntary reaction to the onslaught of my embrace.

At last we get to kiss our own girls. It is a relief by now to hold Marie in my arms again, her figure feels slender and sinuous after the voluptuousness of the other two, and I kiss her at length, a steady-boyfriend kiss, a controlled, protracted pleasuring, the way I imagine it should be in full-on lovemaking when the time for that has eventually come.

"And the winners...!" Jennie rummages in the lady's hat Marlene brought from a peg in the hall, withdraws one of the slips of paper we have written on, "...Oh no, it's me, Jennifer Jane Sloan! And the boys...Paul Armstrong Carroll!" she whoops.

A cheer goes up. I have to kiss Jennie, yes she is a good court, it is certainly no hardship to kiss those lips again as the others applaud our proven kissing prowess, but I only want to get back to my Marie now.

There's a snogging session with our proper girls as the slow summer twilight thickens to dusk and then darkness in the room. Marlene and Mike withdraw to her bedroom across the hall. Charlie and Jennie are on the floor behind the couch where Marie and I are courting. I kiss her with an insistent, earnest, guilty passion; now I am with her, how could I ever even *think* of another girl?

Sinatra and Riddle runs out on the record player and there is just the dark, late stillness of the big house and suburban avenue and the heavy-breathing passion of the warm summer's night.

Strange exclamations and creakings carry faintly from Marlene and Mike in the bedroom. Down on the floor behind the sofa there is a steady rhythmical chugging that ends with Charlie's exhalation of overwhelming relief and Jennie's giggles. It's hand-shandies all round.

Marlene returns and switches on the big standard lamp in the corner. Lighters click and flare, tobacco smoke drifts over the room.

When Marlene goes in the kitchen and fills the kettle, Marie says, "I'll just go and help Marlene with the coffee."

It is after eleven when Marie and I leave. The others are staying the night at Marlene's. I hear afterwards that Mike is consigned to the couch, Marlene has had enough for one night, that's how she treats a fella.

The tennis courts across the way are in darkness. The expanse of lawn, the old winding lane with the high garden walls, the stooping trees, all is very still, dark between the lampposts.

When I put my arm round Marie she stiffens a little, like a cat arching its back.

But she's not a sulker, she comes straight out with it in my face: "Marlene told me you went for her *like an animal*."

I have to laugh at the bloated imagery.

"Paul, I don't think it's very funny." She stops under a lamppost. "Now look at me. Look me in the eye. *Did* you? *Go* for her like that?"

I couldn't help myself then with that image of *an animal*, me with shaggy coat, fangs and foetid breath, and I burst out laughing.

In the blink of an eye, Marie catches me a slap square on the cheek. She is a light, refined figure of a girl, but she can hit okay.

"Aoh, that hurt!" I exclaim, rubbing my poor cheek, though it is anaesthetised by the cider I have drunk.

Marie just stands there, eyes glittering like a panther under the streetlight, staring me out. At last her posture relaxes, she takes my hand and kisses the cheek that is throbbing a little now as the numbness fades.

"C'mon then, my silly boy!" she says affectionately, pulling me after her on down the road, then slipping her arm around my waist, pressing the curve of her hip to mine.

I don't know what to say. The sweet, gentle girl I love has belted me one. Did I deserve it?

Probably: I lusted briefly, drunkenly after another, it is true. Tenderly, I touch the inflamed struck cheek as we walk on, taking a perverse sort of pride in my battle-blow. It is the hard physical proof of how much my girl loves me, with point made and everything forgiven and forgotten in a minute or two.

14

The September rains came in as the summer holiday went out. Marie and I walked to school together on the first day back, cutting through the Waterworks, a miserable damp experience, just us and the ducks under the piddling grey sky.

Entering the school grounds under the high-towered castle frontage of the Victorian edifice, red sandstone cliffs studded with rows of glinting dark windows, we took leave of one another, Marie cutting off to the girls' entrance at one end, I to the boys' at the other, splashing over the puddled tarmac towards the cloakrooms. I cursed the bloody awfulness of it, only wanting to be back in my bed with the cosy sound of the rain on the window.

But combing your hair in one of the mirrors above the long row of wash-hand basins in the bogs, back with the lads again, your mates, you cheered up instantly. You were a part of something bigger out here in the wide world, a member of society, and you needed that too.

We got our new sixth form timetables, Art all afternoon, every day, which pleased us.

"Down to Isibeal's afterwards?"

"Aye! I'll bring Marie."

"Good. Jacqui's's coming." She was Marty's girl, a vivacious blonde beauty.

I pined for Marie through the long school day. We weren't in any classes together this year, she'd moved up a section for maths; I got precious glimpses of her, a few tender words exchanged on the hoof between classes, on the stairs or in the corridors, magic moments. My heart would somersault as I saw her coming, in conversation with some other girl, who'd nudge her, *look, it's Paul*—and a smile lit up Marie's face as she saw me. I wished I could smile like that, like girls can, all total beaming fresh lovely innocent joy at the pure and simple love of being alive. I was too anxious and unsure of myself to ever smile as completely as that, as if the world belonged to you.

After school at half past three we piled onto the red double-decker heading downtown and sat upstairs at the front, Marie tucked under my arm, next the window, *my girl*.

I asked the conductor for "Two halves, please," and got a Belfast blasting, "Whaddaya mean, *halves*, and you sittin' there wi' yer arm round a girl!"

It was full fare from fourteen but you expected to get a half in your school uniform. I roasted and paid up, I hated that conductor to death for making a show of me in front of my girl.

But the feeling was smoothed over in the powerful forward motion of the tall bus, the cockpit of front windows wrapped around us commanding the streets below like a helicopter as we continued on our way, across Carlisle Circus. A right turn at the bottom of the hill and you joined the bustle and glamour of the city centre, crawling along the busy canyon between the high shop buildings, down Royal Avenue towards the green-domed palatial construct of the City Hall, the verdigris-coated old dark statues in its gardens like figures out of Dickens in the September afternoon sunshine.

Here at the heart of town was the quintessence of living. Walking from the bus stop, we crossed into Donegall Square and turned down narrow, high-walled Wellington Street, walking spread out like the Magnificent Seven plus one in our jubilant after-school gang. There was Mike and Charlie, Ralph, Marty and Bob and the two girls, Marie and Jacqui. Frankie got back loaded from the Eastbourne buses, but Jennifer and he kept to themselves after school, one to one, mostly at her place above her dad's butcher's shop. They were too intense a couple for hanging out with the gang in a coffee bar.

Isibeal's restaurant halfway down was afternoon siesta quiet; we filled a long corner table by the big plate-glass window on to the street. Joyce the manageress, a tall, thin, dark-haired South African lady, was easy-going and welcoming.

"Teas all round, please, Joyce!" Our order was unvarying. "That's…eight teas today, please!".

As we settled in Bob said,"Everyone glad to be back at school then?"

There was general agreement: "Yeh, back in the art room after dinner then down to Isibeal's! You have to get your priorities right, that's all."

"Looking forward to the group practice at Frankie's on Thursday!" said Mike. "Hear any good sounds over the summer, that we could do?"

I said, "The Beach Boys, *I Get Around*. Heard it for the first time crackling out of Marie's tranny as I walked her home in the blue summer dusk, it was like a bolt out of heaven, electrifying! We was sent!"

"D'you think we could handle the harmonies?"

"Ralphy-boy there can sing falsetto!"

"I like *Do-Wah-Diddy-Diddy*, I wanna sing that!" said Ralph, chin twisting in his boyish grin.

"You mean you like *diddies*!" said Marty, mordant, bespectacled. "You can't sing that here in Ireland, they'll all be thinking *dirty enough*! It must mean something else over the water!"

Charlie said, "I've got the chords for *House of the Rising Sun*."

"You can show us on Thursday, that's a must for our group!" we enthused.

"The Zombies, *She's Not There*, is really something, jazzy piano and everything," said Mike.

"Marie, what would you like to sing?" I asked.

"*You're No Good* is just beautiful," she said in a sad, sweet little voice, like the song itself.

"Hi, you just watch it, wee-doll, y'd better not be singing that to me!" I joked.

She smiled and babied me, "No, I've got one specially for me and you, wee lad: *Chapel of Love...*"

"*Gonna get married*, are we now?" I was thinking what a nice idea.

"Great harmonies *and* easy to sing," said Marie. "Go down really well with any audience." I liked how there was nothing of the pustular Hitler Youth tendency about her musical taste; good music had bugger-all to do with your age.

Matthew the little waiter, wavy fair hair and rosy-cheeked, round and chubby in his starched white jacket and black dickie-bow, passing with a tray of dirty dishes from a cleared table, took an interest in our big lively circle around the table and queried, "What's all the noise about, you lot?"

"Discussing songs for our group, Matthew!"

"Five boys and two girls?" he counted us.

"Jacqui's not in the group...yet."

"I can't sing and I can only play the triangle!" Jacqui protested.

"That's okay, we've not got a triangle player!"

"We could do with one for the *Chapel of Love.*"

"So you've all these boys to choose from, lucky you!" Matthew addressed Marie.

"I've already chosen one: him there!"

I sat there feeling singled out and special.

"He's the best court, is he now?" said Matthew wickedly.

"Yeh, I've actually tried them all, Matthew," said Marie, "we had a courting competition and Paul won the boys' entries!"

"Well, he's a lucky boy winning the singer of the band out of five contestants!" said Matthew. "Will you sing me something now, while Joyce is out the back? Not too loud now. What'll ye sing me?"

"*Chapel of Love?*" Marie looked round at us. We nodded approval, we all knew it off the radio by now and it was soft and right for genteel Isibeal's.

She began, "*Goin' to the chapel and we're gonna get married...*"

We all joined in, it was a good one to sing a cappella and the more we sang the more it gathered force and the better it sounded, the few other customers there, older people, looking round at us approvingly over their teapots and cream cakes. Life could imitate art and be a musical! When we finished there was mild applause from the other tables.

We sat on there in our corner at Isibeal's chatting, laughing; there were odd discreet snatches of more songs. Time went out the window as you came fully alive in the company and craic. You knew this was the heyday of your youth.

Then home and teatime. The cold black nights of the autumn term closed in. There was homework to be done. A long chat on the phone with Marie. My book at bedtime, Kerouac, *Maggie Cassidy*, the Massachusetts winter snow, sixteen-year old Jack the lad and his mates and the love of Maggie, a dear Irish girl; industrial Lowell even felt like Belfast—literature was universal, speaking the same language to everyone, everywhere, it united us, made us human.

Marie and I would go out Wednesday night to break the long school week; there was the cinema or friends' houses to listen to records. Thursday we all got ourselves on to the train at York Road; the swift diesel hugging the shore of the darkened expanse of Belfast Lough, the lights of the city on the other side that were extinguished as we bored inland to Whiteabbey.

Over the Valley of Death, a momentary winking of cold moonlight on the inky river away deep down through the winter-bare treetops, the river running forever with its terrible secret—*moody river, more deadly than the vainest knife*—poor Sarah Curran, the judge's daughter, murdered there.

We walked the short distance under the tall electric standards up Jordanstown Road, to number 100, the lighted interior warmth greeting us, piling into the big living room, our studio all set up and ready to go. Frankie was getting excited. We'd got a booking in December at the Green Island Hotel down on the Lough shore, the proprietor a golf club friend of Frankie's dad.

"Our first gig!" Frankie exclaimed jubilantly. "We gotta practise hard, get every number just so," he added sternly.

We warmed up with a few old favourites, Kinks, Beatles and Stones. Then Charlie demonstrated the chords for *House of the Rising Sun,* so simple, so profound and powerful; together we hammered out a rough version. The Animals' superbly polished recording of the old blues song had blared out from the radio and record shops all summer. Frankie and I took turnabout to sing the verses, and Charlie and Marie added their harmonies. It didn't sound bad; with our limited instrumentation it was more folksy than the Animals' version.

"Marie: your turn! *You're No Good.*"

"Thanks for that!" she grinned. That song title made us all feel guilty, no joke, it pricked your conscience somehow.

That night Marie wore her hair tucked back under a pretty gypsy headscarf, red-and-white, that emphasised her fair, gentle features and white hoop earrings. Her breasts stood out small and firm in a short, fitted, ribbed white woollen jersey and her blue jeans were skin-tight on the lovely curves of her hips and thighs, flaring out below the knee into bell-bottoms. In performance she emanated that unconscious, intense feminine physical presence that had drawn me to her in the first place.

You're No Good. We had Bob, fair and gangling, on guitar along with Frankie, Charlie on piano; they figured out the chords and showed me a bass guitar line to try and follow; I did my best, I was more of a singer than anything. Marty, handsome in black, thick Buddy Holly glasses, who'd taken over from Mike on the drums for a turn, beat an intro on the bass and we swung in behind him. Marie's voice came in frank and poignant on the superb melancholic fusion of lyric and melody. *"Feelin' better, now that we're through..."*

She meant every word she sang, telling it plain and powerful, yet a little understated, honest and moving and final—*You're no good, you're no good, you're no good...* It brought *t*ears to my eyes, the idea that *she* should ever have to tell *me* those words, *baby, you're no good.* I made up my mind then and there that if I never did anything else in my life, I would make sure I never broke that heart of hers *so gentle and true.* I had to go and kiss her afterwards, as if to reassure her, *you know that could never be me, baby.*

She lowered her eyes a moment, little-girl vulnerable, then looked up straight into mine in a kind of shining, loving appeal. Here was the case for good pop music, unpretentious and unafraid to touch the heart, draw out the simple finer feelings beneath the daily grind; sweet healing music, a true poetry of the people.

Frankie looked pleased with our efforts. "We'll show em what we can do at Green Island. The word will spread now. There'll be plenty of demand for live music coming up to Christmas. And in the new year we'll be moving on to Belfast, to the clubs and dance halls…"

"In the charts by next summer!" I exclaimed, nearly squealing for joy, really getting into it: cutting our first disc, fame on *Top of the Pops*, our heads looming on the TV screens of millions of living rooms across Ireland and Britain. I'd show Nancy Savage I was no guttersnipe!

"Seriously!" I said, "One of Frankie's songs, like *Rockin' On the Buses,* or a ballad like *Missing Jennifer*—sure they're as good as anything you'd hear on the wireless!"

"Ah gee, Paul!" The compliment brought on Frankie's mid-Atlantic accent. "You're real generous!"

15

Marie and I were were stretched out courting on the sheepskin rug in front of the big electric fire with its four long thin glowing red bars and the imitation flame effect illuminating the darkened sitting room at 14 Jacaranda Close, a winter's Friday night babysitting at the Kellys'.

Suddenly Marie moaned and cried out, "Oh, oh, oh, *ooooh*!" She got up and limped around. "Got a bloody cramp!" she said.

There was a crash directly overhead and feet thumped across the ceiling.

"Oh God, she's up!" said Marie.

"Maybe goin to the toilet?"

"No, she's coming down!"

Bang, bang, bang! She was coming down the stairs alright! The door burst open.

"Thought *you* were asleep!" Marie scolded. "It's after eleven and you have to get up for hockey practice in the morning!"

The cross face, puffy from sleep, scowled under its mop of dark bed-hair, "Yous woke me up!" she whined. "I was just driftin' off and I heard you screamin' out like that as if he was stranglin' you or somepin!"

"Don't be rid*iculous*!" Marie fired back. "You just need to mind your own business and go to sleep!"

Thelma twitched her nostrils. "It smells in here," she said, "like low tide at Greencastle!"

"Go back to bed, will you! We don't need your crudeness down here!" said Marie.

103

"Gropin' on the hearth rug!" Thelma sang out. "I'm tellin' Mummy and Daddy, so I am!" And beat a hasty retreat, banging the door behind her as Marie went for her.

"That child," said Marie coldly, "is a holy terror! *I* am telling Mummy on her. She's out of control and they need to send her off to a strict boarding school in the country somewhere that'll teach her some manners! Anyway, that's another romantic evening she's ruined!"

*

The gig came round early in December with the Christmas decorations appearing everywhere. Charlie had just got his driver's licence, soon after his seventeenth birthday, and drove the van borrowed from his father's garage, everyone stuffed in the back with guitars, drum kit, and other bits and pieces of instruments, and the feeling of excitement of our group's debut.

We turned off Shore Road, up a curving drive through winter shrubbery to the Green Island Hotel with its festive lights shining a welcome. We piled out of the van under a starry sky; there was a lovely festive bite in the night air, a coating of frost glittered on the tarmac and parked cars. You could hear the steady laboured unfurling of the waves on the dark shore beyond the sea wall. The lights of Holywood, County Down, studded the farther banks of the Lough.

We humped our equipment up the steps into the foyer with its Christmas tree. Blocks of wood smouldered in an old stone fireplace. The building was formerly the home of a linen lord; portraits of linen lords, presumably, adorned the oak-panelled walls. There was a damp, seedy smell like the rotting underside of straw in a stable.

The colourful poster we had designed in the school art room was stuck up on a door:

Saturday
FRANKIE AND THE FRINGE
From Buddy to the Beatles

Above the legend a line of cartoon figures vaguely resembling us, with Beatles hair and bell-bottoms, Marie's legs in a short skirt, performed a sort of St Vitus's dance.

"You're through here, lads," the tall Hermann Munster of a doorman ushered us into the dance hall. There were hard chairs lined against the wall and a high box-stage. Another group had set up there and as we arrived they began to play. The hall was empty apart from us musicians.

"It's only half seven," said Frankie nervously. "C'mon, we'll get a drink."

The bar was across the foyer, faded furnishings and wilting aspidistras, dim, dreary, and empty.

"You the band?" The barman, who might have been Hermann's brother, looked relieved to receive some custom. "You all eighteen? Drinks are on the house!"

"Red Heart Guiness, please!" was the order of the day. The barman proceeded to open seven bottles and fill seven glasses with the health-giving smooth black, white-collared stout.

We took our drinks back over to the dance hall. The other group, *The Cherries* it said on their bass drum, were going hard at it:

"WEEYPITE!"

Charlie doubled over in hilarity, mimicking the Belfast rendering of the surfing sound, *Wipe out!*

Frankie flashed him a killing look; we were meant to be out winning friends and influencing people, not taking the michael.

"Look at the lead guitarist!" Charlie persisted, pointing at him as if he were a circus freak. "He's an *albino*!" You laughed at people's afflictions back then, especially if you were Charlie.

"Charlie, that is enough!" Frankie scowled. "I only wish we had their instruments!"

They were all shiny electric guitars and big black amplifiers, an elaborate glittering drum kit; we were still acoustic.

"Yous a folk group or somepin?" the albino enquired, observing the paucity of our instruments.

"Bit of everything!" was the answer.

The Cherries played for an hour. It was true that they had better instruments and they sounded more practised and polished than us but it was still just a lot of noise they were making, no soul in it and no stage presence, or so we told ourselves. We were their only audience other than a few helpers who had come with them.

"Wait and see, there'll be an influx after nine," said Frankie hopefully, "after people have had a drink in the pubs and are looking for a dance. Nobody'd want to drink in that morgue across the foyer!"

There was no influx. Only two girls who had appeared and were hanging around, dancing together out on the empty expanse of floor.

"Beatles had the same experience before they got famous," said Ralph encouragingly. "Have you seen that picture of George and John dancing with each other in an empty ballroom somewhere in the south of England and just having a laugh about it? It's how it is, starting out."

Frankie was looking sick but Marie said, "Sure we can just use this like a practice evening, imagine we've got an audience out there."

She proceeded to sing her heart out, We kicked off with her lead vocal on *Heat Wave*—I loved how she sang *Sometimes I stare into space, tears all over my face,* I got a clear picture of her doing just that and a warm sense of the lovely emotional honesty and vulnerability of a girl.

We bashed away on our acoustic guitars, drums, the resident piano, harmonica, maracas, tambourine, bongos, a fizzing concoction of sounds in the echoey space, all held loosely together by our strong vocals.

As advertised there was Buddy Holly, *Peggy Sue* and *That'll Be The Day*, and new Beatles' tracks from *A Hard Day's Night*: *Tell Me Why* and *I Should Have Known Better*.

We did a couple of Frankie's songs and finished with yours truly on lead vocal for John Lennon's *Bad To Me*, that had been a hit for Billy J Kramer. It was the heyday of the Liverpool sound, a heartrending musicality with its subtle chord changes and powerful harmonies, that was a joy to perform.

Our two girl fans joined us for a drink in the bar afterwards. Norma and Valerie said, "This place is too far out for people to get to. We got a lift from Belfast with someone we knew going to Carrick. We seen your poster in Dougie Knight's record shop. We weren't disappointed, yous're the best-looking fellas we've ever seen all in one place at the same time!"

"Well, thanks, and do you like the music?" Frankie queried earnestly.

"Oh aye," they said vaguely, like an after-thought.

"You can have a lift back with us to Belfast," said Charlie. "If you don't mind squashing in. You can come in the front with me, Val."

"Aye, okay!" Valerie wasn't holding back.

Bob had his arm round Norma in the back, both girls looking happy with the arrangement. Marie slumped on my shoulder, exhausted after giving her all to a near-empty hall.

We dropped Ralph and Frankie at Jordanstown and headed back to Belfast. The dark country road spun out till the lights of the city met us at Greencastle.

It was half-twelve when Charlie dropped us at Marie's. I saw her into her house before I crossed the late, deserted Antrim Road and turned down Nettle Soup Lane.

We were pop stars now, all we needed was an audience. Just wait till we cut our first disc!

16

Audrey came home from the college halls of residence for the Christmas vacation. How wonderful it had been at home without her, the days running smoothly, pain-free. Oh to have been an only child, what a different, better person I should have been without the constant crushing of my personality by a malevolent older sibling. We were like Jane Eyre (me) and John Reed (Audrey). What comfort I had found in the opening pages of Charlotte Bronte's classic novel when the heroine finally turns on the nasty little bully and beats him to the floor!

Ma and Da went in trepidation of their daughter. Ma would stand up to her and there were ugly scenes between them, but Da was soft on the only daughter. By way of thanks she'd attack him over some triviality, some inconsequential opinion he'd expressed, any excuse to have a go at him. For example, he said that eating sweets could cause bad breath

"Well, what a load of old rubbish!" she moved in like a shark. "Where did you hear that?" The jaws working, shark-teeth bared.

Once she attacked him with one of his own carpet slippers, belting him across the shins where he sat in his armchair next the fire. He just took it with a dazed incomprehension, he would never show aggression towards a woman, he knew they didn't mean what they said half the time.

For Audrey, education equated to snobbery: how to be superi-or to family and neighbours, the people who paid for you to go to college. She had joined the university Officer Training Corps (OTC)—like most students, for the useful pocket money it provided. She had an army uniform—the inclusion of khaki knickers intrigued me, *killer drawers*—and had to spend a week or two of the summer holidays at an army camp in the Vale of Evesham where a woman private polished her shoes and called her "Ma'm" in a cockney accent. Audrey came back speaking in a silly-genteel anglicised voice, the *"Vellaveevsham"* slipping smoothly off her tongue, like the Garden of Eden.

That Christmas she was reading Guy de Maupassant and loved to repeat his name in the correct French pronunciation, *"Guidamo Passant"*, more like an Italian.

I checked out some of Guidamo's short stories (quite good) and his life—uh-oh! It was with relish then that I reported back to Audrey, "He died of VD, y'know!" That would put a stop to her affectation, I reasoned—no lower death was imaginable.

She flared up in outraged gentility, "Well, trust you to be digging up all the muck from the gutter! You have a lavatory mentality, brat!"

"Not so posh then either, was he, your Guidamo?"

"The private life of a writer has no bearing whatsoever on his work, which is his artistic creation!" She would literally stick her nose in the air as she mouthed her airy opinings.

"Then he's not much of a writer. More of a wanker. A good writer draws upon his own experience, that is what lends authenticity to his *creation*."

"Oh, you know everything, don't you, because you won the English prize at school! But you couldn't get your maths or science or geography—you'll never get into Stranmillis!"

"Just as well if you're anything to go by..." My ripostes were always so feeble and inept compared to the poison darts her tongue could fire off effortlessly.

But I must have hit the spot with that bit of playground *nana-na-nana* —how others can drag you down to their level—because she went for me physically then, the little hard fist in my gut, winding me, the nails of the other hand penetrating my pullover and the skin of my forearm. Not for the first time in my life, but I was bigger than her now, man-sized, and it was my Jane Eyre and John Reed moment; my body seemed to act of its own accord as

I got hold of her arms, pinioning them to her sides, out of harm's way, and propelled her out of the sitting room, across the hall and, a stroke of inspiration, into the little cloakroom under the stairs. And shut the door on her. There was no lock so I leant my weight against the door holding it shut for half a minute while she hammered and screamed inside. We were alone in the house.

"There's a light switch by the door," I reminded her, "if you need to stay in there. I'm not opening up till you say sorry…"

"What fo-or?"

"Everything. Ruining our family life. Nearly putting Ma in the Asylum. Bullying me, making my life growing up a misery, wrecking my self-worth…"

"Lemme out, lemme out! Ah'm sorry, Ah'm sorry! Anything you say, lemme out!"

Satisfied, I walked away then, up to my room to lie on the bed and listen to the thumping of my heart and Radio Luxembourg, letting the music blot out the horror of family life. However, it was better to have taken a stand, I reasoned. Walk tall.

Marie and I would compare notes and empathise with one another on the subject of sisters.

"I've said Thelma can come with us to the New Year's party at Mike's," she said. "She's turned fourteen and needs to learn some social skills before she grows up a total monster, it's best she starts where we can watch what she's up to. I told Mummy we'd both keep an eye on her. Mummy trusts you!"

"So she should, I've looked after her older daughter well enough, haven't I?'

"Trouble is, I don't trust myself with you!" Marie smiled.

New Year's Eve night came with an icing sugar sprinkling of snow and a bright moon sailing over white cloud formations like vast Himalayas above the city.

Ralph came up from Jordanstown in his dad's car and collected Marie, Thelma and me from Jacaranda Close.

'How are you, Ralphy-boy!" Marie kissed his cheek. "Oh, he's like a Teddy bear, you just wanna cuddle him!"

Ralph had this little boy, Bobby Vee handsomeness; he was dapper and stylish, with thick wheat-coloured hair, blue eyes and humorous full lips.

"I'm the boy to pl'ase you!" he exclaimed. "Did you two lovers have a nice Christmas then?"

I told him, "Turkey dinner here at Marie's, turkey tea at Nettle Soup Lane, bum-numbing hours of soporific telly!"

"At least you had each other," said Ralph; he didn't have a girl, but brightened up as he enquired, "Hi, who is this young lady?"

She resembled a large dressed-up china doll now in her bunchy party frock, candy-floss pink, her favourite colour. Her hair had been carefully coiffured and sprayed, like a big black plastic wig stuck on her head, under it the heavily made-up face with its hostile stare.

Ralph stared back at Thelma and joked, "It's not the wee-girl from the third form, is it, who makes eyes at the older boys on the stairs?"

"That sounds like her all right!" Marie heaved a sigh.

Thelma piped up, "Hi Ralphy-boy, can I be your date for the party at Mike's?"

You couldn't help but admire her precocity. She linked his arm, looked up adoringly into his face. He blushed; she *was* a bit young but didn't look it, did she, with the size of those diddies.

"Oh, all right then!" said Ralphy kindly, grinning, always up for a laugh.

"We're off, Eileen!" I called down the hall to Mummy, like the polite and trusted boyfriend I was supposed to be.

Eileen came out from the living room. "See and behave yourselves now!" she half-joked.

"We'll stay for Auld Lang Syne and be back here by one, Eileen," I said. "Ralph has to drive back to Jordanstown too."

"Well, keep an eye on that one, will you now?" She indicated her younger daughter who pulled an ugly face back at her. and said, "Whaddaya think I am, Mummy? A juvenile delinquent or somepin?"

"You certainly have potential in that direction," said Eileen candidly.

"Oh *thanks a lot*! Look, Ralphy-boy's my date for tonight, aren't ye? Wee dote, isn't he?"

"Poor Ralph, that's all I can say!" Eileen laughed.

Ralph smiled, " I promise I'll watch her for you, Mrs Kelly!"

Out at the car Thelma pushed her way to the front and parked her backside in the front passenger seat. As Ralph drove off she leant her head on his shoulder, her body angled stiffly like a toppled mannequin.

Ralph drove carefully, the rest of us in the back looking nervously over his shoulder, it was his first proper driving after passing his test. The city night seemed to crackle with the expectancy and excitement of New Year's Eve, the pubs, dance halls and parties waiting under the stars for us all.

We parked in front of Mike's on Crumlin Road, on the corner where the road forked; a smart semi, well hedged in from the road, garage at the side.

Mike greeted us at the front door, his fair hair combed in a fringe to his eyebrows, deep-chested in a white polo-neck, green corduroy trousers, white slip-ons, always immaculate from head to toe and his movements smooth and precise, almost hieratic— his grandfather had been a butler, he told us, laughing. (So had one of mine—Protestant job opportunity).

He ushered us into the warm, refined but comfortable interior, deep-piled fawn carpeting and yellow lampshades, the discreet, tasteful Christmas decorations still in place. The Dave Clark Five were clumping away on the big radiogram under the window, *Glad All Over!...Yes, Ahm...!*

Gwyneth and Phyllis from school were gabbling on the couch; Bob, Marty and Charlie standing up by the fireplace.

"Hiya, Charlie!" Thelma called out and hurried to his side. Ralph was left standing there open-mouthed, looking deserted for a minute, till he spotted Phyllis.

Thelma insinuated herself under Charlie's armpit, looking up at him like a dog, with eager shining, worshipful eyes as he bummed about flogging off a secondhand car at his dad's garage that morning, "My first big sale!"

"Yah, capitalist!" I jeered.

"Beatnik!" he retorted.

"Billy and Ruby gone?" I asked Mike about his parents.

"Aye, New Year's Rotary dinner at the Malone Hotel. Dickie-bows and posh frocks. Ruby's left us a pile of turkey sandwiches in the kitchen. They assure me they'll not be back till gone one."

Cider and beer were swallowed, clouds of cigarette smoke drifted over the room.

Bob produced his guitar and we put on a bit of a folksy sing-song to warm things up, harmonising on Peter, Paul and Mary, *Take off your old coat and roll up your sleeves, Life is a hard road to follow, I believe,* and the Kingston Trio, *Don't give a damn about a greenback dollar.*

Marie sang Joan Baez *There but for fortune* while Bob's guitar followed her, the chords climbing and sinking, persistent, poignant, dramatic, like a fated life.

"Christ, Marie, that near made me cry!" I told her and kissed her. Her voice, its purity or something, always had that effect on me.

Our parties were never big, maybe a dozen of us at Mike's that night. A bit of dancing then the lights lowered and someone put on Brubeck. Cool. The male to female party numbers were even and we sat round in couples, courting on the three-piece suite and the carpet, spreading out into the smaller back living room.

"You and Marie can have my bed," Mike told me. "Gwyneth and I can go in the guest bedroom." He was an only child.

Gwyneth was an old flame from riding lessons at Glengormley, a big soft strawberry blonde.

Ralph was happy on the floor with Phyllis. Marty and Bob paired with our two girl fans, Norma and Valerie from the Green Island Hotel whom we had invited to the party, they were the nearest thing we had to a fan club.

Holding hands, Marie and I climbed the stairs. We were familiar with Mike's bedroom, past the loo, opposite the top of the stairs. The door was shut, I gave it a push.

Two figures were on the bed, the landing light shining in on them like a policeman's torch.

"Hey!" Charlie protested.

"Thelma!" Marie exclaimed. "I thought you were downstairs in the back room! What are you doing up here?"

"Same as you and him are doing, or going to do!"

"Don't be vulgar, I'll tell Mummy and Daddy. Charlie, can you please take her back downstairs, she's only fourteen, you know."

Marie held the door ajar as they slunk out, Thelma shooting her one of her psycho killer-looks.

We shut the door after them and got under the eiderdown on the double bed in the dark and cold. A lamp post light shone on the closed curtains.

"You'd think Charlie would have more sense," said Marie. "What's he doin' anyway with a wee bag like Thelma? Charlie could have any girl he wants."

I said, "Thelma's been all over him. She's been eyeing him up at school for a couple of years. She went for him tonight like a boa-constrictor to a hog, he didn't have a chance."

"I hope we got here before they went too far," said Marie.

"They still had all their clothes on."

"That wouldn't stop them! Imagine if she got knocked up tonight, at her first teenage party. I know who'd get the blame for it."

"Charlie's not stupid," I said. "We're all terrified of the B word."

"Babies, yeah!" Marie gave a wee shudder. "I mean, they're lovely fat cuddly little bald people, but only when the time is right for their company. Or else it's *shame and dishonour on the famil-ee.*"

I said. "*We're* old enough to get married now. An old friend of mine from my class at primary school, Matt, is married with a kid, they've got a flat on the Antrim Road."

"Sounds cosy!" Marie cheered up a bit, cuddling up. We kissed. "But what's the rush after all?" she said sensibly. "Better finish our education first! We can still have fun, can't we? Then think how good it will feel when we eventually get there, when the time is just right and we can really relax and enjoy it!"

When we came back downstairs, people were up waltzing to Johnny Mathis, *Misty*. Thelma, pissed on cider, hung from

Charlie's neck, her feet trailing on the carpet, like a comedy sketch.

"I love that fellah!" she declared drunkenly to the world at large. "My wee Charlie, Ah won' let no one take him away from me, ever, so I won't, don' care if it's a fuckin' catwalk model, Charlie s *mine*!..."

"Language, Miss!" Marie snapped. She was talking positively of a career in teaching now, and I could just picture her knocking the youngsters into shape.

"*Ooo, Ah'm so sorry, Big Sis*!" Thelma mocked. "Mummy's wee favourite, aren't ye, Miss Goody Two Shoes, with the Perfect Boyfriend, but I know what the two of yous get up to when you're baby-sittin', the fingers and everything, I caught yous at it!"

Marie opened her mouth ready to scream but Mike turned off the music abruptly and announced in his smoothly authoritative voice, like David Jacobs, "Just coming up to midnight now, folks, are you all ready? Join hands everybody!"

The antique chiming clocks in the sitting room and hall went off like time-bombs and we listened as, not quite synchronised, they beat out the slow, heavy twelve strokes to midnight.

And it was a new year! It was an opportunity then to kiss all the girls as well as shaking hands with the mates—the thrill of permitted infidelity, while the male handshakes could be therapeutic, a healer of the year's umbrages and fights.

More booze that we didn't need was quaffed. Marie and I had to support Thelma staggering between us out to Ralph's car.

Ralph had had a few and drove slowly. Blessedly, the streets were empty, he'd have had to swerve into a lamppost or something to have a crash.

"Oh thank God, they're in bed!" said Marie as we turned into Jacaranda Close. Only the hall light glowed in the fanlight of the sleeping house.

Thelma woke up, crying out, "Where's Charlie, where's my boyfriend?"

"Shush! Charlie's gone home to bed and it's your bedtime too," said Marie. "Don't wake up Mummy and Daddy; if they see you like this we'll all be in for it!"

We got her over to the door.

"G'night, Paul!" Thelma kissed me, awkward but lascivious, on the mouth. "Marie, your boyfriend is lush, so he is!"

"Yes, and he is all mine! Now careful getting up the stairs! G'night, Paul love!"

I eased the front door shut behind me. Ralph drove me on to Antrim Road.

"She's a handful, that Thelma!" he said.

"Reckon you had a lucky escape from her, Ralph!"

"Aye, near made a fool of meself, she was comin' on so strong and I started to heat up. Then she took one look at Charlie at the party and disappeared into his arms! *You would cry too if it happened to you!*" He laughed.

"Aye, she'd been going on about seeing him at school, how much she fancied him. She's a bit young, don't you think?"

"I could see that at the party. The big diddies make her look older, and her tongue hangin' out for a good coort!"

"You got Phyllis instead—nice girl, more your type anyway."

"She's a good wee court and all, down on the carpet back of the couch!"

"Dirty enough!"

He dropped me at the entrance to Nettle Soup Lane. The key had been left in the front door for me; they had gone to bed. My parents didn't go out at night. Audrey was sleeping over at a student party on Lisburn Road.

I slipped up to bed in the silent house. I'd had quite a bit to drink but wasn't sleepy, I lay staring into the darkness, wide awake for ages, glorying in the life that had come to me. The neurotic loneliness and melancholia of my early teens had faded to a forgotten blot on the jotter of my life. Now there was the excitement of friends and, above all, my own girl, Marie. I lay there basking in the warm sun of her love, just letting my brain sift images of her, how far we had travelled together from that first schoolboy fixation with her legs under the desk in maths. And there was still the thrill of anticipation, the journey yet to come…

PART TWO

17

"Oh my God, would you look at the long hair on the wee gutty!"

I was back from a summer working holiday on the Channel Islands, just off the night ferry from Liverpool and we were sitting around on deckchairs in the back garden at Nettle Soup Lane, Ma and Da, Audrey and I.

Da had retired from the Gas Board at Easter, after forty-five years' service. He sported a deep suntan from the fine summer spent mostly in the garden, and a week with Ma in a boarding house at Portrush. His hair stood up in a smooth wavy white bush on his handsome olive-skinned head

Ma, ten years his junior, was a self-composed little woman, her reddish hair faded and greying, and the same glasses in hexagonal tortoiseshell frames that she had worn all through my life. Both my parents were always smartly dressed, even just pottering about the house and garden.

It was Audrey who commented on my hair, which I had left to grow long over the two summer months on the distant island of Guernsey. I was too happy being home again, and Marie coming round shortly, to be bothered being annoyed by bitchery.

"We were hanging out with the island beatniks," I explained, to annoy her more. "First we were sleeping rough in the old German Nazi bunkers on the island. The son of the Duchess of Sark was with us, long hair like a girl, a slight, androgynous figure, like a good-looking version of Mick Jagger."

"Hangin' out with the local fruits?" Audrey jeered, putting on her supposed plebeian voice.

"I don't think so," I said. "We were there in the bunker till the fuzz came and moved us on, they're quite heavy on the island, then we squatted in this sort of tenement at Pedvin Square where the beats hang out and the pros ply their trade…"

"Paul!" It was Ma's turn to be shocked, softly. "I don't think that's very nice now!"

"Sorry, Mum, I was just setting the scene: the slummy part of town it was, we had nothing to do with the bad people there. In fact Mike was going out with a really nice respectable girl from the town."

"You stayed faithful to your wee Marie then? Eh, eh?" Audrey mocked in a silly sneering voice as if that made me either a ninny or a liar.

In fact, I had kissed one of the room-maids at the Royal Hotel where we worked in the kitchen, Diane, pretty but clueless and repressed, eminently forgettable, not a patch on Marie; that cheating kiss so insignificant and unmemorable in hindsight that it might as well never have happened and I certainly felt no guilt over it.

Ignoring my sister I went on, "The leader of the beatniks was called Jesus. Kind of a Hollywood version of *the* J C: striking blue eyes, sun-bleached long blond hair and beard; dressed in khaki shorts and shirt, sandals. There were notices in the windows of the cafes over there, *No Dogs, No Beatniks*. We Belfast lads found a small cafe like a sort of hut with those wooden booths inside, down on the harbour; Joe the proprietor was really friendly, like a kindly uncle to us and fed us well—beans on toast for breakfast, egg and onion sandwiches to take away for lunch at the greenhouses where we worked, and a two-course dinner in the evening, pie and mash and a pud."

"Anywhere you go in this life there are those dacent sort of people ready to help you," said Da.

"Our boss at the greenhouses was the same, Tom with a French surname, lived with his mum and dad, brought us out tea and biscuits three times a day. The mother had seen Fisherwick Presbyterian Church on *Songs of Praise* on the telly and felt a connection to us Irish boys she thought must be good

Christians!" I wasn't sneering, I felt connections were important in a more commonly indifferent world.

I continued the tales of our summer adventures to Marie when she came round in the afternoon. It had turned showery and we sat in the front room, just the two of us. The six weeks' separation felt like a lifetime, but oh what a joy it was to be with her again, to kiss her and hold her hand and draw her down on to my knee and hug her waist and see the smooth shapely brown legs hanging down beside my jeans as she turned her bright little face to me and spoke in the sweet, tinkly voice of the Belfast child.

"Did you miss your Marie?"

Kiss.

"You bet I did. Every single moment of every day!"

Kiss.

"Did you kiss any Guernsey girls?"

Kiss.

Little white lie, for it had meant nothing: "Of course not! Whaadaya think I am, a two-timer? Did you kiss any Belfast or Bangor boys?"

"Actually, yeah!" She nodded and looked me dead in the eye. I felt my heart sink, down through the floor. Oh God, was there someone else? I should never have gone away all summer like that, I knew it all along! I'd only sent her two postcards all summer, one when I got there, one coming back.

But I played it cool, the golden rule, as the song said, Billy Fury.

"Who?" Heart turned to a stone in my chest.

"Tony Black." The two words fell like hammer blows.

"Not that wee shite? That dwarf! Marie!" Tony Black with the awful dated Teddy boy hair, strutting his short arse under a maroon school honours blazer. "Was he standing on a box at the time?" These were heightist comments, I appreciate now; I like short people actually, but I had to say something facetious and prejudiced to ease the explosive tension of the jealousy rising in me.

"He came round to Marlene's with some of the First Fifteen, Stan Goudie and Randall Herron, they all have that old Teddy boy hair still. They were pissed even before they got to us. Anyway, Tony saw I was on my own. 'Where's fruity boy tonight?' says he."

"Aye, that's what they call us lads from the art room, me and Mike and Charlie. I hope you told Tony bloody Black to eff off?"

"Well, before I could tell him anything he was all over me, kissing me."

My blood boiled up, I would kill Tony Black—literally, I would seek him out, kick his head in…

"Why did you let him?" I demanded to know. The jealousy sent its deadly venom coursing through my veins, a madness that really could lead to murder and the hangman. Well, I'd get my own back, I'd tell Marie about Diane, say she made me kiss her and I'd let on she was an insatiable nymphomaniac!

"Like I say, he attacked me," said Marie, "I had no choice in the matter! He had thick slobbery lips, like a pair of famished leeches!"

"Och, Marie, Ah'm gonna be sick! Did you not shout help or rape or something?"

"I was wearing jeans that night, and as you say, Tony Black is short, so it was easy…"

"*What was?*" For him to…? Standing up? Oh no!

"To knee him in the bollocks, *wham*! He doubled up, fell on his knees in front of me like a slave, his face turning green and he was about to puke up on Marlene's good carpet but she came running and shooed him off to the bogs."

Only now did Marie's face shed its serious expression as she burst out laughing. Her laughter was infectious and I was swept up in it, the two of us rolling on the sofa in the afternoon.

"Oh God, Ah'm gonna wet myself!" said Marie, clutching at herself.

"You cru-el girl! You might have robbed him of his manhood!"

"Done the female sex a favour… Tell us about Guernsey then," she said. "Did you have a good time with the beatniks then?"

"It was a roughing-it time really, but an experience. There were a lot of other school students from Belfast and there was trouble when they decided on a march to celebrate the Twelfth."

"What for? I mean, away over there who cares about William of Orange and the Battle of the Boyne, 1690?"

"That's what we said but maybe it was going to be a bit of craic and we went along to have a look; they were meeting up in one of the pubs at the farther end of the promenade, so they could parade back down the whole length of it.

"You wouldn't credit it but some of them were wearing Orange sashes they'd brought over with them, no joke, family heirlooms charged with this sort of quasi-religious mystique, it gave me the creeps, the phoney sanctity of it, you know, the dour, dark homes they must come from, that persist in such practices, like witchcraft. And there were reams of orange crepe paper handed out, to wind round ourselves for sashes. It gave you sort of a kick, the feeling that you were standing up for something noble, though God knows what.

"Anyway, the lads and I weren't too enthusiastic and cut off out of it as they set out to march down the middle of the main road along the promenade, there was even a banner unfurled and carried aloft, King Billy victorious on his white charger. We watched from a safe distance, on the path by the sea wall separated from the road by public gardens.

"In no time at all, all hell was let loose, there were the angry blasts of car-horns as the traffic piled up behind the march and the police arrived almost immediately—it's a bit of a police state over there, a tax haven for the rich. They proceeded to arrest the marchers, chasing after the ones who tried to get away. There was an Orangeman up a tree close to us, he'd torn down a big branch to beat off a cop climbing up after him, it was kind of Keystone Cops comical. We hurried on out of it quick as we could.

"Next day at work in the greenhouses the farmer told us the police had been round looking for Irish but he thought we were Scottish and told them no Irish here. We said we were Irish and explained we'd had nothing to do with the trouble in the town the previous night. The farmer was perplexed: what had hit their peaceful wee island? What on earth was it all about?

"It was all over the front page of the local rag. The six named, proudly self-confessed ringleaders of the march had been charged and sentenced within twenty-four hours, with the option of an £80 fine or one week in prison. We bumped into one of them in the town after work; we recognised each other from school, he was upper sixth, Peter Daly, tall, slim, nice-looking fellow, rather refined and gentlemanly, not what you'd expect really, but then Unionism comes from the upper class, doesn't it, manipulating the gullible proles!

"Peter was remarkably sanguine about the whole business. The tanned, sensitive face under the light-brown hair showed no regret for what he had done, it was a holy duty in a glorious cause.

"'*I spoke to my da on the phone to Belfast*', says he, '*and he's been dead decent about paying the fine, he's okay about the whole thing*'."

Proud of you, no doubt, I was thinking, and '*After all, it was the sash your father wore,*' I said, quoting their famous anthem. He gave me a look, '*The Orange cause is no laughing matter, friend. You see these foreigners you meet abroad don't understand us Norn Iron Protestants, that's the real problem*'."

"No, they think you're bonkers actually—I'd like to have told him that to his face but he was in enough trouble already, I didn't need to rub it in."

18

It had been my second bash at O levels that summer term, giving me a total of five now, but still no maths or geography or science, so I could not be accepted for teacher training.

It was Da to the rescue. "I've had a word with Jimmy Mehaffy at the Gas Board and he thinks he could fix you up in the accounts department."

A clerk on the Gas Board, was that to be my fate? To be a clone of Dad?

"Well, the Gas Board served me well," he counselled me. "I have a good pension now. You could follow my example and take night classes for one of the chartered institutes, accountants or secretaries, seven-year course, and you could be head of a department at thirty!"

My heart sank. But I'd outgrown school, I certainly wasn't going back there, my mates had all left and gone into business, and Marie was starting Stranmillis. She'd buckled down and got her maths like a good girl; she would train to be a primary school teacher.

Thinking positively, there was a kind of appeal, a safety, a certitude and security about Dad's office world, beckoning to me now. I had an interview with Jimmy Mehaffy at the Gas Board offices on the periphery of the town centre. An old Victorian factory-like building of grimy red brick, it stood on a corner of the busy main road opposite the back streets huddled in the bad breath of the big rusty gasometer.

Inside it was better, I'd been a frequent visitor here in Dad's time and could still feel his comforting aura about the place, the sense of a cosy routine in a snug, timeless bubble of desk and paperwork, the rounds of the tea trolley and the craic shared with colleagues.

The older women smiled at me, recognising Eric Carroll's lad, but there was a dearth of young people like myself. I felt grown-up in a new, three-piece navy pinstripe suit, my Beatles mop neatly trimmed over the eyebrows, ears and collar. Maybe it was my grammar school education that gave me a super-confident feeling and the belief that the Gas Board would be lucky to get Paul Carroll. The lads, my mates, had sneered at the job, of course, the commodity of gas, I suppose, it was hardly sexy. But maybe they'd be laughing on the other side of their faces when one day I would be Head of the Gas Board!

Jimmy Mehaffy reminded me of Dad with his handsome large grey head, warm tweedy persona and unhurried air, come day, go day, God bless Sunday.

"So you're taking over the family business, eh?" he cracked, then grew a little more serious. "And tell us now, Paul, your father did a great job here but what will you bring to Gas that is parteecular to yourself, to your own individual talents and abilities? What exciting innovations might you envisage here?"

And then the most awful thing happened, it was nerves basically, my brain made a crazy connection between "gas" and "gassing", like bullshitting or worse still, *farting,* like the pong from the gasometer. Whatever it was, I was convulsed by a hopeless fit of the giggles, like some poor child I'd heard once, during the Last Post at a Remembrance Day church service and Reverend Gillies with a face like thunder on him. But Jimmy Mehaffy just blinked his heavy-lidded eyes and stared at me across the expanse of his polished mahogany desk like a big frog, in puzzlement rather than disapproval, or as if I were only suffering a sneezing fit.

"Are you all right?" he enquired.

"Yes...to answer your question, Mr Mehaffy, I think I'd...ha, ha ha!...ho. ho. ho!...I mean, I would, I would...ah-haaa! ha, ha, ha!...I mean, seriously, I have this love...this love of literature... ho,ho,ho, hoho!"— Like g*as on the page*? Or *between your bumcheeks*?—"Aha, ha! Ha! Ha!" Oh grow up, Carroll, for God's-sake! I was sweating profusely, in a fever.

Jimmy, his character cut from the same warm Irish cloth as my da, came to my rescue. "D'you mean 'improve written communication within the department'?"

Suddenly, mercifully, I sobered up. "Yes! Exactly!" And I thought of something good to say: "There is an art to written communication, a subtle and complex *melange* of creativity, accuracy and courtesy, from the longest letter to the humblest memorandum"—I'd heard Dad speak of the latter and I added, "as in literature, from Tolstoy to Enid Blyton..."

Jimmy Mehaffy blinked at me again, simultaneously impressed and perplexed. "Well, aye, Paul," he said at last. "I like the sound of that, yes indeedy! We could just do with polishing up our act. Gas needs new young blood if it is to survive into the coming nuclear age. We can offer you a poseetion as Accounts Officer, commencing mid-October..."

I stared at him stupidly, it had all gone dreamlike, a bad dream maybe.

"What do you say?" Jimmy smiled, thinking I must be over the moon at his offer.

I wasn't, but well, a job was a job for all that.

"Yes, thank you, I'd like that very much," I said, nodding emphatically. It just popped out of me in the end. It was fate.

We stood up and shook hands on it. Dad would be delighted. What else was there for me anyway?

But down on the street, turning back to the city centre, the cold autumn wind and grinding traffic blowing grit in my face, I was overcome with the most awful sense of loneliness and failure. It was as if the job had sealed my fate, dealt the definitive rupture with carefree youth and fun. It was goodbye to all that and forever after it would be long hours stuck at an office desk, in the company of a lot of old people. At the drop of a hat, it seemed, I had become a fully-fledged adult.

Marie was getting ready for Stranmillis now, the real student girl in her big striped college scarf, her cold pink autumn cheeks, cuddlesome in the chunky green sweater she'd knitted herself, full of knots, and orange trews hugging the curves of the hips and legs I worshiped at.

"Oh, I wish I was going to college with you!" I moaned.

We had a few weeks hanging about before starting the new life, and spent each day together, the usual, at each other's houses or trips downtown to the shops and Isibeal's. The lads were working in the middle of town, Charlie at Moon Insurance, Ralph at the Northern Bank, and we'd meet up for lunch. They seemed so happy to be finished school and out at work, they were in their natural element. They looked handsome and confident in their new office suits. Where *they* worked there were lots of other young people, new mates and nice girls.

"Better than the Gas Board then," I said, "it's all oldies there."

"*You*'ve got a girl," Marie reminded me. "You're looking right at her!"

"Sure you're all I need," I told her, "it's true! Long as you don't run off with some other wee student at Stran."

"Nah, the fellas starting college are all spotty and immature, you wouldn't want to run off with any of *them*!"

We were only joking but I breathed a secret sigh of relief at Marie's words. To lose her now would simply be the end, I told myself, my self-worth wiped out. I clung to her like a lifebelt.

We made love in the afternoon sometimes, when we had one or other of our houses to ourselves. It was great to undress in the stagnant grey afternoon light and get into a cold bed together, hers or mine, shivering and holding each other close, our warm skin woman to man. The sex stopped short of the full measure. You could go in a chemist's and buy a packet of frenchies over the counter but just the thought of such a public transaction, almost like a flasher, I thought—it'd be even worse in a barber's shop— put you off ever doing it. There was still an unspoken powerful social taboo on premarital sex. I'd heard of the new contraceptive pill for women now but Marie never mentioned it.

I thought how nice it would be if Marie and I were married, and people did get married from the legal age of sixteen—usually with a bun in the oven—but it was more of a lower-class thing, it seemed, and nice respectable people like us were expected to wait till we were in our mid-twenties, settled and ready for parenthood—sensible enough, I suppose; there was no fate worse for a girl than to be an unmarried mother.

Marie started college and I was the last one left at home, girlfriend and mates all gone out into the wide world. The cold, wet weather had set in and I took the opportunity to stock up with books from the central library and lie on my bed reading by the electric fire in the long afternoons.

Behind the quiet, deeply satisfying pleasure of reading I felt the soul-promptings *to be a writer myself*. But I knew that took time and what was the rush? I knew that I would put myself, my own life, at the centre of my writing and so it behoved me to live that life as fully as possible in the interim. The effect of this was a heightening of experience; the written life had to be better, more alive than unconscious, ordinary, passive living.

I was moving on from the American writers I'd favoured in my early and middle teens, Salinger, Herlihy, McCullers, Capote, Tennessee Williams, Steinbeck, Kerouac, to something closer to home, the English "kitchen sink" school, Braine, Sillitoe, Storey, Barstow, Waterhouse. Those writers, mostly Yorkshire for some reason, like the Brontes before them, and with influences of Nottingham's D.H.Lawrence, the master, chimed with my own situation now in Ireland, a clerk in a provincial industrial town.

The northern English novels portrayed the same sort of reality that I was rooted in, opened your eyes to its own strange beauty and drama surrounding you, a sort of glamour of ordinariness surprising and swelling the heart. You could taste the wholeness of life on your tongue, smell it, feel it, the rain and fog and chill, wet overcoats, crowded buses, the lines of smoking Victorian terrace chimneys and the dominance of the mills and docks, pubs and churches; you could hear it in the unadulterated local speech. It lived and moved and had its being in the earthed sensuality of women.

Not that the reality was all working class, though that was what gave it its strong character; where there's muck there's brass and there was a middle class too, the university, the theatres, concert halls, art galleries, libraries and bookshops, the central new Mod fashion boutiques as well as the local drapers, the smart hotel bars and gee-and-tees besides the spit and sawdust pubs and pints of porter.

Then, not unlike the north of England of those novels, there were the attractive rural surrounds of the industrial town, the hills that enclosed Belfast: Divis, Black Mountain, Cavehill; beyond them the dreamy soft green patchwork hinterland, the Antrim Coast Road and the Glens, the County Down coast. The countryside and its small towns belonged more to a past of steam trains, Sunday School excursions, family holidays, Bangor or Portrush. Growing into our late teens now we didn't bother to look back much, we were townies through and through.

19

The day of judgment must come, and come it did.

Mid-October, pouring rain, chilly now. Ma in her dressing gown, waking me with a cup of tea; her unnecessary cheerfulness grated on me, I grunted crossly, unstuck my eyelids, leant up on my elbow scowling at life over the steaming rim of my teacup. I could hear the unceasing patter of the rain behind the curtain at the window, promising me a good wetting to start the day. The horror-reality of Work congealed in my chest.

The electric fire Ma had turned on for me emitted a low hum as its two short bars reddened like a devil's eyes, with a whiff of singed dust. She had put my clean shirt and trousers over the bedroom chair to warm before the fire. That was the kind of caring, helpful action that Audrey called "petted on the mammy", as if it were *wrong* somehow to care in small ways for the child you had brought bawling into the harshness of this world. Nobody would have dared go near her foul moods first thing in the morning, that was the only difference between us.

I'd cultivated this crisp image of myself going off to work in my new clothes, briskly handsome, the man about town! But in the reality of it now I resented the contact of the new material on my skin, the worsted trousers with their knifelike crease, rubbing against my kneecaps, the clammy pink nylon shirt buttoned to the throat, the pink-and-grey striped tie knotted up pressing on my Adam's apple like a garrotte, then the tailored jacket, stiff and heavy on the shoulders. It was like donning a suit of armour to do battle with the world after the months of freedom, sloping about in the casual clothes I had grown into like an extra layer of skin, the soft worn jeans, shirts and pullovers,

And this was a battle all right, Paul Carroll v the World. All wrong. Downstairs the coal fire burning too bright and cheerful, like Ma, and the wireless tuned to an over-energetic orchestral medley on the Light, the table set for the one going off to work, the man of the house now! I forced down a bowl of cereal, a boiled egg and toast, a cup of tea, feeling almost sick. Ma sat with me supportively, still in her old brown dressing gown, trying to make conversation while I grunted, scowled and hated myself for being this way, beyond all grace.

"Well, have a good first day, Paul!" she bade me at the front door.

The rain was falling mercilessly, I put up my umbrella and stepped out under it. A gust of wind threatened to blow the brolly inside-out and as I struggled to control it a puddle in the lane splashed underfoot and I felt water seep into my sock. It was the assault of an inhospitable, unfeeling world. I came out on Antrim Road to the charging traffic swishing past. There was a queue in the rain for the downtown bus.

I sat damply near the front of the upper deck looking out at the Phoenix pub and the familiar route from school into town . Those were the happy days, riding down to Isibeal's after school, Marie under my arm by the window, our glorious gang all around us.

Now it was *oh, lonesome me*. The familiar sights out the window belonged to better days, they had nothing to do with me anymore. I was a real nowhere man.

I got down by the City Hall and walked it from there, out past the markets, bearing my black brolly aloft like a city gent. The tall commercial buildings of the centre ceded to the artisan terraces, dwindling back like railway lines from the main road, the gasometer looming over them. My heart froze as the dull, dirty brick walls of the Gas Board loomed into view, then I could see the other employees entering there ahead of me, my jaundiced young eyes writing them off as dowdy and uninspiring figures, the kind of dull ordinary people, like robots, who offered no hope. Surely I had been intended for greater things?

I ducked in through the revolving doors that propelled me onward like fate. And here I was then, in prison. Well, at least prison was a dry, warm refuge from the spraying, roaring streets. The tiled entrance hall smelt sweetly of polish. There was a long, burnished reception counter and wood panelling on the walls. A uniformed porter came forward to meet me. I showed him my letter, *"please report to Mr Magill in Accounts"*.

"You're for Kevin," said the pleasant grizzled wee man. "Follow me, Mr Carroll."

Mr Carroll! God, I was grown-up now! Not so bad either, a bit of respect made a change from Nancy's "guttersnipe, Carroll!".

We went through swing doors down long windowless corridors past office doors, penetrating to the heart of the building. Would I remember my way back out of this maze? I wondered anxiously. Worse still, you could find yourself locked in overnight deep in the building, closed up while you'd been sitting on the bogs. Like the horror story, *A Night in the Black Museum.*

We turned in through a door marked *Consumer Accounts*, to a biggish office. The electric lights burned with a cosy feeling and there was a comforting smell of tobacco smoke. But what had this place to do with me? The middle-aged clerks in rows, greying, thinning heads lowered to the Dickensian high, slanting desks with their messes of paperwork.

Kevin Magill stood up to shake my hand, a handsome middle-aged man, with smooth olive skin, bluish about the jowls, fine brown eyes and thick, greying black hair. He was nicely dressed in a green-flecked tweed suit; there was a dignity about him, the general effect was of a sincere, wholesome persona that a boy could look up to.

"You're Mr Carroll's son?" Kevin smiled; my da was a well-liked man with his easy way, though he was sensitive to any perceived disrespect, he was old school *Mr Carroll*, never Eric.

I nodded, swallowed, in an access of shyness.

"Enjoying his retirement, is he?" Kevin enquired.

I cleared my throat but my voice came out a bit squeaky. "Oh aye, sporting a Riviera tan after *living* in the garden all summer! Now the weather's turned he's ensconced in his armchair by the fireside, immersed in his collected works of Dickens!"

"I can't wait till that's me with time to read," said Kevin. "Only twenty-three years to go! I came here in nineteen forty-two out of technical college."

I did a quick calculation of my own prospect: *forty-seven years to retirement, it'd be well into the next century!* It seemed almost in the realm of science-fiction.

"You a reader like your dad then?" Kevin asked me.

"Oh, yes." I said some of the writers I liked and because Kevin looked intrigued I added, "I write too! Short stories, but I'd really like to write a novel."

Kevin's brown eyes dilated in appreciation, a look of enlightenment. He said, "Have you heard of the Belfast writer Michael McLaverty? He was headmaster of Ballymurphy school in West Belfast where I come from. He's a brilliant writer, short stories and novels, oh aye."

I shook my head. "The only Belfast writers I've read are Maurice Leitch and the playwright Sam Thompson."

"Aye, *Over the Bridge*, I saw it performed at the Empire Theatre. Sam was a shipyard worker himself, a good man. McLaverty too takes his inspiration from the ordinary local people."

"It's a movement in literature now," I said, "like the 'kitchen sink' writers in England. Real life. I'll have a look for McLaverty at the library!"

The idea of a true Belfast literary novelist, an older man deeply rooted in the place, fascinated and inspired me. That was where real literary inspiration sprang from, *right under your nose,* the very place you lived in, all the subtle textures and flavours of the life you knew intimately.

Like now, it occurred to me, the pallid spitting void of Belfast sky framed in the high, narrow windows of the old office building, the wavy grain of the dark varnished wooden desk where I sat next to Kevin. *I too would be a writer,* I felt it for sure now, and this would be my subject, or an important part of it, the life of Belfast and its working people.

Kevin was showing me the ledgers I would be working with but I was away out the window, high on the dream of literature and only half-listening, while his supportive presence, the warm, cultured Belfast voice in my ear, was soothing, lulling me into a strange contentment.

Kevin introduced me to some of the other clerks, kindly men and women of the older generation who looked with affection on the new young lad just out of school, perhaps a reminder of their own first day at work. It was like one big family. There was the contentment of a fixed routine in an unchanging, comfortable setting; no real pressure on you, just a steady-going completion of straightforward tasks. You could smoke at your desk and at half past ten on the big clock on the wall above us, Kevin said, "C'mon, we'll have a cuppa tea, Paul!"

A *"cuppatea"*, like a single word in that homely Belfast voice, had never sounded so appealing. I would tell Ma; she and I exchanged and collected cosy local sayings of town and country so they became part of our family vocabulary.

Upstairs in the canteen, the tables laid end to end down the long, narrow room were packed and buzzing with eager chatter. Kevin treated me to the cup of tea and two chocolate digestive biscuits—"One's never enough," he said—it was like having a kindly substitute dad looking after you. I had worked out he was Catholic, they were known to be kinder than us Protestants—it was we ourselves who said so.

At the table we shared with clerks from another office there were a couple of girls about my own age, Mary and Margaret, intelligent and attractive. Beautiful dark convent girl Mary was talking about the Dublin writer Flann O'Brien who she was reading; that impressed me. Margaret was posh, Princess Gardens school, but posh in a cute way with her owlish horn-rims between the curtains of long chestnut hair, she wasn't stuck-up at all. Margaret and Mary became my instant pals. Things were looking up.

But there was the endurance test of the long day till five o'clock. I grabbed a dinner in the canteen, consumed it in ten minutes flat and hurried into the town centre to walk around the shops. It was a lonely, anxious feeling, I grew agoraphobic. In the Arcade I bumped into Ralph with a gang of young trainee bankers, all on an induction course at the Northern Bank.

"Come on with us!" Ralph bade me. I must have looked as lonely as I felt. I seemed to wear my melancholia about me like a cloak. I think it was in my genes, from Gallic islanders on Ma's maternal side. My friends saw it and took pity on me; I never forgot their kindness and loyalty to me, though I'd much rather have hidden my feelings, they were a weakness in you that also attracted malice.

Ralph was cheerful as always, embracing his new life as a banker—"Better than a ——" he jested. He'd just drifted happily through schooldays, emerging with a single O level, English, to his credit. He wasn't academic but he read good books and was clever in a useful way. He always knew he was going into the bank, his uncle would sort it for him. And here he was now, another mate totally at ease in the new world of work.

We walked together, trooping round the town centre in the bankers' group. Ralph seemed to be its leader. His pleasant company and natural confidence buoyed me up. This new life didn't seem so bad really. We were all in it together.

20

I got back to afternoon at the Gas Board in good form after seeing Ralph, notwithstanding a heavy-heartedness creeping back in with the slow, precise movements of the fountain-pen shaped black hands on the big wall clock measuring out the ponderous grey office minutes.

When I had run out of things to do, Kevin said, "Here, Paul, take these accounts records down to the filing room in the basement, would you? They will need to go in their folders in the cabinets, ask Maureen, she'll show you."

You went down a narrow, windowless staircase, along a draughty passageway, past the stores, and came out by the row of offices below street level. The first one you came to was the filing room. Our clerical assistant Maureen, a young woman, brunette and shapely, waved and smiled at me. And oh goodness, she *was* attractive, the sight of her quickening my blood.

Under the luxuriant auburn hair, back-combed and falling about her shoulders, combed in a fringe above her eyes, the pretty face with its dark makeup was striking. The hot room put sensuous colour on her high cheekbones; the wide green eyes held me in a steady, open focus.

I felt my own face flush. She was older than me, in her twenties. Good, she'd consider me too young for her and I'd be left to admire her objectively, as I would a film star like Natalie Wood or Julie Christie. I was safe.

"Hel-lo, Paul," she said. "Settling in okay up there with the Kevin?" She was quiet, self-contained, not warm and effusive like some of the office women, but my name sounded tender on her lips and sent a thrill through me.

"Here, sit down." She pulled out a chair under the long table that ran beneath the window, the girls sitting in a row, filing clerks and telephonists, it was a female room.

She swivelled her chair round, facing me and crossing her legs in the flared emerald skirt she wore. She had the fine womanly fullness of bust and hips, but the legs were coltish, long and slim in dark tights, girlish.

She looked me up and down frankly, said, "You're very well-dressed for this place, I must say!" She was taking stock of me too.

I said, "Kevin has told me not to waste my good suit wearing it to the office! A sports jacket and flannels would do. It's just I feel more *capable* somehow in a suit!" I laughed at my own pretensions.

She stretched out her hand and felt the collar of my jacket. "It's a nice suit," she said.

"P-P-Pierre Cardin," I said. I nearly died at the touch of her slim hand with its long red-varnished nails, rings on her fingers. But I took the gesture as a motherly one.

The next thing she said seemed to confirm that: "*I'm* only just getting back into my normal clothes again after having a baby."

That was the reason for the slightly rumpled, improvised look about her; I'd not yet heard the expression "mumsy" back then. But her status of motherhood only heightened her appeal for me somehow: not a virgin, but a real woman, or something like that.

"What's your baby called?"

"Elizabeth. It was my mummy's name, she died of cancer when I was fourteen."

"Aw, I'm sorry."

"Och, don't worry, it was ages ago. Daddy looked after me, I was their only child. My husband Steve and I have a son also, Robin, he's two. The mother-in-law looks after the kids on the days I come to work. I'm part-time here, three days a week. We need the money and it's good for me getting out of the house and being my own person for a while."

I said, "I remember my poor mother tearing her hair out with the frustration of being stuck at home and feeling everything getting on top of her; that was back in the fifties, with few jobs for married women."

I didn't say but Ma'd had a sort of nervous breakdown, sparked by Audrey's wilful behaviour as she moved into her teens.

Maureen said, "It's not as if either of our two were planned, I got pregnant with our first, Robin, before Steve and I were married. His parents disapproved of me, thought I was a bit low for their son; we ran off to London and married in a registry office. But it was impossible to manage with a baby in a room in London and we had to go back to Belfast Then a year on, Elizabeth was another wee mistake—och, I mustn't call her that!"

It was wonderful to have this mature woman confide in me. It struck me how *physical* a woman's life was, with her child-bearing capacity, how dependent her fate was on a man. I was out in the adult world now; surely the secrets of women and men would be revealed to me. I did have this quality, that people would readily confide in me. Perhaps my shyness seemed to guarantee a respect for their confidences. And I liked to think my face expressed empathy, the broad-mindedness that came from the breadth of my reading.

I was conscious from the start of a sort of hard side to Maureen, if that's not too strong a word, perhaps I mean just her lack of the sentimentality that I was inclined to, and the school of hard knocks that had taught her. You saw it in the set of her jawline and behind her green eyes; there was a sensuality about it too.

She showed me the olive-coloured metal cabinets where the records folders were filed alphabetically in long, deep drawers, under the tall windows below the the road and the wheels of passing traffic. The subterranean room was vibrant with raucous, laughing female voices and ringing phones. Maureen was set apart from the others there, a mother, more solemn and self-possessed.

I went away from her that afternoon full of a strange excitement she inspired in me. The feeling stayed with me through the remainder of the working day, and on the bus home through the evening rush hour, Maureen, Maureen and Maureen again. I didn't believe I had fallen in love with her really, it was more a sublimated eroticism, the idea of a mature woman and how she had taken me into her confidence so readily, the physical sense of her, establishing an immediate closeness between us, that was a compliment to some quality in me, a manliness that had come to me. I wasn't that schoolboy anymore, the one I had so regretted leaving behind that morning as I travelled to my first day at work. In truth, I had moved on; I felt the adventure of growing up, of adulthood opening out to me.

I came in the back kitchen door of home with a spring in my step.

Ma looked up anxiously. "How'd you get on?"

"It was great!" I declared.

She was visibly relieved.

I blurted it all out to her the way I'd done as a boy after school when the two of us would sit by the fire together over an afternoon cuppa.

"I'm working under this lovely man Kevin, he's from West Belfast, family man, four children; he's like a father to me too. And we talked about books; he was telling me about this Belfast writer called Michael McLaverty..."

"Oh yes," said Ma, "I remember Michael as a young fellow, he used to come to Rathlin, and wrote about the island later in his novels and stories."

"Oh, I must tell Kevin you knew Michael!" I said excitedly, it was amazing how everything seemed to come together, the endless connections in this small world of Ireland that we inhabited.

I told Ma, "All the clerks are really nice, they're mostly older, but there's two nice girls my age, Margaret and Mary. And there's Maureen..." Her name on my lips brought me to a gulping halt.

"Yes?" Ma looked up with that bright, avian curiosity in her clear blue eyes.

"The filing clerk down in the basement..." I explained, faltering, embarrassed. What was I trying to say? Tell Ma I fancied this married woman? "Um, she's part-time, got two little kids, her mother-in-law looks after them when Maureen's at work…" I had this sinking feeling that I was exposing myself, giving the game away. "She was telling me all about it…" I finished pointlessly.

"Sounds like there are people you can have nice chats with anyway," said Ma helpfully. "Make the day go better."

"The work's all right too," I said. "I like mental arithmetic, totting up figures, and there are adding machines we can use, it's fun playing with those! And I have to write letters, *Dear Sir or Madam*, to the customers—*consumers*, they're called, of gas, that is. And I sign off, *I remain your humble and obedient servant, P.A. Carroll*! What about that!"

Ma and I had a good laugh.

"Oh Mum, Kevin took me up to the canteen this morning, 'C'mon, Paul, we'll have a *cuppatea*', he called it, real homely like!"

"*Cuppatea*! What a nice man. Catholic, did you say? Sure one Catholic is worth two of our side for kindness and dacency!"

Audrey came banging in for teatime. She was teaching in a secondary school not far away.

"Awful big louts wolf-whistling after me as I went in the gate first thing this morning!" she complained now.

"At least someone thinks you're attractive," I quipped tastelessly.

"Oh, listen to him! The big fellow now he's started at the Gas Board!" she said. "It's well for some people just sitting in an office all day!"

Da had noted my satisfaction with the first day on the job and was wearing his *snoked* face—a contented, cute, happy look—a son sorted for life, following in his father's footsteps! Secure employment was like a religion to Da, the very meaning of life.

"Kevin Magill is a fine man," said Da. "Though he's not awfully keen on the higher-ups on the Board, the discrimination against Catholics."

"Well, he was nice enough to this Protestant boy!" I said. "He was asking after you, I told him you were having the time of your life."

"I miss work sometimes," said Da thoughtfully. "Just the craic, the contact with all kinds of people. Still, I have those characters out of Dickens for company now!"

Marie called at eight. The cold autumn evening air clung about her subtly scented presence, her soft hair and woollen coat. Her cold, kissable little face poked out of a polo-neck jumper and her lovely legs were warmly encased in thick woolly tights under a short tweedy skirt. When I saw Marie all thoughts of Maureen went out of my head, as if I'd never met her and thought about nothing else since.

Sitting on the side of my bed, I plucked at the ridge of Marie's bra-strap through her jumper between her shoulder blades in the lovely matey intimacy we shared, and pulled her to me for a cuddle.

"You still love me then?" she asked softly in a pause, flushed and wide-eyed, the sweetest little face.

"Of course! Do you love me too?"

"Yes. You've not met some other bird at the Board then?"

I felt confident enough in my feelings for her to josh her. "Well, there's Mary, long dark hair, classic Spanish-Irish beauty, or Margaret, cute as a baby, or *Maureen*...!" A stab of guilt as I said her name, I *had* rather taken to her. "Mature, married woman," I teased out the alliteration provocatively, mocking my own adolescent fantasies, "she's part-time, escaped for a few hours from the husband and kids."

Maybe it was mention of Maureen's family, but Marie didn't bat an eyelash at my nonsense. I saw how confident she was in me, and all joking apart, I knew she was the only one for me, ever.

"How was college?" I moved on.

"Teaching practice, observation mostly, Glengormley Primary, it's a great wee school. I was with the P-ones. I love wee kids that age, they're so completely themselves! It'll be nice one day when *we* have a family, Paul!"

She put her small hand on my sleeve, an affecting gesture that touched me with the pure compassionate love I felt for her and our imagined children.

I went downstairs and brought back two mugs of tea, each with two sugars stirred in. Marie was putting my new Beach Boys' *Pet Sounds* album on the record player. We sat on the side of the bed in front of the electric fire drinking our tea, the table lamp casting its shadowy light across the room, Marie a neat, elegant figure, leaning slightly forward, her knees pressed together below the hem of her skirt.

Wouldn't it be nice. What a marvellous opening track, instantly lifting you with its passionate, evocative singing and powerful arrangement. *We could be married and then we'd be happy!* What could be simpler or more wonderful? That song said it all for Marie and me, it was our story, uncannily accurate.

The second track, *That's Not Me,* with its bleak, bittersweet realism, was life before Marie, the adolescent loneliness and depression that was life before love. Yet beautiful too somehow, the way simple truth is beautiful in itself, or can be made so through art.

It was followed by *Don't talk, put your head on my shoulder,* the music pushing poignant loving tenderness to the limit and beyond.

"Beautiful, so heartfelt," said Marie in a hushed voice, listening intently, shaking her head in disbelief. "But so *sad!* Makes me wanna cry, boo-hoo!"

"The song of pure young love," I said, "but heavy with a sort of melancholy ecstasy and fatalism."

"*Listen…listen…listen…*"

Gusting rain in the darkness outside drove at the bedroom window as the strings flowed into the backing mix. The song was a fabulous kind of hymn, drawing out the compassionate heart. I felt the shiver down the spine and the tears prickling, like a man who sees the Light.

21

The Young Marie years were a happy time as she and I settled on the paths of adult life, Marie to her teacher training, I to my career with the Board. With Marie it was effortless, or seemed so; she made choices and simply followed them up, gave herself readily to whatever she was doing. Student life at Stranmillis was enjoyable, they were a gang of mates on the course, the girls and boys mucking in together, unlike school, meeting up in the refectory after classes or sitting out on the high-walled expanse of lawn in sunny weather.

I seemed to know all about the characters on her course before I even met them, living legends she talked about endlessly: Fred and Freda, a couple, Freda a raucous Madcap Molly, swinging from the beam in the college gym, her skirt tucked in her knickers, or downing a pint of Guinness with the best of them in the bars of the Bot or Eg. Niall in his denim jacket and jeans like a workman—a shuffling bohemian cool James Dean. The dynamic blonde thespian Dot in a college production of Sartre's *Huit Clos*, "Hell is other people". Patsy Moore, a dynamic Billie Davis lookalike, *I know something about love...*and so on...

And Marie loved the classroom teaching practice. Not in a phoney, theoretical way—even back then, long ago, the teacher training courses were top-heavy with bullshitting and breast-beating, convenient distractions from poor working conditions, impossible class sizes and built-in pupil resistance to learning—that was purely the teacher's fault now, they were dying to learn but you were letting them down. I think Marie survived because she just loved children, she was a bit of a child herself.

I couldn't honestly say I loved my job at the Gas Board, but there was a certain neat, clear-cut satisfaction in playing around with figures, balancing the books, perhaps I got it from Da. Just the sight of my cuff-links protruding from the sleeves of my jacket as I worked at my desk pleased me somehow with a sense of order and importance in living.

I often had a Players Number 6 small cigarette burning between my fingers or on the ashtray next the enamelled inkwell on the level top of the wide, slanting double-desk out of Dickens that I shared with Ray Milne. The Belfast rain smeared the high narrow windows; it could rain all it liked, the gravelling sound of it thrilled me, reminding me I was dry and safe inside. Ray, thirty-something, in a blue serge suit, lean and pale with a smiling, twinkling blue-eyed charm, was a semi-professional singer in the Sinatra mode; Ray had sung live on Ulster Television. My liking for those old standards was something I could share with my desk-mate.

I took every opportunity to pop down to filing and engage Maureen in conversation. There was always that quickening of the pulse when I saw her. She'd look up at me and sit back relaxed and ready for our chat.

"Paul, you're too clever to be working here," she informed me with her blunt feminine percipience.

"Well thanks, Maureen, but you know I can take a professional qualification and then move on to something better eventually. And I've got my outside interests, the group and my mates…"

"And wee Marie?" she teased. For some reason I seldom mentioned Marie to Maureen, as if I were hiding her away.

"Marie too!" I blushed under Maureen's hard, amused stare.

"You keep quiet about Marie. Do you love her?"

"I think so." I didn't want to tell the truth, a big *Yes*, give the game away; I liked Maureen too and not just as a friend, it was a fantasy to string her along a bit. There was Maureen at work, Marie at home; I needed both to keep me going.

"I was madly in love with a fella once," said Maureen quietly, "I was the same age as you, eighteen, we had our summer in the long grass, I call it, me and Craig. You know that poem, *Splendour in the grass*, that's how I remember my time with Craig. He went to Canada, I was supposed to join him later. It never happened, I never saw him again. I got tired of waiting, got pregnant by his mate Steve, my husband now."

"My husband" sounded a flat note of resignation, duty more than love. I was glad.

Our group played the Jazz Club in the new year, up on the top floor of the tall old building in the heart of town. The podium was level with the dance floor, the ceiling low. We had seen Them play here back in the early autumn; they'd had a Top Twenty hit now, *Here Comes The Night*. Everyone stopped dancing and crowded around the podium to watch Van strut his stuff, there was this real mystique about him, his dedication to the music.

We were playing a Tuesday night, the place a bit empty. We had electric guitars and amplifiers now, and a full drum kit, all picked up secondhand, and the addition of an electric organ to the line-up. We were struggling a bit with the move from acoustic, but our vocals were always to the fore and strong, Marie on lead or driving the backing, Frankie and I alternating my baritone and his tenor, Charlie coming in on the harmonies.

We kicked off with the Stones' *Paint It Black*, a number that raced along generating great excitement. The club provided a psychedelic effect with strobe lighting as we drove the music along recklessly, filling the space with a fearful, imperfectly coordinated electrified racket, Bob's lead guitar runs bubbling along regardless.

There wasn't much mystique about us, no worshipful fans, only a well-dressed Mod couple up dancing while the rest of those present looked on tentatively from the perimeter of the floor. After we finished somebody clapped, one pair of hands, a hollow, lonely sound that was maybe worse than silence.

Frankie and I with some support from Marie harmonised on *True Love Ways*, a Buddy Holly song that had been revived by

Peter and Gordon, and was well within our comfort zone. Its soft charm earned a sprinkling of hands put together as we finished.

A small crowd congregated about the podium as Marie sang *You Can't Hurry Love*. Such a quiet, ordinary, almost invisible little girl in everyday life, she was something else, a fantastic inner Marie emerging when she got up to sing like this, generating an irresistible excitement. She looked wonderful tonight, her hair grown longer, enclosing her face in the student mode, and sporting her trademark leggy mini—the skirts kept getting shorter.

We got a proper round of applause this time and an enthusiastic solid crowd remained wedged about the podium as we relaxed the pace and Marie went into the Jackie de Shannon number, *What the world needs now is love sweet love,* handling it with such an adroit lightness of touch yet somehow a depth of tender sincerity that was utterly engaging. She had an instinctual feeling for the poetry and emotion conveyed by the simplest of lyrics. Our plodding, faithful backing seemed to go strangely well with that natural moving voice. A big cheer went up as she finished and she smiled a lot and backed off with an amusing little curtsey.

We sweated our way through a medley of Frankie compositions that sounded competent and intriguing. Your own songs added a sense of depth and touch of class to the whole performance.

We finished with the Yardbirds, a big favourite of ours that went down really well in the club, *For Your Love,* Ralph's blessed bongos going like the clappers, Marie handling the verses and all of us harmonising like mad angels on the chorus.

We hung around a bit afterwards while records were played; there were soft drinks and chitchat with some nascent fans who ventured over to speak to us. We had worried we might be too poppy for the Jazz Club but tastes were becoming less purist, though none the worse for that, we chose good sound numbers and there were no complaints. Marie seemed to have the makings of her own fan club, boys and girls in equal measure, and I kept my arm around her possessively, *the girl is mine*!

Gigs and clubbing generated a sweaty sensuality; I wished Marie and I could go and just be together somewhere afterwards, but where? It was too late and dark, cold and dreary, with work in the morning. We didn't have our own car. So we just kissed goodnight and crawled off to our separate beds. The answer had to be marriage, I told myself as I drifted off to sleep on my own.

22

In the summer things went a bit pear-shaped and I was led astray.

It started with the bank holiday weekend at the Kellys' caravan on the County Down coast. We got down there on the Friday evening. The caravan was a recent acquisition, replacing the Bangor holiday let. We booked in at the big caravan site spread across a field above the sea and made a beeline for the pub just down the hill.

There was a TV up near the pub ceiling with the summer soccer cup madness in full flood, the pub packed, cheering the games along. I might as well have been in hell, I felt only a revulsion for the football frenzy, could barely lift my head to look at the figures chasing the ball on the TV screen and I was outside all the sporting prattle and bonhomie around the big packed table where we squashed in together and Reggie Kelly held court, *the fella in the big picture,* to use his own expression, sweating and swilling, roaring out belly-laughter and wisecracks over the deafening racket. I was stuck there mutely between Marie and Eileen, there was no point of contact, everything subsumed into the vacuous collective.

The greater part of the weekend was spent in that way down the pub, including Sunday—they'd evaded the sabbatarian licensing hours somehow, or they'd been waived for the new religion of football. Everybody was pissed most of the time— politely pissed, the caravan site was select, the retreat of well-heeled Belfast business people like Reggie and Eileen.

One figure stood out in the lunchtime bar, a strikingly handsome, dark young man with the fashionably longer Mod hair and a big navy-blue and white polka-dot kipper tie under a blue and gold striped silky jacket, a vision out of Carnaby Street.

"Gorgeous-lookin' fella, isn't he?" Marie whispered to me. "He's James Young's new acolyte!"

Though there was no sign of James Young himslef, an older man, a local actor famous for his one-man shows at the Ulster Hall that combined stand-up comedy and storytelling with the serious address of social issues like "mixed" Protestant-Catholic marriages, the more decent, liberal view delivered in a sentimental style that could move his audiences to tears.

After the pub we staggered back up the hill in the after-ten dark, stopping off at the caravan of some friends of the Kellys, latter-day local showbiz people, a harmony group in the Four Freshmen style, who were glad of an audience these days.

Eileen, a Gallaher's mill girl from Ship Street, had sung with bands in the 1950s, modelling her style on Peggy Lee. A social elevation accompanied her celebrity and she was married at just seventeen to Reggie who was a few years' older and building up a successful business. Eileen, quite the lady now, just looked on appreciatively as the caravan quartet put on a spontaneous little show for us, anecdotes of their bygone days of local celebrity interspersed with a cappella bursts of perfectly honed vocal harmonies.

"Sing the Whiffenpoof Song!" the request came insistently from Reggie and his bachelor mate Noel. "Aye, the Whiffenpoof Song! *Ooh please, sing us the Whiffenpoof Song, would ye, ooh go on!*"

It seemed to be the only one they knew, or they just loved the sound of its name, repeating it like a mantra. Their faces, flushed with booze, shone with happiness as at last the quartet obliged, first their perfect a cappella, and finally everyone singing along:

> *"We're three little lambs who've lost our way,*
> *Bah! Baah! Baaah!"*

The last line said it all for me:

> "Oh Lord, have mercy on such as we,
> Bah! Baah! Baaah!"

More Scotch (the men) and vodka (the women) was drunk and I have no memory of crossing the grass and getting into bed in the caravan that night. Lucky *I* didn't end up like a whiffenpoof!

My next memory is muzzy hungover sun-bathing on the grass beside the caravan on the Saturday afternoon. I got my head in a paperback I had brought, by J.P. Donleavy—it caused heads to wag and tongues to tut-tut though I don't think anyone else there except Marie had read a book in their lives, but Dublin-based Donleavy's reputation as a pornographer had gone before him.

Reggie's friend Noel staying with us was a shop-boy, so-called, though in his forties now, at a well established Belfast department store. A bachelor and long-term mate of Reggie's, he had a relaxed, accommodating way with the Kellys, always keeping well-in with Eileen, that served to lighten the constant tension between husband and wife, their endless bickering; with Noel around, it all got swallowed up in a lake of booze, afloat with belly-laughs, the *big picture* and Whiffenpoofs.

Noel was a stocky, black-haired man, straight nose, dark brows, with a touch nasal, effeminate quality in the voice, like James Young. I didn't imagine shop-boys earned a lot but I guess Noel Bunting had only himself to worry about and was always well-dressed and deep-pocketed, waving a tenner—two weeks' pay to me—at barmen to pay for another colossal round of drinks.

We sat round sweating in the hot sun on the grass. I got a little distracted from my "porno" book at the sight of Marie moving about or lying down un-self-consciously in her bathing costume, her smooth bare skin and erotic curves, a pure kind of lust overwhelming me. What a shame we were stuck here with her family and the football.

The evening's drinking started soon after four, and by seven Marie and I were sitting in the back seat of Reggie's car going somewhere. Where? Why? Why only the three of us? Don't ask me, detail was lost, it didn't matter, I was blootered and so was Marie, her head sunk on my lap.

"Oh my!" she cooed. "What is going on down here?"

"Wait!" I whispered. Reggie at the driving wheel was glancing round over his shoulder.

Marie sat up and let out a moan, "Daddy, let us outta here, willya? I need some fresh air, I feel a bit sick!"

Reggie pulled in to a lay-by above a stretch of the coast. Marie and I tumbled out into the sea air and the sound of the tide slopping in and out.

"Pick you up on my way back," Reggie called to us. "Half eight here, okay?"

I expect he was pissed too. No one worried much about drink-driving back then, with the accident statistics to prove it.

Hand-in-hand, Marie and I made our tottering way down on to the rocks. She wore a cardigan over a light, floaty summer dress, her bare legs glowing and creamed after the day in the sun.

The pale-blue eyes and straight white teeth shone in her sun-kissed visage, the curtains of her hair lifting gently from it in the sea breeze. The state of her inebriation was in the forthrightness of her speech.

"We need a private little place now, Paul, for you to make love to me!"

She wobbled a little and tightened her grip on my arm to stay on her feet.

I cast about desperately for somewhere sunken and hidden where we might be together, down among the rocks. The situation brought a fleeting sharp memory of Naomi on Islandmagee.

We came to the water's edge. Calm and burnished by the lowering sun, the Irish Sea sloshed in lazily over the rocks. The deserted evening bay curved to low grassy headlands at either end.

We turned back, along the bank of a brook that ran down to the sea. We were exposed to sky and sea but hidden from the road above and it seemed no one came here anyway. We lay down on the rabbit-cropped grass and began to make love.

Marie clutched me to her in a drunken passion.

In a short time her knickers lay tossed aside on the grass, my trousers down as I pushed up under her skirt, between the soft spread of her thighs.

"Oh Paul, we'd better not!" she said, suddenly sobering up and scared. "I want to, but not now! Not yet! You'll get me in trouble!"

The idea of *getting a girl in trouble* brought a sense of the whole world crashing down around your ears and Marie's words were enough to stop me in my tracks, even at the last moment, as it happened now. I rolled off her and zipped up. She pulled her panties over her shoes and up her legs under the skirt, wriggling her bottom securely into them.

She laid her head on my shoulder and we sat there close and contented, safe and secure now in the level golden rays of sunlight on the grass and rocks and sand and water, the endless rhythm of the sea in our ears; there was a time for every purpose under heaven.

Tuesday morning, Reggie and I went off to work in Belfast, leaving the women to return later in the day. He dropped me outside the Gas Board.

"Thank you!" I called to him as I slammed the car door cheerfully behind me, relieved to get away from Kellys.

I went through the revolving doors into the building with a satisfying feeling of its almost homely familiarity to me now, its calm, safe, sober welcome, Fred the porter nodding to me from his cubby-hole. Kevin already at work in his corner of the office under the window. Now why couldn't Kevin be my girlfriend's dad instead of Reggie Kelly? "Mixed" marriage or no!

"Dad says you didn't speak all the way into Belfast in the car," said Marie.

It was the bank holiday post-mortem.

"Oh yeah?" I bridled. I felt annoyed, picked on, I said, "It was really early, I was just waking up and a bit hungover, anyway I don't recall a single word *he* spoke to me *all weekend*. He had his pals and the football, that seemed to be enough for him."

Marie was trying to stay neutral. "I think he thinks you're a wee Latin-speaking grammar school snob, looking down on the likes of Reggie Kelly, haulage contractor."

"Marie, that is just *ridiculous*! He's a successful business man for God's-sake; I am a clerk on £4.18s a week, it's less than a charlady earns."

"Don't be cross. Daddy's just funny like that. Pulled himself up by his own boot-straps kind of cliche."

"Oh and I'm *privileged*, am I? Childhood on a housing estate till we moved to that shabby-genteel dump on Nettle Soup Lane. And I had to stay on after school every day for a year and then work hard at problems every night till suppertime to pass the eleven-plus and get to the grammar school *to speak Latin*!"

"Paul, your dad is a retired accountant, a professional man, and your ma the daughter of a Church of Ireland clergyman. It's a different world to York Street, Gallaher's mill and the docks, that's Mummy and Daddy's background. They both left school at fourteen."

"So, they've done really well in life then, haven't they? Above all, they gave me *you*, didn't they?" I kissed Marie, it wasn't her fault, but I was annoyed that I had been wilfully misunderstood, branded a snob now, there was no justice in it.

I reacted very badly to criticism. Maybe it was the persecution I had suffered growing up under the claws of Audrey, that had left my skin flayed raw and hyper-sensitive. At the same time I had this warm ego from caring parents and it didn't like having cold water poured all over it.

Marie was having another, late break, before the new term began, a week youth-hostelling in Scotland with her college friend Lorna; I'd been fine with that when she proposed it early in the summer, but I found myself resenting it after the wasted weekend at the Kellys' caravan with me feeling left out of it the whole time then criticised for not joining in. I blamed Marie a bit. Now the prospect of her seven days' absence felt like a betrayal, me working every day while she had fun with someone else. It should have been Marie and me—I couldn't afford to go away on holiday that summer. There would be other boys where she was going too—I felt the rabid bite of the green-eyed monster.

The misgivings just got worse, turning to resentment and growing anger as the day of her departure approached. When I confided my concerns to Maureen at work, she said, "I tell you what, I think I can get away on Saturday, if you fancy meeting up for a cup of tea or something, and it won't be so lonely for you?"

My heart seemed to stop, the flame of desire igniting in me, *Maureen wants me!*—then there was the dissembling to myself that this was a simple, happy offer of companionship from an office pal. And maybe it really was that anyway.

"I'd love to, Maureen!" I responded in an affectation of pure innocence. We must start like this and then keep it that way, friendly, safe.

"Steve's working and I can have the car," she said, "we can go for a drive and stop off somewhere for lunch or afternoon tea."

"Brilliant!" Then I had an idea. "We could go across to the island, how do you fancy that?"

She'd been very taken with my descriptions of summer weekends with the gang at Mike's cottage on the island, her exclamations of "Oh, I wish I could go with you, Paul!" piercing me like Cupid's arrows.

I spoke to Mike, he wasn't going to the island this weekend but I could have the key to the cottage. Maureen and I could make a cup of tea there and bring something to eat with it. I said I was taking a work friend to see the island; I never let on it was a woman, what did that matter anyway, she was still a friend, wasn't she?

I couldn't quite believe the way it was all panning out, like a plot in a novel, everything conspiring to bring Maureen and me together. I felt jubilant and terror-stricken by turns. But it'd be alright, life wasn't a novel, in reality you played safe and everything was alright in the end. My hands were shaking as I put the plan to Maureen, leaning over her desk and speaking quietly, no one here must know. There were looks from the other girls, Cherie with her huge wing-framed glasses, always avid for a bit of fresh gossip.

"Oh Paul, that sounds wonderful!" Maureen responded and it touched me the way her face coloured a little.

23

Maureen picked me up at Cromac Square, close to work, and we drove out past the markets and the Electricity Department, across the Lagan bridge into East Belfast and on to the Newtownards Road. The interior of Maureen's Austin car was messy, kids' things strewn in the back; it smelt of kids, though not unpleasantly so. I didn't mind anyway, after all it was what a woman did, it was her fecundating sensuality; it was real, it was good. It was Maureen.

We passed the grounds of Stormont and suddenly we were out in the countryside, cutting through the patchwork fields of County Down. It was a grey day of summer's end and the approaching onset of autumn, the hedgerow and woodland trees just waiting to change colour and shed their leaves. We travelled in silence mostly, mesmerised by the motion of the car, the hum of the engine, the pages turning on the picture book scenery.

She drove briskly, a steady fifty mph on the open road, looking pleased with herself, revelling in the taste of freedom and adventure, hands casual on the driving wheel with their slender ringed fingers and the nails a glossy dark-red today. Under the driving wheel the curves of her hips, thighs and calves were relaxed in weekend blue jeans. Her auburn hair, soft and freshly shampooed, fell about the polo-neck of a beige jumper, her ample maternal breasts warm, living things pushing out under the wool.

Exhalations of her perfume modified the car's homely smell of pushchairs and feeding bottles.

As she drove I turned my head enough to drink in her profile, the thin, delicate nose a little tip-tilted and the high cheekbones, the green eyes under long mascara'd lashes fixed on the road ahead. She delighted in her resemblance to the actress Raquel Welch.

"Steve has the van today at work and his mum has the kids, I told them I was meeting up with the girls from the office for someone's birthday lunch."

"Oh yes?" So this was a secret assignation? What did that imply?

I acted the innocent anyway. It cannot be, I told myself, that this mature, married mother of two, Mrs Maureen Jones of Dundonald, could possibly have anything in mind today other than a friendly outing with a colleague, a decent young fellow at work who took the trouble to listen to what she had to say...

But there would be just the two of us on a desert island. And after all, I was a man, wasn't I, nineteen now, one year past the official definition of an adult, and as I thought of it, I felt it in my body sitting there next to this woman, it was in the spread of my thighs and the breadth of my shoulders on the car seat. A good-looking young man, why wouldn't an older woman want me? It was a classic situation, she could teach me something of adult life, that I knew I lacked, while I could give her back something of her lost youth. That sounded great, but inside I recoiled from the intense physical and psychological reality of it.

We parked the car down by the harbour and I took her round to the Spar grocer's where we bought bread rolls and cheese slices, a fruit cake and a carton of milk to take to the cottage. Any awkwardness between us evaporated as the food-shopping bonded us; after all we were only whatever we wanted to be, good pals, boyfriend-girlfriend, mother and son, all rolled into one; there was an intimate sweetness between us in the shared purpose. I thought how wonderful it must be to be married, to feel this ordinary closeness to a woman all the time, it was spiritual as well as physical.

Trimble's ferryboat, a medium-sized fishing vessel, sailed at two; we passed between the pincers of the harbour walls, under the round white lighthouse which that good old Irish rebel Brendan Behan had painted once, and out to sea. There was a handful of Saturday afternoon trippers, mostly birdwatchers headed for the farther Lighthouse Island with their beards, binoculars and anoraks. I was into a different kind of birdwatching altogether. There'd be a few walkers here for the big island too, but nobody I knew, I noted with relief, nothing to come between Maureen and me now.

Out on the bottle-green, furrowed expanse of sea the breeze picked up, blowing Maureen's long hair wildly in her face, painting dabs of fresh colour on her cheeks, the eyes marked out in their dark liner like little jade mirrors in the cold skin of her face. She put up her hood, the blue wind-cheater she wore gave her a fresh schoolgirl look. I ached to put a protective arm around her, to stop her blowing away.

Her eyes narrowed into the distance. "Is that it, your island, Paul?"

"The big island, yes."

The long, low shape, like a sleeping dog, stretched along the horizon between sea and sky.

"It looks so mysterious! This is an exciting adventure you're taking me on, Paul!" she said in a wee baby voice.

Our eyes met and hugged.

As we drew nearer, the indistinct grey shape of the island turned to green and the details emerged like a painting in progress, hedged fields, scattered dwellings, the grazing sheep fixed like white eggs.

"They're all summer holiday cottages now," I explained. "The last family to live on the island, the Cleggs, left in nineteen forty-eight. Only the sheep have permanent residence here now."

The island coastline came up to meet us, barren and lonely; Trimble steered the boat in alongside the makeshift landing stage. You had to jump then from the side of the rocking vessel. I had done it often before, I landed safely now and had the thrill of Maureen's cool, soft hand clutching mine, as she took a nervous leap. She landed cleanly, laughing and clinging to me for a heart-stopping moment, that was all, both our faces blazing with the closeness and excitement of our shared adventure in the open air.

A few walkers disembarked here and then the boat moved off around the bay towards Lighthouse Island. I led Maureen along the track that ran by the seashore for a hundred yards or so, the waves piling in over the banks of shiny brown sea-rods. We turned inland, through the gap in the high straggly hawthorn hedge and up the field towards the farm buildings on the hilltop.

"Bunny-rabbits!" Maureen cried out like a child. Their white tails flickered away mischievously through the long grass. dockens and thistles.

"We shoot bunnies here," I said, doing a Hemingway, macho man. "Mike has a shotgun. Then we eat them, except the myxy ones—myxomatosis, the poor things crawling around blind."

"Och, that's cruel!"

"They're such a pest though, digging up the place, devouring all in front of them, and there's the seagulls too, they'll attack lambs or an injured sheep. It's a savage world out here!"

She gave a little shiver. Looking round, she asked, "Where have the others gone? There was an older couple and a solitary man got off the boat in front of us."

"Most walkers follow the shoreline right round in a complete circle."

"It's awful lonely. Feels like there's only me 'n' you in the whole world, Paul!"

What a nice idea!

"It's different in the middle of summer with all the crowd over staying in the houses, meeting up for ceilidhs, drinking and singing, strumming along on our guitars, every night's a party!"

"You don't know how lucky you are, all of you," she said. "All that great craic with other young people is what you miss when you're married with a family and it's all about looking after them and you have no life of your own anymore, it's hard work right round the clock."

But, it occurred to me, *I envied her*! It was my little fantasy at that moment that Maureen was my wife, walking beside me.

I couldn't imagine anything better. Having kids together would just complete the glorious happy intimacy of the scenario.

At the hilltop we passed the deserted stone farmhouse; it huddled in the sparse shelter of a few tall, thin trees that bent and creaked in the wind. From this eminence you had a view of the whole length of the island, north to south, the green, sheep-dotted fields sloping down to where the white surf broke over the jagged black rocks of the shoreline. There was another farmhouse some distance away on the grassy central ridgeway and another one among trees in a sheltered dip at the south end.

The sky had darkened and the wind blew harder, chasing the streaming smoky clouds. The mainland had disappeared.

"Let's get down to our place before it rains!" I said.

As we dropped down the other side of the ridge, looking out on the Irish Sea, we saw Trimble's boat on the grey water below, approaching Lighthouse Island, like a toy in a bath. Beneath our feet the broad, wind-combed, tussocky back of the field dropped away steeply, making our feet run. The startled sheep *bah-ah*ed and went bounding off with clumsy, stiff movements.

Maureen, taking nervous little running steps to keep her balance, stuck out her hand to me with a squeal of "Help!"

I grasped it manfully, supporting her. As the field bottomed out she kept her hand in mine. There was no one to see us here and we walked on together like that, till we stood on the edge of the headland looking down on the slate roof and chimney of the whitewashed old fishermen's cottage tucked in a corner of the cove.

Maureen held on tightly to my hand as we followed the faint narrow path down the grass hillside, past the well. Down in the bay the waves ran into a natural harbour between the rocks. The green rowing boat we fished from was pulled up on the grass above the sand and pebbles of the little crescent of beach.

It was hidden away, secluded and sheltered down here at the back of the island. A portion of grass field above the shoreline was fenced off as lawn around the cottage. We entered by the small wooden gate, I turned the key in the front door and in we went.

The place had lain empty the past few weeks and it felt cold and damp. The first thing I did was light the fire. There was a pile of dried-out driftwood in a box by the hearth, a packet of firelighters and an old newspaper I tore and scrunched into balls. It only took a minute or two, the driftwood catching and the tongues of flames rose, licking hungrily till they fairly roared up the chimney and the small room glowed.

Maureen was smiling round at the homeliness of it, the one living room, the daylight entering through its three windows, with a solid table and chairs, a couch and armchair and a rocker, the divan under the front window, the small prints of Irish scenery on the walls like a railway carriage.

"There's a bunk room through there," I indicated the doorway off, "with coat-pegs and a wash-hand basin."

"I could do with the loo," said Maureen.

"That's outside," I grinned. "You go over the rocks, down below the tideline, that's the flush! There's paper here."

I handed her the bog-roll, a little embarrassed for her. The island soon got you back to basics. But Maureen had changed too many nappies, I guessed, to be funny about the natural human business of pissing and shitting.

Sneakily, but with affection, I watched her progress from a side window as she went up and over the grass and rocks down to the waterline, till she ducked out of sight.

She hurried back inside. "That makes your bum cold!" she cried, with a wriggle in her jeans. "And it's starting to rain."

Drops hit the window and soon the glass was weeping in a downpour, while the wind rumbled up and down the short chimney and the wood-fed flames burned fiercely.

"Oh God!" I exclaimed, it was all quite dramatic.

"We just got here on time," said Maureen, arms folded, peering out the window as if she were in her own sitting room. "We'd have been washed away coming down the hill!"

"And swept out to sea!" I joked.

It was dark in the cottage. I put a match to the oil lamp on the table. Lighting things gave me a sense of control, with Maureen watching, dependent on me, the man of the house! I got the pail, the rain had eased and I ventured back up the hill path for water from the well.

"I'll stick on the kettle!" I said, returning with the half-filled pail, going through to the tiny scullery. There was an old black oil-fired cooker under the tiny square of sea-facing window.

Maureen was humming to herself, *I Can Hear the Grass Grow*, as she got the crockery from the cupboard and laid the table for our repast.

"This is cosy!" she declared in her cosy little voice.

I'd never seen her so happy, there was usually this cloak of discontent about her, with touches of a wicked dark office humour, always the sense that things were never quite right, that she had been cheated of a life somehow.

Cheated of her youth. And here she was now, freed of her responsibilities for a whole long Saturday afternoon. She had put the sea between herself and duty.

"The sea air makes you hungry!" I said, biting into a cheese roll.

The tea steamed in its cups, the fire was blazing up with fresh wood I had added crackling and spitting, lighting up the room. The rain intensified again and drummed hard on the roof. It really was a cosy feeling, shut in, far away from civilisation.

"I'm famished!" she sighed.

We ate in a comfortable sort of silence, quite relaxed in each other's company now.

She broke the silence, speaking in her soft sort of baby voice, "Imagine if we could stay here for a week, Paul, just the two of us, completely away from it all, it'd be heaven!"

"Could you come over for a weekend sometime maybe?" I asked her stupidly, knowing it'd be impossible. *And here was the problem with Maureen: the impossibility of it all, of her and I together...*

I must have looked crestfallen as she shook her head sadly. "Not a chance, unless I ran away, and I could never leave the kids." She made it sound like a real immediate dilemma.

And we looked at each other.

"Sit over by the fire?" she said when we had finished our fruit cake and tea.

We pushed the small, low, faded leather couch closer to the flames and sat down side by side.

She took my hand, held on to it. It was a wonderful feeling but I was unsure what it meant, it might have been motherly, sisterly, how could you tell? Maybe just that we were dear friends.

What if I kissed her now but she didn't want me to? *"Paul, what do you think you're doing? And I thought you were a nice boy, I trusted you to bring me here!"* Her tears! *T*he image of it, the shame and horror of my self-exposure, paralysed me.

Then she spoke: "Paul, I'd love to know how you kiss!" Sweet and playful like the game we'd played with Marlene and Jennie, just a bit of fun, nothing to be taken too seriously?

And I kissed her. *Was* it only a game to her? A light-hearted re-living of young teenage parties? I kept on anyway, moving my open mouth on hers, with the increasing feeling of drowning in the mad ecstasy of it rising and burning up like the driftwood fire, till she broke off softly and whispered, "C'mon, we'll lie on the bed."

There was the deep joy of being handed a precious gift you'd not dared even to imagine, the impossible dream of making love to Maureen, but my heart was walloping against my ribs, my stomach was aching and I was shaking all over.

We made our way the few steps to the narrow divan bed, the wet daylight falling through the window above on to the pale-green candlewick spread. Maureen stretched out under the window, half on her side, her hip curving in the blue jeans, ready for me. I lay down, leant over her, she closed her eyes and raised her slightly parted lips to mine. We put our arms round each other and kissed.

"Oh, Paul," she exclaimed softly as we paused for breath, "you kiss just like that fella Craig I told you I was mad about before Steve..."

I kissed her again, harder, not to be outdone by any other fella. I felt her soft bosom crushed against me and I stroked under the woollen jumper over the smooth warm skin of her ribs till I felt the cups of her bra and the heavy curves of her breasts resting in them. I reached behind her and fumbled ineffectively with the clip on her bra-strap. She gave a little derisive chuckle at my inadequacy and reached back to unfasten the clip in an instant. The stiff cups fell away, the rounded weights of her breasts came free and I filled my hands with their incredible soft fullness of naked woman-flesh, the firm nipples pressing into my palms.

Both of us breathing heavily, I undid the metal button on her jeans, unzipped them and tugged on the waistband, down over the swell of her hips. She lifted her bum to help me along, the coarse denim of her jeans ceded to lacy panties, then her bare skin, the soft buttocks still cold from their sea-airing, the spread fullness of her thighs open on the dark-thatched entrance to her body.

With our clothes off we were under the bedspread and I was kissing down the length of her body, brow, lips, throat, breasts, belly, drowning in the lavishness of her femininity. But impatient of my kisses, needing the fulfilment of what we had begun, she took hold of me and drew me between her legs.

I had both longed for and dreaded this moment of a man's life, entering a woman for the first time; Marie and I had discussed it and agreed it must be excruciating, too big into too small, tearing at the flesh like a knife, we were happy to postpone it, but now Maureen took me inside her effortlessly—was it easier after you'd given birth? I wondered—till I rested in the softness deep between the moist walls, and I had come home at last, oh thank God!

There was an urgency now as she moved under me, sliding her hips to and fro on the under-sheet, while her raised knees gripped my sides in a sort of gallop to the finishing post.

I thought I should make this ecstasy of pure living last as long as possible, the man was supposed to do that, wasn't he; I tried to empty my mind, to be cooly in control, masterful, but the woman drove at me hard and insistent in an increasing intensity, till she let out a strange cry and that did it, I was pouring myself into her, groaning and gasping, collapsing on her like a man with a bullet in his back.

We lay there very still for a time, my body across hers, like two felled trees or fatalities on a corpse-strewn battlefield. The rain had eased at the window, there was the ticking of an old clock on a shelf, the constant rhythmical rolling and dragging of the tide below. The anxiety had gone, the sick fear in my stomach, nothing really mattered now, there was only this closeness to the woman, the "little death" they had called it.

"You don't need to worry, Paul," she said from under me. "I'm on the pill, I've had enough of getting pregnant."

I told her, "I love you." I started to kiss her, my blood rising again, pressing into her thigh.

She kissed me off, "You're sweet! What time is it?" she said and reached down for the black lacy knickers in the pile of our intermingled clothing discarded on the floor. I put my hand out and stroked the lovely full curves of her bum as she bent over but her knickers went on quick, pulled up *snap!* The fun was over, it was back to a lesser reality.

"What time's the boat?" she asked me.

"Five," I said. "We'd best get on, get there in good time. Miss it and we're stranded here till next Saturday!"

The driftwood had burnt down to grey ashes. I extinguished the oil lamp, we rinsed the cups and plates and knives, warm water from the kettle added to rainwater from the butt, stashed them on the draining board.

I locked the door behind us. The rain had stopped, the Saturday afternoon had a washed freshness, everything green and shining as the sun struggled out intermittently.

The wet grass seeped through our shoes. It was a struggle up the long, steep rise to the farm at the top, my knees trembly after our performance on the bed, though Maureen's legs were sturdy in their tight denim, her small steps firm and sure on the grass. I thought of how she had carried two unplanned children growing in her belly for nine months each, delivered them squalling into the world, the tremendous power of a woman. Why did we speak of them as the *weaker sex*? What would we men be like carrying an ever-increasing load around everywhere for nine months?

The silvery running sea glittered in the fitful, glancing sunshine; across the corrugated metallic water the long line of the County Down coast was emerging from the rain-mist. The ferry was approaching round the north point of the island. Maureen linked my arm, the simple womanly gesture melting my heart again as we walked down the hill and along the shoreline, but she separated her body from mine as we neared the landing stage, "You never know who might see us," she explained. It was the sensible, obvious precaution to take, but I felt it like a blow to me, a rejection.

As we stood together in the crowd on the ferryboat pushing out to sea, I wondered if it was obvious anyway that we were together, and whether they could tell *we had made love*. I basked in the awesome awareness and strange peace of my lost virginity, the sharp recall of the woman's body moving under me. It was a torture to stand there beside her and not to touch her anymore.

We drove back to the city, mostly in silence, Maureen looking anxious and preoccupied. But our action that afternoon had said it all. I kept glancing round at her profile above the driving wheel, her face showing the strain she must be under now; I felt terribly in love with her. It was a sort of gratitude above all.

There was still the tenderness between us but I could tell her mind was fixated on home again, Steve and the kids, the mother-in-law, they'd all be waiting for her like a reception committee. To save her time, I told her to drop me on the road opposite the parliament building gates, she lived near there and could be home sooner. I waited at the stop for the bus into town.

The rest of that weekend I was filled with the glory of Maureen, of what had been between us. I went over our time together again and again, striving to recall every detail, as if to convince myself it wasn't a dream, it had really all happened; it would always be with me and I could never be the same again. Maureen, Maureen, Maureen, her name embodied a pure magic that had come to me, a great gift in my life.

I didn't dare ruin the spell, spoil it all by wondering where on earth it was leading to. I lay awake a long, long time in bed in the dark that night, floating on the warm waves of ecstatic recall, and again waking in the morning, while church bells chimed, going over and over every detail in my mind's eye, my brain high as a seagull over the grass and rocks of the island.

24

Work on Monday morning brought the first vague misgivings.

I had no moral qualms about being an adulterer or anything. Love was love. Love was the law. The Bible told me so.

But where did the agony and the ecstasy of forbidden love fit into another wet Monday morning going off to the Gas Board? Suddenly life was all complication now. It had been so easy before, so simple: Marie, Mum and Dad, the group, the office, working with Kevin, the harmless flirting with Maureen...I wished in a way I could have all that back, the innocence and ease of it, a calm sea around the safe harbour of loving Marie.

Overcome with shyness, afraid to show my face in the filing room where Maureen would be waiting for me, I hid away at my desk in the upstairs office, head down poring over ledgers like Scrooge. Till eventually she came to me, under the pretext of some filing query, and there was no problem after all, she was smiling as she breezed in, all morning-fresh and good-humoured, putting me instantly at my ease.

"You'd better come and see," she said over the made-up query and I followed her out of the office.

Our footfalls echoed in the dim, empty corridors, till we stopped at a remote hidden corner by a window overlooking the backyard outbuildings, the vans and trucks coming and going on a damp grey Monday morning.

"Was everything okay for you getting back on Saturday?" I asked her.

"I think so," she said. "Steve was looking at my face, where you kissed me, but I got in a remark about being caught in the wind and rain chapping my skin...out walking by the sea with the girls of course!"

She grinned, happy at the memory of being kissed. "What about you?"

"Well, Marie's away and all I could think about was you, all through Saturday night and Sunday, I didn't go out at all."

"It'll be a while before I can get away like that again," she said soberingly.

There was no cold rejection of me, the thing I had dreaded now she'd maybe had enough of my hypersensitivity; there was the warmth of a new familiarity between us, but also a little sadness, for something that could never be.

"I love you," I said quietly, unable to help myself. It was a way of telling her thanks really.

She half-smiled and looked up and down the empty corridor, in case anyone was coming, before she said, "Paul, just be careful now, you're a sweet fella, I'm glad I met you...I'd better get back now. See you later then."

I realised that was it and it hurt.

"Hal-lo!" It was Marie on the phone. You know, wee Marie Kelly, your girlfriend. Sings in your group, remember? You told Marie you loved her too...

Marie had a voice that smiled at you down the telephone line, gladdening your heart, reminding you that the voice and you shared something very special. In your mind's eye a comic strip thought-bubble with her sweet cute face in it, the laughing blue eyes and layered Mod haircut, popped up with the voice.

"Oh, hallo!" I replied, strangely shy. There was the funny feeling every time she phoned that you were falling in love with her all over again, as if you'd just met and were still at the chatting up stage. Say something cheery...

"How was Scotland?"

"Wet, cold. Blisters on my feet after all that walking." Then her little-girl voice, "I need a warming cuddle!"

"Come on round then, it's here waiting for you!" I'd not planned to say anything like that; I'd thought I should be distant with her after Maureen, making up my mind between the two of them. I persisted in the belief that I could have Maureen if I tried hard enough, kids and all, and we'd have another one, of our own...

"You can come here," said Marie. "They're all away tonight with Auntie Gladys in Coleraine. Bring your toothbrush, that's all you'll need!"

"Dirty enough."

"Yes, quite!"

It was the Saturday one week on from Operation Maureen. I told Ma I was staying overnight at Charlie's on the Oldpark Road, put a few things in an overnight bag and glancing over my shoulder like a spy, I walked the short distance to Jacaranda Close.

Marie opened the door to me and flung herself around me as I entered the hall. She'd bathed and her hair was still wet, she was in her dressing gown, all scented and soft, it did things to me. Her wee face was vivid with the joy of seeing me again, her very own first real steady boyfriend!

"Oh, I missed you!" she declared, kissing and kissing me till my head spun. "I just kept thinking every minute I was away, *I wish my Paul was here!*"

"I missed you too," I said, meaning it. "How was Lorna then?"

"Oh, all right. I'd had my fill of her by the end of the week. Girl friends only go so far. If you want a true friend, find yourself a fella—the right one of course!"

"No other fellas in Scotland then that took your fancy?" I joked nervously, thinking that would serve me right after Maureen, but would kill me in the process.

"Oh, there were a couple of fellows interested, students at Glasgow University, they were, scientists!" She pulled a face. "Real geeks! Lorna fancied the lanky one, Andrew, so I had to entertain his wee fat friend, Dennis, studying molecular biology, a must for conversation at dinner parties! Don't worry," she added, looking at my face, "I wasn't tempted! Dennis played the guitar and we'd sing and generate a bit of craic in the common room while the other two were busy having a lumber on the bunks.

"But I got enough of tramping the Trossachs in the end, anoraks and leggings, really sexless, and peeing behind bushes, trying not to get it down the back of your boots. Wet coats, sweaty socks and smelly feet in the hostel. Not really my scene. I couldn't wait to get home and get really clean again and all dolled up just for you. Hang on there, will you, the fashion parade is on its way!"

She went flying up the stairs and I went in the sitting room and looked through her records, put on the Lovin' Spoonful, *"Do you believe in magic In a young girl's heart?"*... They were singing about Marie for sure!

She was gone a while. I could hear the continuous agitated creaking of her steps on the ceiling above my head. The evening was fading at the window.

"De-daaa!"

Marie made her entrance.

"Oh God, Marie love, you look fantastic!"

It was the shortest dress I had ever seen, the waist gathered in with a thin leather belt like a snake, it scarcely covered her bum that stuck out in all its perfect pert charm, cheeking me, the lovely length of legs descending from the miniskirt in horizontally striped red-and-purple tights. Her breasts were small compared to Maureen's but definitely all there, pointing at me under the moulding of red jersey.

The helmet of boyish brown-fair hair enclosed her pale little face with the light-blue eyes that were made up with greenish shadow and eye-liner; she wore a pale lipstick and she was posing with the expressionless vacuity of a mannequin, a look that, however, was simply irresistibly *cute* on her. Steady on stiletto heels, she stalked to and fro a minute like Jean Shrimpton on the catwalk; it struck me how a girl simply walking could be an art form. Then before it could all get too serious, she burst out laughing, "Ha, ha, ha!" and collapsed into my arms.

In the midst of all this fun I was thinking hard about my life. Over the week of Marie's absence I had entertained all kinds of febrile, fantastic plans around Maureen and me, how I must persuade her to run away with me, kids and all, to London maybe, how I would have to confess everything to Marie when she got back, the drama, both our tears…But now Marie was here with me everything fell into place as before and I could see sense again.

Suddenly I realised the truth about my whole life: that *I could never, would never hurt Marie*. Actually, I would kill myself first, lie down in front of a train, before I should cause a single tear to run down that dear face, and if we *were* ever to part, it would have to be Marie's doing, she was a free agent, I didn't own her and would never hold her back, but it could never, ever be my doing. Of course I'd foreseen this long ago when she had joined the group and sung *You're No Good*, the memory cutting through me now.

"Oh Marie! I love you so much!"

And it was *my* tears alone, hot, salty, rolling. I fell on her neck to hide the contortions of my face but my body was shaking uncontrollably. I experienced the most tremendous sense of relief that I was not going to destroy what we had and wreck my life. I thought there must be a God watching over me, caring for me, stopping me doing terrible destructive things.

Marie hugged me to her, like her little child. "Oh what's the matter, Pauly? Oh never mind! We're back together again, forever now!"

"Say you'll never leave me!" I sobbed pitifully.

"Of course I'll not leave you! There's no one else for me but my Pauly, you should know that by now!"

She patted me better, then softly added the blessing of her lips, "Come upstairs?"

I let her lead me by the hand, like her pathetic child.

Upstairs in the fresh, pretty bedroom with its Julie Driscoll and Scott Walker posters (Marie was a strange hybrid of the two singers), she unclasped the snake-belt, pulled the red jersey mini-dress over her head and off, and laid it neatly on the bedroom chair. Her slip followed, then her red-and-purple tights, rolled down the ivory legs with their faint tracery of blue veins and kicked away.

Usually, getting down to bra and pants, she would shiver down between the sheets and wait for me. But tonight, first the white bra, then the little white aertex pants, came off, and she stood there *quite* naked, as they say, with the beautiful tits, curved hips and and inverted triangle of dark-fair bush. There was no embarrassed modest averting of her face or shivering rush to hide her shame between the cold sheets. Rather, she stood there a minute, posed plain as an artist's model, looking me straight in the eye, brave and proud with womanhood.

She lay supine on the bed, watching me undress. I saw her face darken with desire when I stood there naked, erect. I went to her on the bed now, empowered by the sense of my experience with Maureen, knowing what to do. Marie took me in her arms and opened herself to me; I entered her easily, felt her legs wrapped around my back and her curving softness under me, cleaving to me. With the rhythm of her body against mine, within a few fevered minutes I felt myself coming and withdrew neatly, ejaculating on her tummy.

We lay there in each other's arms in a deep peace, nothing more to say, as if we had died happily together. Then she turned her face to me on the pillow and said, "That was good! It was easy after all! You were so confident and firm with me!"

"Only because you made it easy, you were ready for me."

"Because you made me feel that way. Shame we waited so long really, we've missed out on years of full-on lovin' pleasure!"

"Could have gone wrong though, maybe it was better to wait."

"Oh Paul, I loved it! I love you!"

"I love you, Marie!"

"I'm hungry!" she declared. "C'mon, I'll fry some leftover potatoes for supper. Watch TV for a bit then we can sleep all night here in my bed and wake up together as if we're married already! Oh, heaven!"

25

"Pleased to see Marie again?"

I nodded, "Oh yes!" I smiled.

And Maureen smiled back at me, relieved, I think, that I had come to my senses.

I had given her back a bit of her youth, the sense of expansiveness and liberty denied her by that early pregnancy, the excitement of a boy mad about her again, it was enough to be going on with at any rate. Maybe we could do it again sometime, but clearly there was no question of ditching her husband and running off with young Paul.

For my part, I would never forget Maureen. She made a man of me. She'd felt enough for me to give me that, and satisfy her own need to be loved, not taken for granted. Was it love? On her part, I doubt it. She wasn't free to give me love. Affection and fun, yes, that was all. That was good.

But I had certainly loved her. Or loved being in love with her. How do you tell the difference? I loved anyone who loved me, which made me an egotist, I suppose. It was a big ego-boost to have an older woman wanting you. Though how old was twenty-three to my nineteen really? Both those ages look awfully young to me now, as I write this in middle age; how could twenty-three ever have seemed old or mature? We grew up quicker then, it's true.

But the love of Maureen had brought me pain too, left me unfulfilled and missing her, needing her desperately for a time, and it nearly wrecked what I had with Marie, the true love of my life. Yet it was nobody's fault but my own.

Anyway, Maureen's temporary contract with the Gas Board ran out at Christmas. She asked a few of us younger ones she'd worked with along for a farewell drink on her day-before-last, at the Black Bull in Cromac Square. Afterwards I walked her down past the markets towards the bus station and in the dark under the railway bridge by the river we had a final goodbye court—just a kiss but with the drink taken I got carried away, prolonging it till she laughed and protested, "I have to go, Paul, I have to go!"

In the end my brief little affair with Maureen—as it seems now, though such a big thing for me at the time—only served to confirm my love for Marie. That was the best thing Maureen did for me. After Maureen my love for Marie just grew and grew.

There were so many facets to Marie. There was Marie the Taurean homemaker, baking trays of mince pies and flapjacks, a strong nurturing instinct and womanly caring; then another Taurean trait, the earthy sensuality that developed as we matured and grew together, the liberation to an unfettered expression of her femininity, the pleasuring of herself and her man in the deep intimate sharing that binds the couple, not for a minute, an hour, or a day, but forever.

There was the glamour and talent of Marie. Back in the maths class, when she was still only fifteen, it was those legs that had fixated me; the face when I looked, almost an irrelevance, was attractive after a plain Jane fashion, though with a pleasing soft femininity. But in the time since then, in the advance into full womanhood, Marie had grown *beautiful*—an inner quality that shone through in her natural love of life. The sense of her woman's intrinsic beauty, the love she brought into the world, was expressed in her physical appearance, the cultivation of her natural feminine charms, hair, make-up, clothes, fashion that does what art does, improves upon reality, upon nature, enhances and invests it with meaning and beauty.

Being the singer in a band encouraged this art of living in Marie. The band, or group, as we said back then, survived for quite a few more years. We secured a weekly spot at the Pound, a trendy new "wine bar"—furnished in pine, clean-smelling and more girl-friendly than the old pubs—located just off the town centre near the docks—and gathered a faithful long-term following about us there who would shout out requests for old favourite songs by the Beach Boys or the Mamas and the Papas, the harmonies we were known for, that we had polished up over the years.

Beyond that, it had soon become clear to us that although many were called, few were chosen in the fame game of pop, and we had shrugged our shoulders and got on with the real business of being alive and *making music*. Frankie continued writing his songs, over a hundred at the last count, though they remained pretty firmly in an early sixties bubble that yet had its own perennial charm, the era of the Bobbys—Vee and Rydell and Vinton, the ones before Dylan though we did him too, *Masters of War* and *Mr Tambourine Man*. Frankie's blonde Jennifer was replaced by brunette Anne; then we heard that Jennifer had got pregnant by someone else. Frankie wrote a song about it, how their love had gone the way of old hits.

When Bob shipped out with the merchant navy and Mike and Marty had had enough of the drums, we found a brilliant guitarist, Brian, and drummer, Sheridan, to take their place. Brian at eighteen though looking older, short and stocky, blinking studiously through horn-rims, his fair hair already receding, mustard cardigan with leather buttons, brown slacks and scuffed Hush Puppies—like the civil servant he was in his day job at the Ministry of Agriculture. Art student Sheridan parked like a tank behind the drums, his torso poured into a big red T-shirt, arms and legs working with machinelike precision, face deadpan-beaky like an owl glaring out between flopping sheer curtains of long light-brown hair.

Brian, influenced by Cream and Hendrix, became a popular turn with the solos he played on his shiny red Les Paul guitar, the love of his life. drawing an attentive crowd about the stage. The accelerating, dramatic run-in to Vanilla Fudge, *Keep Me Hanging On*, was really something in Brian's hands. Charlie opened on the keyboards with a delicate, eerie touch, the notes descending as Sheridan knocked out time on the bass drum, my bass guitar creeping in then Brian making his entry on lead guitar, the sound building, building, and we were off in the hammering frantic race of the instrumental introduction, *faster, faster*, STOP!

And Marie was at the mike, *Set me free, why don't you, babe?...* and jumping up and down, remonstrating, pointing, *Get outta my life*—belting out the lyric with her whole body as we surged along all together in a frenetic sort of charge of the Light Brigade—the Light of love.

It was Marie who came closest to making a name for herself. The manager of a visiting minor band from over the water, Psychedelic Soma, who we were supporting at the Queen's student hop one dead midweek midwinter evening, signed her up and got her a recording contract for a cover revival of the oldie *Hold Me, Thrill Me, Kiss Me*. Sessions musicians, not us, would provide the backing. We weren't too deeply hurt by that rejection, we all had steady jobs in Belfast and planned to keep them.

Marie flew to London for the recording at Abbey Road, together with a refurbishment of her wardrobe at Carnaby Street and King's Road, hairdo at Vidal Sassoon's salon in Bond Street and publicity photos. We were all very excited for her. There was a promotion with write-ups and pictures of her in the Belfast papers, some of the English tabloids, and in New Musical Express and Melody Maker: Marie the "Belfast girl-next-door" hits the big time!

Then glory of glories, back to London for an appearance on *Top of the Pops*! And wasn't she fantastic on the small black-and-white screen, so radiant and living, vivid and passionate in her plea to be held, thrilled and kissed down lovers' lane, the dear face of my precious pet filling the screen, *my* Marie singing *to me*. Tears filled my eyes. The camera swept down the full length of her neat, shapely figure, then closed in again, crawling up her miniskirt, lingering on the rhythmical thrusting of her hips and thighs, the legs I loved become public property now.

I didn't mind at all, she was mine, *a-a-all mi-ne*, as Jim Morrison gloated, I liked the idea of being a pop star's boyfriend,

And your bird can sing! I would trendy up my own image to go with hers, shock the Gas Board with my long hair and loud kipper ties, flared maroon pants belted low on the hips. Out on the street the Belfast girls would see me and tell each other, "*See him, he's whadayacaller's fella, Marie thingy, Gawd he's lush!*" The girl, the gear, the hair, the aura would do it for me! An easy vicarious celebrity, oh and by the way, you can see him singing at the Pound every Tuesday night!

I supposed we *might be rich* too! Nipping over on the plane to our Chelsea weekend pad? Hanging out with Mick and Marianne—or was it *my singing bird adieu* for her already, left a junkie rotting on the streets. I wasn't jealous of Marie's success in any way; I resolved to go with it, enjoy it, to travel with her whenever I could, world tour coming maybe, U.S., Australia, I'd take unpaid extended leave from the Gas Board.

There was so much excitement!

Then...nothing.

The proposed tour of Britain and Ireland cancelled. Initial record sales disappointing and recording contract not extended to a second release. Too many girl singers coming on the scene now, they said. A lie, there were only five, I counted them.

Brian and Sheridan had followed Marie over to London, and played at the Marquee in their own makeshift band, Rat—Steve Winwood had approached Brian afterwards to praise his guitar playing. But a short time later Brian, caftan, flares and granny glasses replacing his civil servant uniform, his receding platinum blond hair swinging about his arse now, had become an alcoholic junkie in a Fulham squat and attempted suicide with an overdose of sleeping pills, while Sheridan under pressure from his father had found a barber's shop and a white collar post with the Greater London Council.

Marie's verdict on the music business was, "Bullshitters and conmen—just capitalists out for themselves, doing as little for anybody as they can get away with, only in it for the quick buck, not interested in cultivating talent. Promises, promises, then nothing, sweet f-a. The phoneys coming in the windows, as Holden Caulfield said. I'm glad to be out of it!"

I kept the copies of her record—a Frankie composition on the B-side, *Goodbye My Baby*—I'd bought up with my savings to give away and help put it in the charts, and the cuttings and posters that had gone with it; the skimpy-glittery dress like chainmail she wore on *Top of the Pops* hung in the back of my wardrobe, she didn't have room in hers and I wouldn't let her bin it. I liked to sniff it. The records could be given away over the years to selected friends and family and one day our children would be interested in Mummy's moment of fame.

26

I had settled into a career at the Gas Board. It wasn't so much a choice, it was just happening to me, the way life does. I was taking the seven-year part-time Institute of Secretaries qualification at the Tech, attending there two nights a week, a soporific two hours' endurance test, but the promise of a secure profession, guaranteed promotion, in charge of an office at twenty-five, a department at thirty, would be my considerable reward. And there was nothing to stop me going on reading good books and doing a bit of writing and sketching and making music with Frankie and the Fringe.

Marie completed the three-year teaching certificate and got taken on at the nearby Ligoniel primary school where she had done her last teaching practice. There was no shortage of phoniness and utter bullshit in the teaching profession either, it was rampant throughout society, but she liked the youngsters and without making a religion of it, heavy weather or a song and dance about everything, she got on best as she could with teaching them the old-fashioned things they needed to know in life like the three Rs and the elements of music and drama and hopefully a few social skills and emotional intelligence along the way. She breezed through the working week and was ready for the *craic* when we met up midweek and weekends, romantic twosomes, cinema or Chinese, or with the group, or get-togethers in friends' flats in the university district or, in season, trips to the island.

When I wondered if my life was a bit boring and broke out momentarily and wrote to the local papers asking if they needed a cub reporter, an old fantasy of mine, after Hemingway, I got an interview with one of the editors, an elderly locally famous character, in his office at the top of the *Telegraph* building in town. He had a pleasant way of putting me at my ease and I relaxed completely in his company and talked really openly, enthusiastically about myself; he was a good listener.

"Oh, you don't want to abandon all that to become a newspaper reporter," he advised me finally. "From everything you have told me here today, Paul, it is clear that you have made a wonderful life for yourself: the trips to the island, the music and so on, friends, girlfriend, a secure position with the Gas Board, so you need never starve! Frankly you'd be mad to give all that up for the lot of a newspaper reporter!"

Was he just saying all that to get rid of me, as a friend suggested later? But what struck me at the time and ever after was the rightness of his advice to me, a sincerity and wisdom of advanced years coming through against the hideous reality, the killing materialism and filthy microbe life of newsprint. Who'd have known it better than a successful editor?

I went back down in the lift feeling very pleased with myself, my life *exactly as it was*! The editor had simply confirmed what I knew already, that in truth my life was perfect and I only needed to wake up to the fact.

So much of that was down to Marie. It was a blessing in a way that the distraction of fame had only been temporary, that we had been destined for the good simple life, an easy security and a kind of basic, tried and trusted human decency, the love of one woman and one man, a family one day, all the things you probably sneer at when you're younger and know nothing.

There was the sense of rootedness in our hometown, our own country where we had lived all our lives, where you belonged in a way you never quite could anywhere else; you were intrinsic to the culture, the streets that were as familiar and part of you as extensions of your own body, the local speech, its colour and vitality that the Oxford Dictionary could never match; the local humour turning everything to a sense of fun because the world was a ridiculous place, only the rest of the world couldn't see it somehow.

And what would you be if you moved away where there were big opportunities, climbed the cosmopolitan ladder of success? Apart from being a phoney, you'd be nothing, that's what, all strangled vowels and statistics, and the convenient butt of xenophobia with its moronic ignorance of your culture.

Reggie Kelly seemed to get over his aversion to me or my alleged snobbery. The harshness left his speech and he spoke to me kindly, like the son-in-law I would be to him soon.

"And does the Gas Board and the night school leave ye any time for your writing?" I could hardly believe my ears, that he should even be interested in my writing. I expect Marie and Eileen had had a go at him, *just show a bit of interest in the fella, would you!*

"Oh aye," I assured this lover of the arts, "a page a day's the most you need ever write, that's a fair fat volume at the end of a year!" I explained. Not that I had got that far yet, but what was the hurry.

"Och, sure ye'll be the next Harold Robbins!" said Reggie with a hoarse belly-laugh. It made me smile but I saw the pained expression on Marie's face.

"You mean JD Salinger, Daddy," she corrected him. "Paul writes *literary fiction,* not sadistic thrillers!"

"Or what's her name," said Reggie, not to be outdone on high culture, "the Dublin woman: Joyce!"

When we all laughed cruelly, he said, "What's so funny about that?"

"You're trying your best, Reggie, that's good enough for me," I said, suddenly taking to this unpretentious working man.

Reggie and Eileen had enough on their plate with Thelma. She had finished school with three O levels and got a basic desk job at Moon Insurance, where Charlie worked, back of the town hall.

"She drinks like a fish!" Eileen complained. "After work down Hannegan's or Kelly's. Then round to the Maritime Hotel for dancing. Gets back here all hours, slaughtered."

Reggie snorted, " What kind of friends has she got anyway that would let a young girl get that drunk?" His question revealed a touching naivety.

"Indeed they're all at it, Daddy," said Marie. "It might be different if she had a steady boy to look out for her, like my Paul does for me—not that I ever get slaughtered of course, but generally, I mean."

Afterwards Marie told me, "From what I gather, Thelma has been round all the boys in the office, and I don't think it's just a kiss and a cuddle, I'm surprised she's not pregnant by now or got VD. I suppose it's one way to get a fellow if you look like the back of a bus, hee-hee!"

"She's not that bad-looking," I said kindly. "Bad attitude is the problem really. A bloke will go for a girl with a nice personality before one who's just pretty but vapid, honest, I've seen that again and again."

"Pity you can't just go out and buy someone a new personality then," said Marie coldly. "I'm fed to the back teeth with that sister of mine, like a canker on society and a life sentence for our family."

"You can get books now," I said, "American ones, that show you how to change your personality, how to win friends and influence people."

"You've got to actually want to do that in the first place though," said Marie. "Just to read a book at all would be an achievement for that young lig!"

We'd escaped to the local Phoenix saloon bar for a quiet pint on a weary winter Thursday evening.

"How's Audrey these days?" Marie grinned. We were the Twisted Sisters Sufferers' Support Group at times.

"The Bitch 666!" I exploded bitterly, just letting off steam. "She's only back the odd time, still cuttin' straws with her backside as Da says, she's settled in her flat with two other girls, all teachers."

"Jesus, that must be fun!"

"There's a steady boyfriend she abuses now, Robin, a bank clerk. Nice well-dressed good-lookin' fella too, thinks the world of her, love is blind as they say, and she just treats him like shite."

"Keeps her off your back anyway!" Marie smiled at my vicious hyperbole. "Why do the children of perfectly nice, reasonable parents like ours turn out so bad sometimes?"

"It's not the parents' fault, whatever the head-quacks may say," I suggested. "It's something in human nature, will, wilfulness, it's in the Bible. The need to be top dog, it could be in a family or the whole world like Hitler. Jealous as hell of everyone else, the worst passion of all...Then the kindly parents let them get away with too much, when a stricter approach would do better."

Paul and Marie were growing up for sure.

27

Then came the evening when Reggie and Eileen returned from their Bingo at the Linfield Supporters' Club in Sandy Row and found the note Thelma had left. It was uncannily like the lyric of the Beatles' song of the day, *She's Leaving Home*. Right down to meeting a man from the motor trade, as it transpired.

Eileen nearly fainted when she read the note left on the kitchen table. Then she read it aloud in a trembling voice to Reggie.

> *Dear Mum & Dad,*
> *By the time you read this I will be in London. Monty and I are in love and are moving away to make a new life for ourselves, away from his wife and I know that you would not approve of him either as he is a married man but he doesn't love Anita his wife anymore and Monty and I are in love now and have to be together.*
> *I am sorry to do this but I am eighteen and an adult and must begin to live my own life the way I choose. I will write soon to let you know how we are getting on, I am safe with Monty who loves me and there are plenty of rooms to let in London and plenty of office jobs that I can do so please do not worry about me,*
> *Love.*
> *Thelma*

Reggie caught Eileen before she could collapse on the kitchen floor.

"Holy Jesus!" she moaned in a half-faint. "I can't believe this is really happening to us. Reggie, *what did we do wrong*?"

Reggie struggled to stay strong and manful.

"Ach, the stupid wee bitch!" he said. "I'm gonna ring the police! Get that bastard Monty whoever he is putt behind bars where he belongs, away from the daughters of men!" Then, on second thoughts, "Is Marie gone to Paul's? We'll speak to those two first, they might know something more about it all!"

We got the call, it was clearly something serious, we were to go to Jacaranda Close immediately.

It was half-ten at night. The house was all lit up like a party going on. But inside Eileen was in tears, Reggie looking grim. Without a word he handed us the note. Marie read it aloud, her voice faltering as its message got worse.

"Well fuck me!—Oh sorry Mummy, I couldn't help it. Is she trying to kill you and Daddy or what?"

"She's a wee eejit, a nutter, that's all!" said Reggie. "Well, I tell you one thing, she is coming back home as soon as I get my hands on her. And as for that bastard, my lord bloody Montague of Beaulieu, he is dead meat! Monty, she calls him. Do you know him?"

Marie and I looked at each other and we both said, "Montgomery Clark, of Clark's Garage? He's a customer at the Moon. she says he's a 'lush-lookin' fella'. He's a good bit older than her, in his late twenties, I'd say."

"Och, it's too late to do anything now," said Reggie. "I'll call at Clark's first thing in the morning..."

I don't believe anybody slept much that night.

At Clark's garage in the morning the abandoned wife Anita was there too, in floods of tears. They had two young children.

"Don't you upset yourself now, Missus," said Reggie, "I'll see your husband goes back to you, soon as I have an address in London."

That didn't take long. Mr Clark Senior had an idea they would be staying with English friends in the motor trade, at

Neasden in North London, and sure enough, a phone call confirmed it.

Reggie and Eileen flew out on the next plane from Aldergrove. What followed was not quite what you might have expected. Reggie and Eileen spent a couple of days at the house in Neasden with Thelma and Monty; it turned into a bit of an impromptu holiday, they all went sight-seeing, ate out at a restaurant in Chinatown and went to the West End theatre to see *Guys and Dolls*, the best of pals together.

But, but, but…they all came back to Belfast together on the plane, Monty and Thelma with their tails between their legs, he back to Anita and children, she back with Mummy and Daddy.

And it was acting out a kind of make-believe then as if nothing had really happened. "Except for Thelma's foul mood," said Marie. "She hasn't spoken since she got back. The Moon's been dead decent and given her back her job and she goes in and out to work with a face on her like cold porridge and never a civil word out of her, but I'm sure it's over, there's no word of Monty Clark anymore."

"He had his fling, I suppose. Young girl mad about him. Lucky the wife would have him back, but she has the kids to think of, even if he doesn't," I mused.

"Maybe another one on the way, withThelma preggers?"

"Oh dear God, don't say that. A married man with three kids, you'd imagine he'd have a packet of frenchies handy."

"Here's hoping and praying…"

28

Thelma's little escapade gave Marie and me the idea of a weekend break in London. Why should the bad people have all the excitement?

"Dirty weekend?" she grinned.

"I hope so," I rejoined gaily.

It was funny, in our twenties now we hadn't yet moved in together. We had a nice safe conventional bourgeois idea of saving up to get married in comfort.

Marie had a passing acquaintance with the Big Smoke now, following her meteoric rise and fall as a pop star. *Hold me, thrill me, kiss me* hadn't done badly in the end, edging into the charts Top 100 at 99 for a single week.

Marie had to laugh. She said, "Most of all it promoted the original American recording, everyone went out looking for that instead!"

"Yours is better," I said, meaning it.

"Well thanks, Paul. It's great that you believe in me. I tell you what, you can do it to me tonight."

"Do what?'

"Hold me, thrill me, kiss me!"

"All right, if you insist!"

We were booked into a small hotel on long, ruled, terraced Gower Street. The tall trees were stripped bare around the elegant Bloomsbury squares, in a dim grey-and-white frosty winter world, the figures moving stiffly in anonymous crowds like a Lowry painting.

"You can imagine Virginia Woolf strolling here," said Marie fancifully.

I wanted to see Charlotte Street with Dylan Thomas's old haunts, the Wheatsheaf pub and Bertorelli's restaurant.

"Dylan and the 'knickerless girls'," said Marie.

"Caitlin and he met in the pub here and had it off the same night in one of those rooms above the shops," I said. "Love at first sight."

"You make it sound very romantic!"

We visited the bookshops down Charing Cross Road. Marie picked up a novel by Jane Howard; I chose Henry Williamson *The Dream of Fair Women.*

"Sure you've got one now!" said Marie in mock protest.

"Aye, no need to *dream* anymore," I agreed, giving her a squeeze, her little face all winter-cold and cheeky like a London urchin.

We found the Greek restaurant she knew, Jimmy's in Frith Street, Soho. You descended to a basement with tables laid out plainly. Marie ordered for us, stuffed vine leaves and a bottle of *Retsina*. It was served with chips, green salad and crusty bread and butter, utterly delicious. And all so simple and unpretentious, not intimidating in any way. And cheap! We sat on finishing the sharp red wine because it was alcoholic, screwing our faces with each sip but enjoying the inebriation creeping over us like a spell.

The world closed in around our two presences face to face across the small table in deepest Soho. We were self-contained in our little love-bubble, in tender-heartedness and the worship of eyes, our voices sweetly caressing each other.

Got back up the stairs, half stumbling out on to the pavement. It was dark now, the night streets lit-up and busy. Jazz floated out from Ronnie Scott's directly across the street.

"Ornette Coleman or one of the greats," I said, "they all play there! You'd have done better as a jazz singer, Marie."

She shook her head, *maybe, who cares?*

I let Marie lead me by the hand, through the strange night crowds in the narrow garish streets, feeling dizzy and lost. There were neon signs for *Striptease*. This was the Soho night, sleazy!

But I was a writer, I fancied a closer look and Marie did not demur when I suggested,"What about a nightcap in one of these dives, the full Soho experience?"

We went down steps behind railings and past a nodding bouncer into the cellar club, busy, mostly men. We stood at the bar with our Scotch and sodas. A fine-looking woman came out on the podium and performed a striptease dance to *Big Spender.*

When she had stripped to just a thong, she sauntered down through the audience, smiling and natural, big pointed breasts she carried before her like proud trophies of her femininity. As if there was some kind of telepathy between her and me, she paused momentarily to primp my tie. I could smell her fresh sweat and perfume commingled like the scent of spring hedge-blossom, and looking her in the eye I was surprised by the sweet, innocent beauty I saw there, she was only eighteen or nineteen and there was nothing corrupted in the face yet, just this naive assured public offering of herself —*Love for sale.*

"Do you like her?" Marie asked, smiling, as the stripper moved on through the attentive, admiring crowd in a sway of soft buttocks and the dusty-gold long hair thick and wavy down her back to the waist.

I nodded, feeling relieved that my girlfriend didn't find the performance distasteful in any way.

"Striptease is only a form of dance," Marie explained afterwards as we hurried through the cold dark streets to bed, "clothes only get in the way; why not dance without them? So it's titillation for the men, but it does the same kind of thing to me, to be honest, I identify with the woman and the power her body gives her, *she*'s the one in control, you can see that in the confident way she moves and the look on your face like a pleased, polite small boy when she fixed your tie.

"It's just an acting out of the preamble to sex after all, it's not hurting anyone to take your clothes off, is it? You could see it as something dirty and demeaning, down in a seedy Soho cellar, and so on, if you were that way inclined, but they didn't seem like bad people in that place, they weren't disrespectful of her, of women, truly they were in awe of the stripper, you could see the kind of worship in their eyes and feel the love in the room, she wasn't a piece of meat to them, she was a fantasy of their own girlfriend or wife for that short time she danced for them and moved among them without her clothes."

Marie was always a loving partner to me but, whether it was the romantic weekend aura, the Greek food and Retsina, the neon-lit London night, the stripper, it all came together when we got back to the gaunt hotel, and had climbed the stairs to the warm bedroom with its low lights and long drop of velvet curtains, the rushes of the late Saturday night traffic under the window.

Slow build-up is best as a rule but we couldn't wait that night, clothes discarded the minute we shut the door of our room behind us; up on the bed, Marie on her hands and knees, opened to me, her ecstatic cries as our bodies locked and moved as one in the rhythm of love, eternal like the sea.

When I have finished, the light out, lying on my back, she cuddles up to my side, her nipples and bush brushing me, and she wants to speak the intimate dark, obsessional, fulsome words of love in my ear. Questions:

"You're *big*, aren't you?"

"Is that good?"

"I like to feel you deep inside me, filling me up."

She runs a proprietorial fingernail gently measuring the length of the shaft.

"It feels like velvet!" she declares. "What's the most sensitive part of it? Oo, it's growing again! What shall I do?"

And this sweetly cloying intimacy, like warm treacle poured in my ear, is something just for the two of us in the dark and dead of night, special words that speak of a profound respect for the life-force. I answer her questions quietly, seriously, in the masculine pride she rouses in me...*yes, yes, there, like that*...she makes me both her master and slave, tender and powerful, this beautiful naked woman who feels almost physically attached to me, paying homage at the shrine of my manhood, as I worship the woman in her.

In the morning I remember something and tell her, "I forgot to put anything on last night."

"Oh!" She just smiles. "Bareback rider? I *thought* I could feel you inside me better but I was too carried away to say!"

"Me too. Do we want a little baby?"

I worry for a minute but Marie doesn't seem bothered so I forget it. We're old enough now to have a baby anyway. There is Speakers' Corner and lunch at Selfridge's in Oxford Street before the evening plane back to Ireland.

29

"Yes, I am pregnant, the test is positive! Twelve weeks gone!"

"Are you sure? Just the one night with no protection and it makes you pregnant?"

"Yeh, got this potent, powerful man, really gave me his all that night, three times, no nonsense! Remember?"

"You seem okay about it?'

"Of course I am, it's our child inside me, it's everything I could ever want!"

"That's how I'm feeling too. Oh, Marie, it's wonderful! Congratulations, Marie and Paul!"

I kissed her. We were strolling through our old haunt, the Waterworks, on a Saturday afternoon of early spring, the trees suddenly bursting into leaf. There was a background music of bird twitter and little children playing that seemed all of a piece, the same animal life.

"Be *our* child soon!" I said.

"I was just thinking that." she smiled. "What a long way we have come since the maths class! And that first kiss here, over there. What shall we call him or her?"

"*Not* Audrey or Thelma, that's for sure!" I said. "Nor Reggie or Eric!"

"Wee Elvis? Cher for a girl?" she joked.

"Maybe! You know, you look different already," I said. "Definitely radiant, as they say!"

"At just three months, really?"

The fresh complexion and clear eyes were like a happy child's. As long as she wanted this baby, I was over the moon. It was sexy too, I felt a heady rush of desire, an urge to take her in behind the bushes, do it on the grass in the fresh air. Her face burned as if she could read my thoughts.

"We need to get married now," she said, matter of fact.

"Is that a proposal?"

"Aye! You know, man and wife, wedding rings? We're bringing a child into this world. I'm sure he or she would like Mum and Dad to be a proper item, a permanent fixture. There's not a lot of free love going on around here."

A new kind of intimacy bound us then, as if we were married already, in love till the end of time, there was nothing to quite match the grandness of that ideal. The silly love songs said it all, that two hearts became one and you would never be lonely anymore. It seemed you had come to the whole purpose of your life on this earth, not alone spiritual, but also in a physical way that was equally meaningful, the fulfilment of your biological destiny, the continuation of the human race.

We didn't mention our pregnancy to the folks when we informed them of our intention to get hitched, it seemed unnecessary to embarrass them with this revelation of our sex life. 1960s or not, premarital sexual intercourse was still a sin, or some other word, not religious but with the same meaning.

"Do you need to save up first?" was my dad's initial response, ever the auditor, his grey eyebrows knitting above the horn-rims. "Setting up house will cost a bob or two. Obviously we will help you as much as we can, but…"

"I've already got us down for a Trust house, Dad," I said. "The rents are reasonable and you can furnish a place cheaply secondhand."

"We want to start a family while we are still young enough to enjoy it," said Marie, flashing a winning smile of her straight white teeth.

Ma and she exchanged knowing womanly simpers.

Reggie and Eileen were less enthusiastic. He gave me a look as if he knew rightly where we were coming from. Eileen tilted her head back and narrowed her eyes at her older daughter.

"You're twenty-one and Paul's twenty-two, that is young. Do you not think you should wait a couple more years?"

"Aye," said Reggie. "Sure what's the rush? There's time enough for screaming kids and debt."

"But why wait?' said Marie. "We're in love and all ready to go now, enjoying life together!"

I said, "We've looked at the finances and reckon it'd be cheaper living together."

"Well if you've both made up your minds anyway, we can't stop you," they said. "We'll speak to Reverend M'Nirey about a date."

"Soon as possible," I said a bit too hasty and got another old-fashioneed look from Reggie.

On our own afterwards, Marie said, "I think they guessed what's happened. They'll know anyway when the baby comes! But we'll be married ages by then, no one'll care. I'd just rather say nothing now, or it looks like a shotgun wedding."

"They don't need to know," I agreed.

Marie said, "I don't think their experience of marriage was too wonderful. They lived with her ma, Granny Campbell in Ship Street for a while, not a good start. There were lots of rows, Mummy hated it when Daddy went off drinking with his mates round Sailortown. The pair of them settled down after I came along, Daddy working flat out to build up the business, Granny told me. They still quarrelled a lot, for years, I think it affected Thelma, that's why she's the way she is: a pain!"

"How come you're so…normal, if that's not a boring word, but, you know, not at all neurotic, just my nice lovely Marie!"

"Cause you're not like Daddy to Mummy, you put me first, not your mates and beer and football!"

I had to give her a hug. The thought of my child inside her thrilled me to the marrow. I wanted to cry for the love of her and this new life that had come out of our love.

We were so careful of our unborn child that we stopped penetrative sex.

"Like being sixteen again." Marie murmured, the curve of her distended belly pressed up to my rigid length and her cool hand, clutching possessively, fingernails impressing gently, caressed me rhythmically.

30

The wedding service in the Presbyterian church by our old school took place in April with the traditional showers sweetening the fragrance of the new season's blossoms on the avenue trees. April love is for the very young. Family from both sides and our friends from the group and our workplaces filled the church.

We'd rather mocked the idea of the religious wedding ceremony—neither of us had darkened a church door since confirmation at fourteen. But I was shocked into a kind of great awe and powerful sense of the drama and deeper meaning of the Creation as the organ blasted out Grieg's Wedding March that I knew as *Here Cones the Bride*. I had to fight back the tears of an overwhelming poignancy as the strange figure of my bride in her flowing virginal white made its way up the aisle on the grey-suited arm of her portly little dad.

Mike, with Marie's inexpensive ring in his waistcoat pocket, nudged me into the aisle to join her. I was stiff with self-conscious awkwardness, my face frozen with the strain of not crying. When I could see her face clearly under the veil, it wore the sweetest pixie smile I had ever seen in my life, and although the tears stood in my pupils now, I felt only this immense happiness flooding my being and the whole world.

The reception at the hotel on Antrim Road with the Zephyrs, the 50s dance band friends of Eileen and Reggie playing and the drink flowing like the River Lagan down to the Lough was a lively affair. Mike made a witty speech, recalling schooldays and the group, Reggie a tearful tribute to the daughter whose welfare he must now entrust to another man, Paul, a good man he had total confidence in to that end, and I could see the real human being there for a moment back of the barroom, football terrace bluster.

The Kellys' side was very boozy and backslapping, outgoing business people with loud voices and deep pockets, our Carroll side reserved and mostly teetotal, quiet little auditors or teachers, forever watching the pennies; we must have seemed dull and stingy to the Kellys.

Tina Hookey, the pissed and garrulous jewellery-dripping wife of a millionaire bookie seemed to take a shine to me, "Come on, Paul, me 'n' you'll fut the floor, can ye jive?"

"Not very well!" I gulped, trapped.

"Give us a wee waltz then! Listen, they're playin' ould whatsisface Humperstink! Come on, ye boy, an' give us the *last waltz*! I have a son your age, another Paul, married at eighteen, aye, got the wee girl Rosie in trouble and had to do the right thing by her, or his da was gonna kill him. You'd never have done a thing like that now, Paul, wud ye? I can tell ye're a clane, dacent fella!"

What did the woman know then? Paranoia gripped me momentarily, I blushed and shook my cheeks stupidly. *Was it all going to come out now, about Maureen, and wreck my marriage, sin had a way of catching up with you*!

"And would ye credit it," Tina went on, "the same boy's chasin' other weemin now behind wee Rosie's back. She tould me! Ye'll always be true to your wee Marie now, won't ye, son?"

I was overwhelmed and claustrophobic in the roaring room. I had a tendency to get cornered by bores, too polite to extricate myself from their clutches. I couldn't take any more of Tina's blabbering confessional account of her no-good promiscuous errant son, the shame of her existence; I managed to hide when she went off to the loo. I watched from the cover of some other guests as she came back looking for me.

It was a relief to get away from the reception. A taxi took us down to the station and we caught the train to Whitehead. We exited from the little station in the spring evening light with a cold wind sweeping the almost empty promenade, white horses on the cold navy-blue sea.

Our seafront hotel bedroom window looked out towards Scotland. We had a light evening meal then it was early to bed, we were exhausted, but in a happy way. Your wedding day was a public celebration of your love; uniquely it put love at the heart of community.

Marie came out of the bathroom with no clothes on and looked down at her swollen tummy as she rubbed it, "Look at our wee baby!"

"I love your pot belly," I said. "Don't you look cute!"

"He-she is kicking away there," she said, then, "Oh, look at you!" I was undressed too, and she came to me, the bride stripped bare, catching her breath as my stiff length gently prodded her belly-button.

Relief came quickly by her hand and we were soon falling asleep in the quiet hotel, lulled by the sound of the waves running in beyond the sea wall.

She opened her eyes and smiled at me in the gloomy morning light filtering around the curtains.

"Hello, Mrs Carroll!"

"Hello, husband!"

"Am I that boring, 'husband'? Husbanding my resources kind of thing? The Chartered Institute of Secretaries."

"I think 'husband' is sexy, the gravity and respect in it, sort of thing. Husband and wife. Perfect. Now we can do what we like! It's all legal and aboveboard!"

I kissed her but she patted me as if I were a big friendly dog and announced, "Don't know about you but I am *hungry!* That was a long night!"

We bathed, dressed and descended to the dining room. Off-season in the faded little resort, there weren't many other guests. The waiting staff smiled knowingly, indulgently at us, what a sweet young couple, and brought us big oval plates of Ulster fry, and toast and jam and a pot of tea.

In the sunny forenoon we took the bus out along the green peninsula of Islandmagee, my trip down memory lane. As we got down at the stop for Granny's, as it had been, the wind was blowing in the fresh green foliage of the tall roadside trees. The half-empty bus roared off in a stink of exhaust. The sun-dapple swayed beneath our feet. The shady loneliness of this stretch of road hit me again, it was unchanging.

I'd told Marie before but now we were here together I was excited like a child, jabbering on about my granny's.

"There was some girl?" Marie smiled, putting her finger on it, indulging me; she wasn't the jealous type, you could tell her things from the past, she knew it was only her I loved now.

"Naomi!" The name, never to be forgotten, filled my mouth pleasurably. It conjured up bare brown legs, a flash of cotton gusset, the bladelike, darkly beautiful gypsy face with the intense black eyes, her deft angular movements and quick intelligence.

I took Marie's hand and we crossed the road and went up the lane that climbed past the small housing estate. But I experienced a sinking apprehension with every step now, sensations of guilt and loss for what had been and was no more.

"Yeh, up there! Up that loaning, see the trees at the top, the big house, Blackhall Farm. That's where she lived, next door to Granny's! *Naomi was a witch!*"

"Och, go on with you, I'm sure she wasn't that bad?" Marie tittered.

"No, no—a *nice witch,* I mean."

"Like that song by Sinatra? *Witchcraft!*"

"Well, like that too but I mean a real witch. It's like a tradition hereabouts, taught her by an older woman. You've heard of the Isandmagee witchcraft trials at Carrickfergus? Well, it didn't end there, the black arts get passed on down forever, an old woman called Peggy, I met her, and everything, *she* taught Naomi!"

"Omigod, Paul, you're scaring the shite outta me now, scuse my language! Sure it's not one of your stories you wrote?"

"Honest Injun! C'mon we'll have a dekko at the old place!"

As we passed the cream-coloured council estate, I said, "That's where Auntie Mary and Uncle Frank lived then. After Granny died they moved away to an old cottage in Glenoe and Frank died not long after that. Mary went a bit odder and more reclusive then and wouldn't answer the door to visitors. Ma and Da invited her to our wedding but heard nothing back; when they called round looking for her a cat came running up to look out the dusty window, that was all; Mary was in there hiding from the world, just her and the cats now. Sad what becomes of people. I always really liked Auntie Mary, though no one else seemed to. Maybe cause I'm a bit odd myself."

As we came over the brow of the hill, the past ran up and slapped me on the face, the wind seething in the high treetops and the sea stretching away below, wrinkly green and white-capped.

"Gobbins that way," I pointed. "The witches' caves where they found the black candles they use in their masses."

"Oh Paul!" Marie hung on my arm. "There's something creepy about this old place!"

Nearly ten years had passed, a decade seemed a long time back then, but the place was still the same, Granny's neat cottage and the tall, faded farmhouse and its outbuildings, *the barn*—what memories! Did the big house look even more rundown? I was half hoping for a glimpse of Naomi, half terrifed of seeing her again.

"C'mon, we'll walk to the shore," I said.

We picked up the lane at the back of the houses where the fields sloped to the clifftops.

I jumped when Marie cried out in alarm, "Look, *people*!" My talk of witches had spooked her.

They were coming towards us up the loaning from the sea; gradually you could make out the figures of a woman and three young children. It was my turn to feel fear. As the figures drew nearer I saw they looked a bit wild, windblown and poor, gypsies maybe?

As we squeezed past each other in the narrow way the woman lifted her head to acknowledge us with a momentary, abstracted look and call, "Keep in now!" to the children, two little girls and an older small boy who turned dirty faces to gawp into ours in the way of country kids not used to strangers.

I saw the refinement on the children's faces and the beauty of the woman. I heard the voice and looking into her face I registered the faint familiarity of the high cheekbones and the jet eyes hard and glittering in the thin yellow face under the lank black hair.

Naomi had never really looked young. The angular frame in the old raincoat was thicker at the bust and hips from childbearing, that was the only real difference now.

Focused in on her three young charges, lost in her maternal preoccupation, she didn't appear to recognise me at all. Her eldest, the boy, was about six. So she had married at sixteen. Not unusual back then and she had been *advanced*, so to speak! I smiled to myself at the memory. Thank God for girls like her. She'd looked like an urchin back then too, like her children now; posh country folk like the Blackhalls could be terribly badly dressed, I supposed they had nothing to prove. She looked mentally ill but then she always had. I thought of the book *All of Them Witches* in *Rosemary's Baby* and shivered.

"Marie, *that was her!*" I whispered when we had put the little family group safely behind us.

"Who?" Marie looked cold in the hard wind coming off the sea.

"Naomi! She didn't recognise me at all!"

"Thank God for that, she mighta put a spell on us, on me maybe outta jealousy!"

"Too busy with her own family for that now," I said.

"They look underprivileged," said Marie. "Could do with free school dinners!"

"That's how poshies are," I said, enjoying being privy to the vagaries of social snobbery, learnt at the knee of my clergy-daughter mother.

"It's an upside-down world," Marie sighed.

The rain was coming over the water, stippling and darkening the face of the deep, an Old Testament sort of image. I said, "Hi, shall we turn back? Don't think the weather's right for the shore, we'd be sheltering in some witches' cave!"

"Heaven forfend! Maybe Naomi was coming from there, a meeting of the local coven!"

"They're not all bad people, you know," I quoted the young Naomi. "They know herbal cures for diseases and help people too."

"Oh, I expect Witch Naomi taught you a thing or two about human biology," said Marie archly. "She's pretty, right enough, in an interesting gypsy fashion."

We came back past the rear of the farm, the gaunt, scabby walls of the old house and the mucky sprawl of the yard, no sign of life about the place in the intensifying rainfall now. Naomi would be in there in the damp, dark old rooms, feeding her children as once she had fed me; there must be a husband around, some farmer, and the brothers maybe living there still, what woman would want them? I had a good look at the barn where I had first learnt at least something of the art of lovemaking, on just such a pouring wet afternoon as this.

"What are you staring at?" said Marie.

31

Before long we got settled into our Trust house. A new one had come up eight miles out of town at Green Island, on the Lough shore, where the group had played the hotel that Christmas time. There were regular buses and trains to Belfast. Marie had acquired a little Fiat car. She was unmistakably preggers now and still rushing around, comical matchstick legs under the big round belly, what a wee dote!

"Love the view!" we told each other. We were on a bit of a hill overlooking the Lough. The new development was constructed in a soft red brick, with covered entries through to the backs, two reception, three bedroom, sloping gardens front and back, the perfect nest! The blessing of public housing.

"But awful quiet," said Marie. "Semi-detached suburban Mr and Mrs Carroll! The neighbours seem to be preparing for the Zombie Apocalypse. Well, you never see or hear them. Working the night shifts at Courtauld's, I suppose."

"No neighbour-noise can't be bad," I said. "And we can make our own entertainment, I'm sure!"

"Dirty enough!"

Our wee girl was born in October. She was in no hurry to come out of her mummy, a whole long night's labour. Marie was past caring by the time she popped, she passed out and I got to hold the baby first. Caitlin we called her, after Yeats' Ireland-woman, ni Houlihan—Kevin at work, a Gaelic scholar, had educated me in Irish mythology—though Caitlin soon became Katy.

Marie was poorly for a bit. I took part of my annual leave from the Board and helped Eileen with the baby's feeding and nappy changes, an intense, packed 24-hour routine. Mike, Charlie and the mates called by in the evenings after Marie had retired to an early bed and I was on my own with Cairlin, we drank wine round the fire, listened to records and passed the baby round from lap to lap; the lads were soon fighting each other to hold her, the baby seemed to enhance the laddish proceedings! I'd take her upstairs to Marie's breast after the lads had gone.

I took Katy for walks in a sling on my chest, tucked under my coat like a Joey Kangaroo in a pouch, down to the local shop and along the shore. When Marie was up and about again we stepped out together in the cold wind, pushing Katy in the new red pram, a lovely floaty sensation, giggling like the kids we still were really. The pram pulled us down the hill, so we had to run to keep up, singing the *Runaway Train*. On a safe stretch of unimpeded flat ground I sent the pram flying off in front of us and we ran to catch up with it, till Marie protested, "Stop! We'll have an accident! You'll push her into the sea!"

"That's impossible!" I protested, I had developed such a surety of touch with the baby.

I loved the feel of the pram handle in my grip, or the baby secure in her sling on my breast, or dandled on my knee by the fireside, or kicking her wee legs on the hearth mat propelling herself along till I had to save her from the fire. This was a new, emotionally satisfying, tactile experience for me, the warm living weight of my child in my arms.

My parents came to babysit while we had our first night out since the birth, at a Van Morrison concert.

With her return to complete wellness following the birth, Marie experienced a powerful resurgence of desire. Quiet evenings after tea, the scene of perfect peaceful domesticity with Katy asleep upstairs in her cot, curtains drawn shutting out the freezing winter dark, Marie comes to me where I sit reading my book by the fire, lifts her skirt and climbs onto my lap, lies prone across my knee and the chair-arm, head upside-down as I stroke her. We abide there suspended in the deep evening silence, only the flapping of the flames among the burning coals, the glory of each passing moment that ticks away with the contact of our bodies, the beating of our hearts and the ticking of the mantelpiece clock.

When she is good and ready, naked below the waist, she leads me up the stairs behind the swing of her hips, to kneel on the bed for me and draw me into her cleft softness. Her cries of fulfilment pierce the dead silence of the Sunday evening dark over the row of terraces above the Lough.

"The neighbours will think I'm strangling you," I say afterwards as we lie there together in recovery.

"I can't help it," she says, seriously, and explains, "it's a postnatal surge of hormones or something, I can't seem to get enough of you, I'm just dying for it all the time!"

"Don't worry, baby," I tell her, "I don't care about the neighbours; I mean who knows, we might be an inspiration to them!"

At Marie's suggestion, inspired by a French novel she is reading, we devise a little private game to keep me on the job assuaging her fizzing hormones, it's a rule we must both follow at all times: Marie is forbidden to wear knickers in my company; the idea is that she must be ready for me at all times and instantly, to simply lift her skirt and do it without negotiating the obstruction of underclothing. It is also the green light to me that she is ready to go whenever I please; she might be washing the dishes, polishing the table, down on her knees scrubbing the kitchen floor. If I come home unexpectedly, say, or she has forgotten our rule at any time—I may lift her skirt to spot-check—she must remove her knickers immediately.

For my part, I must be ready, willing and able to satisfy her needs at a moment's notice. Knowing my wife is always ready and waiting for me is my spur to action.

"Obedience requires discipline," she announces, her voice hardening, the schoolmistress. "If I forget to be knickerless and ready for you, you must deal with me as a disobedient wife."

It's not long till she transgresses. In the nearby Church of Ireland we've taken to attending Sunday mornings, to be part of the local community, Katy in my arms as we singalonga Moody-Sankey, Marie pulls a face at me and mouths, *"I forgot!"* and points down at her hips as she mouths, *"Knickers!"*

I put on an angry husband look. This is worse than Wink Martindale's *Deck of Cards* and I will surely punish her as no woman has been punished.

Back in the house she apologises in mock hand-wringing pleading for a pardon she doesn't want.

"I am so-o sorry, my husband, we were in such a rush getting out to church with Katy! Look, see my shame!"

We have shut the front door behind us and are still in the little hallway with an interval of wintry sunshine falling through the frosted fanlight. Marie lifts her loose, pleated kilt, unbuttons the stockings from the garter belt she wears now to facilitate our game, and slips her panties down her legs on to the floor.

"Is that better now? Does that please you, sir?" she begs me. "Now I am ready for you anytime you like! Do you forgive me for my disobedience, forgetting your rule, my master?" She shakes her head to cue in my answer, "No!"

Rising to the occasion, I respond, "You know the rule by now, my wife, you *do not* wear knickers in my company, ever, you must be ready for me at all times. You leave me no option now but to discipline you."

"Ooooh!" she wriggles her hips. "I'm going to get a sore bum!"

"We will go up the fields this afternoon and you will help me select a fine sally rod!" I say sternly.

"Yes, sir," she murmurs and buttons up her stockings, knickerless in perpetual readiness now. Both our faces are burning in the charged anticipation, it is all so silly but such fun!

In the grey light of the afternoon we walk up the cold, desolate farm-fields that spread in a green patchwork quilt up the mountainside. Katy sticks up out of a superior framed carrier on my back now, Marie and I hold hands as we walk. It is a walk of love, the couple and the child of their desire. In the hedgerow by the full brown stream that tumbles down the mountain to the Lough the sally rods stick up, hard, bare and winter-cold. We must select the right one.

Marie has to approve it: "Not too thick or thin, heavy or light, short or long," she decrees, "it has to feel just right across my bare b-t-m. I want you to beat me nicely, because you love me, husband!" She smiles into my face. "Look, this one's perfect! Smooth, light and flexible but firm the way I like!" She switches it at the curve of her hip like a jockey.

Returning to the house in the deadening light of the December Sunday afternoon, as if the end of the world is nigh, we settle a slumbrous Katy down in her cot, going sound asleep after her outing in the fresh air.

Now the wife kneels up on the double bed with her skirts about her waist; the husband stands over her, wielding his rod. The long mirror on the wardrobe door holds their reflection.

Switch!

"How's that?" he mumbles thickly. It's scarcely more than a tickle, it's just a game and he'd never really hurt her.

"Harder!" Her voice sounds half-buried, flat and strange to his ears.

Switch!

"More!" She wags her tail. "That's better—that's just right! Again, go on! Spank me!"

The light playful switches of the pliant sally rod warming her bottom is a bonding foreplay before they make sweet love and go downstairs afterwards to get the tea like any normal happy married couple.

Their little game seems to express a deep need in both of them, her essential femininity and his valuing of it in some acute, primal way, the need to possess and be possessed, totally. The little rituals they devise bring a story, a purpose and compulsion to their lovemaking—and also a sense of fun, the comic absurdity around tradition and the solemnity of the marriage vows, the promise to *"obey"*!

In that time following the birth of Katy, Marie and I spun a warm cocoon of all-consuming eroticism around the two of us, binding us closely woman to man. The fantasising and frank sensuality after the birth of Caitlin entailed a complete trust and mutual respect, it deepened our love in a total binding commitment, and most of all, paradoxically perhaps, a profound *tenderness*, a kind of fabulous secret and intimate sharing. Marriage was a sexual union; the recognition and celebration of this simple, beautiful natural fact was the secret of a successful marriage, of satisfaction and fidelity, everything in life turning around that central raison d'être of the relationship .

32

Marie sings, *"And when the evening comes, we smile..."*

The quiet, beautiful lyric sums up the essence of new married life, the simple promise marriage brings of lifelong homely, intimate sharing and emotional security, as well as the excitement, the fun and games that enliven the settled flow of the days, weeks and years.

Tara was born two years after Caitlin. The two wee ones brought Marie and I incomparable joy. Of course there was discomfort and exhaustion attending to their needs, shredded nerves and drop-down-dead fatigue, occasional rows, yet somehow you wouldn't have missed it for all the tea in China, the quiet satisfactions and closeness of family life. But also the adventures, the excitement the children brought to trips and treats, the vicarious re-living of your own happy childhood days and the elevating sense of your vital place in the wider community of mankind, your stake in the future of humanity.

The passion of Marie and I never died, it went on being expressed in changing nuances, piquancy and experimentation, that was all. Practice makes perfect and there are no exceptions to the rule. Marie and I as a couple were lucky to have grown up in the time of comparative sexual liberation that came out of advances in family planning. We weren't those sad promiscuous types you hear too much of, as if their superficiality represented achievement; rather, we found love in each other, in monogamy, and practised it fearlessly.

Maybe the liberated sex went with the great music, the love songs of the day, the ones we performed in our little group. After all, I had married a singer of the period, Marie Kelly, there was the 45 rpm record, the press cuttings, the still faintly-scented dress, the memory of her appearance on *Top of the Pops* that remained vivid.

"Top of the flops, in my case," she laughed now. Being nearly famous was one of the things she least regretted in her life. Me and the kids meant most to her. She was a good teacher and all that virtuous stuff but at the end of the day teaching was just work, like any other job, with added bullshit, like public life generally.

Private life, the marital/lovers' bedroom, family and friends, books and music and theatre, the arts, the creation of a good, caring, loving life here and now in the everyday reality, that was what Marie believed in and taught me. The band still got together now and again whenever we could manage it—Frankie, a civil engineer, was often away. There were charity and birthday dos, and the like. A small circle of old fans, becoming old hippies now, turned out to see us, and our kids were impressed. There was plenty of demand for the incomparable 1960s' pop we still played mostly—the kids loved it. and we were into the late 60s too with Steve Miller and Crosby Stills and Nash.

I didn't stay at the Gas Board in the end. I knew all along, in my heart of hearts, that accountancy or secretaryship just wasn't me. Yet I stuck it out for some years, till Tara started secondary school and I felt that I had more room to grow.

My progress had been slow on the Chartered Institute classes and in the end I dropped them, took an A level English Literature at the Tech and got accepted as a mature student on an English degree course at the new polytechnic. I got a grant and was around home more to help out while Marie worked compulsory unpaid overtime at the chalkface.

Believe it or not, I *missed* the Gas Board to begin with, perhaps I still miss it in a way, that cosy corner of the office I shared with Kevin and the other nice homely sort of people I worked with, the cups of tea and chocolate digestives, the desk-world, the rain on the windows, the fixed routine under the big wall-clock, like a tradition laid down by my father before me.

The old man shuffled off this mortal coil at seventy; just five years after retirement the heart stopped beating. He'd got hooked on the poison of the news in the long hours and isolation of retirement, the endless hopeless conservatism of the newspapers, wireless and TV. Reading good books got squeezed out in the end by all that materialism screaming for attention. The liberal attitudes he'd brought me up on seemed to go out the window with the good books, in the name of that same controlling, steamrolling materialism of corporate greed and the profit motive.

Ma went another ten years, she was that much younger than he; the grandchildren kept her busy. There were Audrey's two as well, Wee Jimmy and Willie—Big Jimmy, the architect she had married, had turned out to have a gambling addiction, it ran in the family, and gambled away their limited middle-class prosperity, first his business, then the car, then the house—the boys and she had moved back in with Ma and travelled by bus, while Big Jimmy, penniless, unemployed, went home to his widowed ma and his old betting shop mates in shebeens back of the Shankill; the marriage was finished.

And Thelma...in hindsight it was hardly surprising that she bore a child out of wedlock, and could not tell who the father was, though Marie and I suspected Charlie. But the child, Charles—yes indeed, what a coincidence—came as a complete surprise. Thelma had appeared to be putting on weight, that was all; she tended to run to fat anyway, the bump in her belly concealed by a corset, as it turned out, it must have been excruciating.

Close to the Christmas of her twenty-fifth year she had woken up in the morning *giving birth*, the child pressing out of her, unstoppable. The baby nearly strangled on its umbilical cord; quick-thinking, practical Eileen saved it. Coming out of the blue like that, it was a shattering blow dealt to the whole family, but Eileen and Reggie gritted their teeth and helped Thelma look after Charles, and he was growing up a happy enough wee fellow.

Thelma met someone in the civil service where she worked now and there was talk of an engagement.

"Things have a way of panning out," I commented unoriginally to Marie as we walked on White Park Bay on a couple-only weekend away, Katy and Tara gone to Eileen for two blessed nights.

On these odd occasions that we could get away, just the two of us, we would reflect on life's little conundrums.

Marie agreed, "I'll be glad to see Thelma married and settled in her own place before she has another surprise baby!"

"Our twisted sisters ended up with twisted lives, but not through any real fault of their own," I sighed with the rolling waves expiring on the long, windblown crescent of yellow strand with no other humans in sight.

"You think not?" Marie gave me a look. We had always been hard on the two of them, when we talked together like this, a form of therapy, getting the frustration off our chests. "Even Thelma?"

"No. I blame the bloke, Charlie or whoever it was, she was always stuck on him and we saw her with him at that party at Brent's bungalow in Carryduff, musta been around nine months ago, they'd been out the backyard..."

"Up against the drainpipe?" Marie pulled a face. "So romantic!"

"Fancy just shooting off inside a girl like that!" I shook my head in disgust.

"You'd never do that then?" Marie smiled. "To me?"

We both laughed. "We were engaged, or as good as, we were using frenchies, but didn't quite get it together that one night, did we? Got carried away. You said you liked it bareback. And Katy was a joy and got us married and settled down like proper grown-ups."

Our minds emptied as we strolled on, arms linked, along the waterline. I said something about the "deep-throated background roar of the ocean, with the faint blue outline of Kintyre across the channel".

"When are you going to finish that book and send it to a publisher?" Marie asked me. "You describe things so well."

"Oh my book, it's not really the kind of thing they publish anymore," I said. "But I'll get it finished anyway soon, maybe get it photocopied and passed round any friends who can still read."

"The girl Flora in it, is that me? The sexy daughter of the fisherman?"

We laughed. I explained, "Every girl whom the hero, Anthony, falls in love with is at least a bit of you. You're the only girl I've ever loved or even really known."

"Your wee plain Marie, the 'Irish girl-next-door' as they called me!"

"You are beautiful, Marie, it comes straight from your heart and shines out of your lovely kind eyes. And it's in your singing."

"What about your gypsy queen Naomi! You were somewhat taken with her, before me, I can tell!"

"But she was a witch!" I grinned. "You saw her, remember?"

"And how do you know I'm not? *A witch!*..."

Marie made her light-blue eyes bulge crazily; momentarily I shivered and had to look away.

"Poor Naomi, she looked half-mad when we saw her that day," I said. "They were a weird family, the Blackhalls. Big Unionists, though she didn't care about any of that crap, I don't think so, I hope not..."

Cows had wandered down on to the strand by the stream that ran over it down to the sea. We jumped the stream and clambered over the rocky debris at the foot of the cliffs and up on to the road with the line of houses, second homes now, tucked under the big bosky headland, the old salmon fishing port, where we had hired a cottage for the weekend.

We were the only people staying in the houses that weekend. Indoors, we climbed the stairs to the bedroom with its low window overlooking the sea, and undressed in the afternoon light. Marie had kept her slim but shapely, womanly figure, her breasts and hips a little ripened with child-bearing, more appealing than ever, her fair skin very white, the dark-fair triangle of pubic hair trimmed back neatly now.

Undressed, I lay on my back on the red eiderdown on the saggy old brass double bed under the low boarded ceiling. The waves beat rhythmically up on the rocks and sand of the disused harbour below. The west lighthouse of Rathlin Island on its high clifftop shouldered into the horizon framed in the window.

I was plainly ready and Marie settled herself on me, sighing as her body engulfed mine. Her cheeks burned now, she rolled her pale eyes as she moved on me.

"It's great, going to bed in the afternoon like this," she said, her voice thick in her throat. "Like old times."

"I love you, Marie with the laughing eyes," I said. "I always will."

Our eyes met, held, locked in the love and trust of the moment and all of time.